STRUMMIN' UP LOVE

A COUNTRY MUSIC STAR WESTERN ROMANCE

MUSICIANS OF LONG VALLEY ROMANCE
BOOK ONE

ERIN WRIGHT

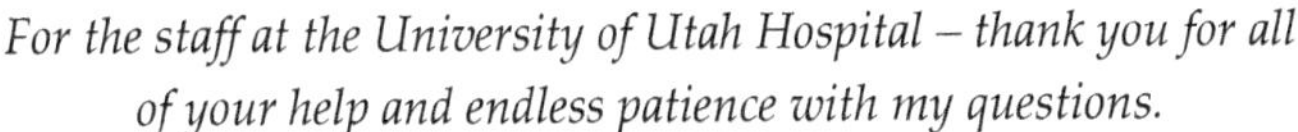

For the staff at the University of Utah Hospital – thank you for all of your help and endless patience with my questions.

Graham, you're gonna make a superstar physical therapist someday soon.

And to my family – love you always.

PROLOGUE

ZANE

November, 2017

Z ANE RISLEY RAPPED IRRITABLY on the door of his wife's bathroom. If Tamara made him late for the CMAs, he would kill her with his bare hands. The most important night of his life and there she was, holed up inside of the bathroom for hours—

"I'm almost done!" Tamara shouted through the closed door. "Stop banging on the damn door. This is all your fault. If you'd pay for a hairdresser and make-up assistant like Faith Hill has, I wouldn't have to do this all by myself. I swear you *want* your wife to look like a hag in front of everyone—"

But Zane had already walked away, the blood pounding in his head as he clenched his hands in rage. If he had to hear one more time about how he wasn't helping Tamara live up to the standards of Tim-God-Almighty-McGraw, he might be tempted to plant his fist through a door, or a wall, or Tamara's snide face, and God knew how the gossip rags would love to go crazy over *that*.

"I'm ready," Skyler hollered as he clattered down the stairs to the front drawing room.

At least one Risley can get ready on time.

"Be there in a minute, Skyler," Zane called out casually over the railing to the main floor, trying to keep his voice as even-keeled as possible. Just because Zane and Tamara could hardly be in the same room for more than 32 seconds without a shouting match ensuing didn't mean that Skyler had to bear the brunt of it.

He was just a kid – a kid with a bitch for a mother, that was, who'd done her best to poison him against Zane.

The things she said within earshot of Zane about Zane, taunting him, trying to get a rise out of him…he could only imagine what she said when he wasn't there.

He quietly slammed his fist down on the elaborately carved railing, as much anger as he allowed himself to show in front of Skyler. After his current tour was over, Zane'd take Skyler out on the town for some father-son bonding time, doing…

Zane stared blankly at the hideous painting on the wall that no doubt Tamara had spent tens of thousands of dollars on, trying to think of what he could do with Skyler. Something fun. Something…male. And bonding. And shit.

Hmmm…Didn't Skyler like soccer? Yeah, now that he thought about it, that seemed right.

Well then, Zane would play soccer in the backyard with him when he got back off tour. Hell, he could call the landscaper and ask him to put in a soccer field. They weren't using the running track much anymore anyway. In fact, he could invite a bunch of boys over and they could play a huge soccer game – have a big tournament. He could offer cash prizes and maybe slip a little green into the right hands to make sure that Skyler made a goal – or seven – and Zane could cheer him on from the sidelines.

That seemed like a very father-like thing to do.

At least, that's what happened in all of the Disney movies,

and that was about as good of a role model as Zane was going to get.

But first, he had to drag Tamara away from her mirror and her makeup and her hairspray, and get going to the CMAs. He'd make plans with Skyler for a soccer tournament later. He strode back down the hallway, his long legs eating up the distance easily, and through his wife's bedroom to stand in front of her bathroom.

"Tamara Raine Risley, if you don't come out of that bathroom *right now*, I'm going to leave without you!" he hollered, banging on the door with his fist. Dammit all, *should* he just leave without her? That'd show her. She'd be spitting nails if he left her behind; he'd just love to see the look on her face when she realized that he'd actually carried through with his threat.

Except…showing up to the Country Music Association awards ceremony without his wife would mean the gossip rags would go wild. They already liked to take every little spat and blow it out of proportion. If he wasn't holding her hand and smiling gently into her eyes and handing her a dozen roses every time they went out into public together, the media made it out like they were on the verge of divorce.

He let out a string of swear words under his breath that'd make a priest faint.

It was just like his self-centered, bitch-of-a-wife to pull this kind of stunt. Screw it. He needed to make an appointment with his lawyer on Monday. See how expensive it would be to just divorce her already. Hell, according to the gossip rags, he'd already divorced her ten times over, so why not actually make it happen?

It'd been a couple of years since Zane had looked at his wife with anything remotely akin to love, and this whole staying-together-for-the-child bullshit was getting real damn old.

"I'm done," Tamara said haughtily as she yanked the door

open and strode past him, her glittering high heels only rivaled by her glittering dress. There was a slit up the sheath of gold that ended at the top of her thigh, but instead of making her look sophisticated and beautiful, Zane thought she looked like an aging has-been, desperately clinging to the little fame she used to have.

Which, funnily enough, was exactly what she was.

He stomped down the staircase behind her, the air frosty and bitter between them. Their butler, long on the talent of feigned deafness whenever a fight was brewing between Zane and Tamara – in other words, whenever Zane was home off tour – stepped forward and opened the front door for them with a slight bow. "The limo is outside, sir," he said blandly. "Best of luck tonight."

"Thank you, Frank," Zane murmured distractedly as they headed out into the freezing November air, his breath puffing with every word. They'd hit an unexpected cold snap and the resulting skiff of snow on the ground was the talk of every party and meteorologist. It snowed each year in Nashville, of course, but not normally this early in the season. It was going to be a hellacious winter – Zane could feel it in his bones.

Good thing he was heading out for California in the morning for the next leg of his tour. At least San Diego would have the decency to still have fall weather.

He heard Skyler's shouts of delight as he practically threw himself inside of the limo, intent on exploring every corner of it. Zane was stumped for a moment – why in the hell was Skyler acting like he'd never been inside of a limo before? – when he remembered that actually, his son probably hadn't been inside of a limo before. Tamara had refused to let Skyler go on tour with Zane, saying that he should stay home and go to school and play with his friends – all of those things that every boring, normal child did. She didn't seem to understand that her son could always go to school later, but that the chance to tour with his father was only happening *right now*.

Just one more topic that they argued about.

One of many.

Zane slid into the limo after Tamara and the driver hurried to shut the door behind them when Zane stopped him. "Step on it tonight, okay? My *wife*," he sneered the word, "felt like making us 45 minutes late would be a superb plan."

The driver nodded his understanding, closed the door, and then took off at a jog for the driver's side, clearly taking Zane's request to heart.

At least someone *listens to me.*

"Did you have to tell the *driver* that you think it's my fault that we're late?" Tamara hissed. "Anyone else you want to tell? Want to rent a blimp and fly it over Nashville?"

"If I thought it would do any good, I'd do that *and* take out an ad in *The Tennessean*," Zane shot back. "Is that what it would take to actually have you get ready on time?"

Tamara opened up her mouth to fling something back at him but a tug on her arm made her look down instead. "Mom, Mom, check it out!" Skyler said, pulling at her arm and pointing. "A fridge! Inside of the car! Can I see what's inside of it?"

"Sure, dear," she said vaguely, patting his hand.

"Come look with me, Mom!" Skyler said, tugging at her hand. With a sigh, she unbuckled her seat belt and followed their son across the huge space. Zane almost barked at them to sit back down and get buckled in, but swallowed the words instead. Skyler hadn't been in a limo before. He needed to let him have his fun. God only knew he didn't have a lot of that with Tamara as a mother.

He felt his phone buzz and pulled it out of his tux pocket. He groaned. It was Heidi Marshall, the liaison for the potential winners of the awards ceremony, and her text message was in all caps, leaving no doubt as to the state of her mood.

WHERE THE HELL ARE YOU?

Yeah, not much doubt there. He was sure if Heidi could reach him in that moment, she'd wring his neck. They should've been there ten minutes ago, and, he took a quick peek out of the window, they still had a ways to go.

On our way. See you soon.

He felt the anxiety mixed with anticipation rush through him again at the thought of what just might happen that night. When he'd received the news that he'd been nominated for *Male Vocalist of the Year*, he'd literally stopped breathing for a moment. The rush of emotion at the knowledge that he'd *finally* made it…

And now, the awards ceremony was happening. Tonight, he'd find out if he'd actually won. He could already hear Brad Paisley and Carrie Underwood, the co-hosts for the event for years, reading his name together at the microphone. He would stand up, acting humble but knowing all along that of *course* they'd read his name, and then he'd stride confidently up to the front, every eye in the place on him, clapping and cheering for—

There was a screech of burning rubber as the tires went skidding and the limo was fishtailing and Skyler screamed and Zane's seat belt went taut, holding him in place as the world spun upside down and right side up and upside down like he'd somehow been deposited into a dryer when he wasn't looking. There was crunching metal and breaking glass and when it finally stopped, Zane just sat there, frozen, his seat belt tight against his chest, cutting off his air, and he didn't know what just happened or where they were or—

"Mom. Mom. Moooommmm…"

His son was moaning; he was in pain. Zane had to get to his son. His hands were scrabbling at his seat belt but it was jammed and his fingers weren't working right and—

His wife. He couldn't hear Tamara. Why couldn't he hear her? Why wasn't she calling out for help?

All of the sudden, he wanted nothing more than to hear his wife bitch and moan at him that he wasn't home more often, or that her hair wasn't right, or that the maid wasn't doing a good enough job cleaning the master bathroom toilet.

Anything was better than nothing at all.

Zane finally wrenched his seat belt free, gasping in the suddenly available air. He registered in a sort of detached way that at least the limo had ended right-side up so he hadn't been hanging upside down by his seat belt, and then he was pushing his way through the wreckage towards the moans of his son.

It washed over him then.

He didn't know how he knew that his wife was dead. It was a certain knowledge that would come back to haunt him later. Maybe if he'd tried harder in those first few minutes to search for her and stem the flow of blood from her head, maybe she would've lived. Maybe his certainty hadn't been right at all, and he should've tried harder.

But in that moment, amongst the creaking and groaning of metal against metal, Zane was working his way towards his son because he could hear his pleas for help.

Pleas for his mother. His mother who was already gone.

"Mom, where are you?" His son's ten-year-old voice was high and reedy with pain, not yet having begun the transition to becoming a man.

"I'm coming, Skyler," Zane grunted, trying to remember why he'd thought a stretch limo would be just the thing for the CMA Awards. If he'd chosen a regular car, he would've made it to Skyler's side already.

Stupid Zane. Always needing to show off. Only wanting the best—

Skyler's thin, childish hand slipped into Zane's and tears of relief began trickling down Zane's cheeks. His son was here. He was alive. He was clinging to Zane's hand and that was all that mattered.

"Dad," Skyler choked out, and Zane knew that his son's pain was almost swallowing him whole and Zane wanted to take it on himself, make it his own, protect his son from it. There was metal wrapped around Skyler, trapping him in place, and Zane's gut told him that it would take a miracle to have his son come out in one piece. "Where's Mom?"

But Zane never answered that question. The firefighters and first responders showed up just then, pulling at the doors, prying them open, the horrendous screech of metal against metal like the claws of a giant ripping at the car, making it hard to think.

But even if they hadn't arrived, he still wouldn't have answered that question, because he'd failed his son, and there was no answer to give.

He'd lived, while his wife had died.

And for that, Skyler would never forgive his father.

CHAPTER 1

LOUISA

May, 2019

(18 months later)

L ouisa did a full-body stretch, not wanting to open up her eyes because somehow, she knew there was something waiting for her that she didn't want to face up to, something she didn't want to confront. If she kept her eyes shut, then she could push it away a little lon—

Her outstretched hand whacked the coffee table and just like that, everything was back.

She'd played by the rules and kept her eyes shut, dammit, but it didn't matter. She knew the truth anyway. She wasn't at home in her bed, sleeping away the rare morning off. She was on her mother's couch and it was her mother's 1970's relic of a coffee table that she'd just inadvertently punched.

Well hell, the sharp corners of the coffee table had given her the scar that ran across her forehead, courtesy of learning to walk before parents realized that sharp edges and toddlers didn't mix, so the coffee table probably had it coming.

"*Mija*," her mom said, her soft voice wrapping around Louisa like a warm blanket in the middle of February. Just for a moment, Louisa reveled in it, content to play the part of a small child in need of comfort, and ignore the fact that she was 28 years old. When Matthew had come home 12 days ago with his big news…

Well, she'd become a daughter in need of comfort instantaneously. Funny how she could emotionally revert back to her childhood in the blink of an eye.

With a quiet sigh, Louisa finally forced her eyes open, a living room she knew as well as the back of her hand swimming into view.

"Are you okay?" Her mother's face appeared just inches away from her own, and Louisa jumped. This wasn't an easy feat, honestly, considering she was lying down, so it really was more like a whole-body jerk, complete with a wild swing of the arm and another *whap* against the coffee table.

"Yes, I'm fine," Louisa groaned, running her hands over her face and then rubbing her hand gingerly. "Nice and awake now."

"Sorry, sorry. I was talking to you about the bathroom, and you were not answering."

"You were?" Louisa searched back, trying to figure out if her mother's words had registered even on a subliminal level, but came up with nothing.

Huh. Maybe she wasn't fine.

Scratch that. She bloody well wasn't fine at all. Who was she kidding?

"Em is making breakfast burritos in the kitchen," Mom continued, "and Alex just got out of the bathroom. If you hurry, you can squeeze in there before Frizzy realizes no one's using it and hogs it for the next two hours." She gave her daughter a wry smile.

"Thanks, *Mamá*," Louisa said, reaching out and squeezing her mother's hand. It'd been a good long while since she'd had to jockey around younger siblings, trying to make her way into the bathroom before anyone else did, but it'd all come back to her soon enough.

Stupid Louisa. You thought you'd escaped all of this, but you didn't. Living in a too-small house with too many siblings is your life. It doesn't matter how many medical degrees you get – this is still where you'll end up.

Emilia shouted for help, and Mom hurried off, leaving Louisa to swing her legs off the couch and make a dash for the open door of the bathroom before the twins, Francesca and Isabel (or Frizzy, as almost everyone called the pair of them) seized their chance and clogged up the bathroom for the rest of the morning. They'd just discovered makeup last year, and according to everyone who had the bad luck of sharing a bathroom with them, now spent most of their waking hours either applying or removing it from their faces.

Was I ever that vain? That self-absorbed?

It seemed impossible, honestly.

After using the worn, 1970s avocado green bathroom that perfectly matched the coffee table, Louisa headed for the kitchen, the smell of eggs, salsa, and beans drifting on the morning air.

Mi casa.

This was her home. She'd been stupid to think that she could make a home in a white man's house. Matthew had told her that she made him into a better person; that just being around her made him want to try harder, but apparently he hadn't finished that sentence. *Try harder to find someone else to love* was what Louisa had actually managed to convince Matt to do.

Not the most useful talent on the planet, turns out.

And now he was happy with his white girlfriend and their incoming white baby, and Louisa was here. Right back where she'd started.

Back where she belonged.

The chatter, loud and happy and enthusiastic, switched

seamlessly between English and Spanish as her siblings dished up their burritos and argued over whose turn it was to do which chores that day.

"*Tia* Carmelita called, Louisa," Mom said, cutting across the argument over the last person to scrub the toilet. "She said you should call her back. Wanted to talk to you."

Louisa arched an eyebrow at her mother, trying to divine the point of this. *Tia* Carmelita, her mother's sister, lived up in the mountains of Idaho, north of Boise, far, far away from the potato fields and cheatgrass and lava rocks of Pocatello. Carmelita visited them once a year, understanding that it was easier for her to drive across the state to visit them than it was for her sister, brother-in-law, and six children to trundle across the state to her.

Once-a-year visits…well, Louisa knew her aunt well enough to be able to pick her out of a line-up, but they weren't close by any stretch of anyone's imagination. They certainly didn't have cozy little chats every Tuesday morning.

Mom just shrugged her ignorance at the look Louisa was sending her. "She wouldn't say why; just said that it was important and to call her as soon as you had a chance."

Curiouser and curiouser.

Louisa hurried through her breakfast burrito and then dug into the side of black beans and salsa as quickly as she could without being rude. Alex slid into the chair next to her, sending her a grin as he dug into his food.

"Want to go outside and play *fútbol* after breakfast?" he asked around a mouthful of food, the scrambled eggs from the breakfast burrito spraying the table in front of him.

"Alexander Vargas," Louisa scolded him. He had the good graces to look ashamed and wiped hastily at the tablecloth. After a big swallow of milk washing down the remaining food in his mouth, he tried it again.

"Wanna go kick around the *pelota*?" he asked eagerly. He was 13 and just starting to hit that stage in life where he'd become much too cool for his oldest sister (or anyone in the family for that matter) but apparently the desire to play *fútbol* won out over being too cool to be seen with family.

Oh, the struggles of teenagerhood…

"I have to call *Tia* Carmelita first," she told him. "Then we'll see."

His face dropped and he dug back into his burrito without another word. Louisa sighed as she stood up, ruffling his hair as she passed to take her plate to the sink. She was the oldest of the six Vargas children; he was the youngest. She'd been a second mom to him – hell, she'd *been* his mom – after their mom had almost died giving birth to him. Their mother had been weak and shaky for months afterwards and by the time she regained her strength, it'd seemed natural to everyone that Louisa simply continue to take care of Alex. When she'd left to go work at the University of Utah Hospital down in Salt Lake City, Alex had cried for days.

And now I'm letting him down by not kicking a ball around with him for an hour.

Whatever *Tia* Carmelita wanted, Louisa would get it done and then go play with Alex. It was only right.

Louisa snagged the cordless phone off the cradle – her mother refused to get rid of the landline and only have a cell phone like everyone else in the civilized world – and hit the speed-dial for the Miller's house. Carmelita was the housekeeper for the Miller family – had been all of her adult life – and often joked that God didn't send her kids or a husband because he knew she had enough people to take care of in the Miller family.

Stetson Miller, the youngest of the Miller brothers, was only 18 months older than Louisa. The last time she'd seen him had been at his father's funeral. She'd heard that he'd gotten married since then, which pretty much destroyed every one of her fevered teenaged dreams. Not that he'd ever even realized she was alive but Louisa vividly remembered that he was tall, lanky, and handsome as sin.

All of the good ones are taken. It explains why I stuck with Matt for so long.

"Miller residence," her aunt said in her softly accented voice, a dead ringer for her sister when they were on the phone. It was a little creepy how similar they sounded, honestly.

"*Hola, Tia* Carmelita," Louisa said, slipping easily into Spanish. They chatted for just a moment and then, ever efficient, Carmelita dove into the heart of the conversation: She had a job for Louisa.

"You *what*?!" Louisa said, so startled she switched back to English without meaning to.

"A singer," Carmelita said, making the switch effortlessly and following Louisa's lead. "His son is a…how do you say… he cannot use his legs…"

"He's a paraplegic?"

"Yes, that is the word. He is only 12 and he cannot walk. Poor boy." *Tia* Carmelita sounded like she was on the verge of adopting the kid herself and Louisa chuckled under her breath. Carmelita was never as happy as she was when she had someone to cluck over, and since the youngest of the Miller boys was now probably pushing 29, she was likely going stir-crazy. A paraplegic child was just the person she'd love to mother-hen.

"His dad is Zane Risley," Carmelita continued. "Have you heard of Zane?"

"Ummm…no?" Louisa said, quickly searching her memory for any mention of that name, and coming up blank. "Did he graduate from Sawyer High School?"

"Oh no. He is a famous country music singer, at least according to Stetson. I do not know – I do not listen to such stuff. But Zane and Skyler got in a car wreck and now Skyler cannot walk. They flew here from Tennessee to attend Dr.

Whitaker's horse therapy camp but Zane needs someone to help take care of Skyler. Dr. Whitaker's wife, Kylie, called me after hearing from Abby that you might be available. I told her that you know far too much to be a nursemaid to a little boy but Kylie...she is stubborn. She insisted I ask."

It was on the tip of Louisa's tongue to ask who the hell Dr. Whitaker and Kylie and Abby were, but decided to let it go for the moment. She had to focus and figure out a tactful way to say thanks but no thanks. She was an RN with a bachelor's degree in nursing, dammit. Before she quit, the hospital had been training her to take over in preparation for the charge nurse of their floor retiring, at which point Louisa would've been in charge of a crew of over 15 nurses.

She had not gone to four years of school just to hold the hand of a little boy and blow his nose, no matter how sad his story was.

"He cannot walk because of...how you say...his back. No, his spine—"

"His spinal cord?" Louisa supplied, perking up. The unit she'd worked in was one of the premier spinal cord injury units in the US; people from all over the nation flew to Salt Lake to be treated by their unit. *Sounds like a crushed vertebra, or three. I wonder which ones. Did they do surgery? What was his prognosis? How long ago did this happen? Have they been doing therapy on him since then?*

"Yes, that is it," Carmelita said with satisfaction. Her aunt's English was superb, but Louisa doubted she had much reason to learn technical medical terminology. "His spinal cord. It was hurt. Over 18 months now, and he still does not walk. Poor boy."

"Which verte—" Louisa caught herself. Even if someone had told Carmelita all about the injury, it was doubtful she would've understood a word of it. *Tia* Carmelita was a housekeeper for a rancher, not a specialized doctor at a hospital. "Huh," Louisa said instead, tugging on her earlobe as she thought. "Do you know what happened to the last nurse?" It seemed awfully foolhardy to fly across the country to attend a horse therapy camp without the proper staff in tow.

"He did not like Idaho, I do not think. He is already gone back to Tennessee."

Louisa chewed her bottom lip. She was so overqualified for this job, she could do it in her sleep, but hell, hadn't she been thinking just a couple of weeks ago how nice it'd be to take a little vacation? Taking care of one small child would be a vacation, honestly, after being in charge of a whole floor full of needy patients.

And shit, a famous singer? He probably had loads of cash. She'd make sure he paid out of his nose for her specialized care. This could make a nice dent in her student loans. Maybe even wipe them out.

Damn, that'd be nice.

"Tell them I'm interested," Louisa said finally. "Let me know what I need to do next."

It was, Louisa thought as she hung up the phone and stared dazedly at the wall, not at all what she thought Carmelita would be calling her about. Not that she had any idea what Carmelita would be calling about – recipe exchange? discussions about the price of beef? – but a job was definitely not on the list. She'd planned on spending the day applying for jobs at hospitals across the country but suddenly, this easy-as-pie position had just fallen into her lap.

Never one to question her good fortune, she sought Alex out. They could play a little *fútbol* after all.

CHAPTER 2

"Y OU FOUND A NURSE for me?!" Zane repeated, stunned.

On the first day of camp – was that only yesterday? It seemed so much longer – when Zane had confessed to Dr. Whitaker's wife, Kylie, that he needed a nurse for Skyler, he'd done it mostly because they kept expecting him to know how to help Skyler transfer from his wheelchair to the saddle on the back of the horse, and he finally confessed that he just didn't help with that sort of thing. His gone-forever-back-to-Tennessee aide usually did.

The nurse had not only gotten a ride back to Tennessee on Zane's private plane at no cost, he'd done so with a six-figure check in his pocket – his payment to keep his mouth shut about what a horror Skyler was.

The nurse'd lasted a whole eight months – a record – but apparently salt in his coffee was a step too far.

Zane had already called the staffing agency and demanded a replacement, but they'd sounded dubious about their abilities to convince yet another nurse to take a stab at being Skyler's assistant. Apparently, Skyler's...difficult nature had made the rounds at the agency and no one wanted to take him on.

No shit, Sherlock. He's a hellion. Of course *no one wants to take care of him, least of all me.*

He was, without a doubt, the worst father on the face of the planet. Not only could he not take care of his son himself, he couldn't even convince anyone else to do it either, not for love or money. Or the love of money.

But now, the veterinarian's *wife* was telling him that she'd found someone for him. Was this for real?

"But…who?" he finally got out. There was *no way* he could hire some rando that some chick was recommending to him. He needed the nurse to be vetted and FBI background checks and the whole nine yards.

But still, he was a little bit curious who they'd found in the backwoods of Idaho to take care of his child. Some high school student who wanted to be in the medical field someday? A 97-year-old woman who was in diapers herself?

Licensed, professional, skilled nurses did not simply sit around No Name, Idaho, waiting for someone to come along and hire them.

"Well, Adam's best friend is Wyatt Miller," Kylie began. "Wyatt is married to Abigail. Abigail was visiting Jennifer and Stetson last week, which was when Carmelita, their housekeeper, mentioned that her niece had quit her job at the University of Utah Hospital and had moved back home to Pocatello. So when I mentioned to Abby that you needed someone to help you, she knew just who to call."

Kylie smiled angelically up at him, her thick blonde hair in a long braid over her shoulder, acting for all the world as if that game of telephone that she'd just rattled off should make total sense to him.

"This…uhhh…what was her name?" Zane asked, keeping an eye on Skyler, who was apparently throwing some sort of tantrum over the saddle they were using. Adam seemed to have it under control for the moment, but Zane wasn't taking his eyes off the scene, just in case.

"Louisa," Kylie supplied.

"Louisa," Zane repeated absentmindedly. "What was her position at the hospital?"

He was ready for Kylie to say administration or bookkeeping so he could dismiss the idea out of hand and get on with his life, when she came back with, "She was a nurse in the spinal cord injuries unit at the University of Utah Hospital, which, Carmelita informed Abby who informed me, is one of the top hospitals in the nation for spinal cord injuries."

Zane wrenched his eyes away from the power struggle playing out to stare, slack-jawed, at Kylie. "And this nurse wants to come take care of my child? Doesn't she have patients of her own to take care of?"

Kylie shrugged. "Abby didn't seem to know why Louisa wasn't at the hospital anymore, but it sounds like something personal happened. You'll have to ask her. But honestly, if she's Carmelita's niece, you couldn't do any better. There is no finer people than Carmelita."

Zane searched his mind, trying to remember if he'd met this paragon of virtue, this Carmelita, since arriving in Idaho, but came up blank. He'd never been great at names, and it was really starting to bite him in the ass.

"Hold on, did you say that Carmelita is a housekeeper?" he asked. Maybe he'd screwed up the story. Maybe this perfect soul was someone else completely.

"Yup," Kylie replied cheerfully. She did everything cheerfully. Zane tried not to let this fact grate on his nerves. "She's been the housekeeper for the Miller household all her life, from what I've been told. Her parents helped take care of the Millers and then Carmelita took over as soon as she graduated from high school."

"And the housekeeper's *niece* is – was – a nurse at one of

the top spinal cord units in the country?" He tried not to slather the sarcasm on too thick. Somebody was playing a practical joke on him, and he couldn't say he exactly appreciated that.

"Isn't that the American Dream?" Kylie asked softly, her light green eyes piercing through him. "That if you work hard, you can be whatever you want to be?"

"Right. Of course. I just…" He scrambled around to find words that wouldn't make him sound like a bigoted asshole. "I was just surprised," he finished lamely.

"I think you'll be really happy with Louisa," Kylie said with finality. "I'll tell Abby to tell Carmelita to tell Louisa to send over her resumé. I'll make sure it's here when you two come back for therapy lessons tomorrow. Will that work for you?"

Zane opened up his mouth, tried to think of a reasonable – and non-assholish – excuse to give as to why that would not work, came up with nothing at all, nodded, and closed his mouth.

"Good," Kylie said, pleased. "I'm going to go check on my daughter, Ruby Carol. I think Skyler might need a hand." She nodded towards his son, which Zane saw, with a sigh, was yelling at some Mexican kid. She headed towards the house while Zane moved over to the squabbling pre-teens.

"Dad," Skyler whined, drawing the name out to two syllables, "this kid won't let me ride Midnight. Says that he's the only one who rides her. I told him that my dad pays good money for me to be here, and I can ride any damn horse I want to."

Zane raised one eyebrow in silent rebuke of his son's profanity, and then turned towards the Mexican kid. "Hi, I'm Zane Risley," he said smoothly, putting out his hand to shake. He found over the years that his name, height, and demeanor tended to get him what he wanted, and knew that some scrawny 12-year-old was no match for him. "And you are…?"

"Juan Miller," the boy said, hesitantly shaking Zane's hand and then whipping his hand behind his back. "I am Dr. Whitaker's assistant," he added proudly. "This is my second year of being paid to work here, and I say no kid rides Midnight except for me."

"Is she your favorite horse?" Zane asked, delicately feeling out the reasoning at play here.

He shrugged. "I like her. But mostly it's because she's not always nice. If she gets riled up, she'll throw her rider. Skyler isn't good enough to ride her yet. He just started riding earlier this week."

Zane nodded thoughtfully and then turned towards his son, who had his bottom lip stuck out so far, it'd probably collect water in a rainstorm.

"But I want to ride her!" Skyler yelled. "If *he* can ride her, *I* can ride her."

Right. This wasn't going well at all.

Zane looked around for Adam, hoping to spot the tall veterinarian close by so he could come to his rescue. Alas, he was busy saddling up another horse for a little girl with pigtails. Why in the hell did Zane pay all of this money for this camp if his son wasn't even going to be taken care of? Adam needed to hire more employees – there needed to be more than just him and a little kid running the joint.

This camp had seemed like such a good idea when Zane had first spotted an article about it online. Horses? What kid didn't just love horses? And since Skyler'd already been kicked out of a music therapy camp *and* an art therapy camp, Zane had been looking at a summer calendar empty of anything even vaguely entertaining for Skyler to do. A horse therapy camp out in the middle of nowhere?

Why the hell not.

But now…

"IIIII wwwaaannnnttttt tttoooooo!!!!" Skyler was really

working up a head of steam now. Zane looked back at Juan desperately, but the kid's jaw was set as hard as stone.

"Can't you just have Skyler sit on the horse's back while you lead it around?" Zane hollered over the noise. Anything to get his son to stop yelling. "Just right here in the paddock. The horse can't do much here."

He was practically pleading a twelve-year-old boy for permission to ride a damn horse. What had his life come to?

"What's going on?" Dr. Whitaker asked, unruffled, as he joined the little group. Juan and Skyler fought to talk over each other and get their side of the story out, but Zane just closed his eyes with relief. Dr. Whitaker could take care of the situation. He'd know what to do.

Zane walked away, heading for the shade of the barn and rubbed his temples, trying to smooth a pounding headache away. Suddenly, this Louisa chick sounded like a gift from the gods. As long as she passed a background check, he'd hire her sight unseen. Anything – anyone – was better than this. She had to know how to deal with Skyler better than he did. God only knew it wasn't possible to know less.

CHAPTER 3

LOUISA

C HECKING HER PHONE for directions again, Louisa turned right onto a deeply rutted road and began bouncing along it, gritting her teeth in an attempt to keep from accidentally biting her own tongue from the sheer force of the jerking of the car. Why, for heaven's sakes, did one of the biggest stars in the country music business live on a road like *this*? Didn't he make enough from his record deals to be able to pay for a road grader to come fix this mess?

She'd signed a summer-long contract sight unseen, which meant she was stuck in this job for the whole summer. How many times would she drive this road in the next 105 days? Did her contract cover car repairs, like her transmission falling out of the bottom of the car after it hit its 19th pot hole? Somehow, she didn't think it did.

After what seemed like an eternity – or seven – her phone began chirping excitedly that she had arrived at her destination just as a monstrously oversized house came into view. Louisa couldn't help gaping at it as she slammed on her brakes to stare up through the windshield.

This was…

She used to make fun of the McMansions – huge, grand

houses out in the middle of a farm field; farmers or ranchers doing their best to show off how very big they were in their very little pond – but this house was more than a McMansion. It *was* a mansion. Who would build a house this big outside of Franklin, Idaho, for heaven's sakes? Her parents were from Sawyer and even she only barely knew where Franklin was at. A house like this should be in the hills of California, not on the outskirts of a tiny mountain tourist town.

Finally realizing that parking smack-dab in the middle of the open parking lot in front of the mansion probably wasn't appropriate, Louisa slowly crept forward into a parking spot and killed the engine. In the silence, she could hear birds chirping and squirrels chattering as they swooped from giant pine to giant pine, busy with their lives, industriously working away.

Squirrels can find a purpose in their lives. Why can't I?

Shaking off the thought, she pushed herself out of her car and began walking briskly towards the front door, up the paving stone path laid in a curve that ended at the oversized wooden front door. As she went, she instinctively kept track of the accessibility of the place, noting with surprise that there were no steps for someone in a wheelchair to struggle over, nor was the path too skinny or bumpy for a wheelchair to be able to easily navigate. From what Louisa had been able to gather, Zane had just shown up in the last week or so, and was only in Long Valley for a horse therapy camp for his son. Surely he hadn't had this mansion built for him beforehand.

Which meant that he'd somehow managed to rent (or buy, she supposed) what appeared to be a handicap accessible mansion in the wilds of Idaho.

What are the chances that something like this would be on the market?

If you had enough money, you could make almost anything happen, she guessed.

She rapped on the dark wood, the decorative carvings so

elaborate that her eyes had a hard time figuring out where they should rest, and then the door swung open noiselessly. There stood Zane Risley. Louisa knew it was him because she'd done a quick Google Image search after she'd been informed that she'd been hired, wanting to know *something* about the man she was about to go work for, and the man in front of her…

It was definitely him. Blond hair that ran in curls and waves to his broad shoulders, and bright blue eyes that had been so captivating on her computer screen, she'd been sure that they'd been enhanced through Photoshop.

But now she knew they hadn't been. She'd never seen such intense, such brilliant blue eyes in her life and every bit of her professionalism, her training, seemed to drain away in the face of it. This was a bad idea – a *very* bad idea. He looked much too much like Matthew. When she'd looked at the pictures on Google, she'd thought maybe it was just a trick of the camera, of the angle, but now that she was standing in front of him, she realized he could easily pass as Matthew's long-lost brother, but an upgraded version.

While she'd always thought Matt was a cute guy, next to Zane…well, Matt's hair had been a little shorter; his eyelashes not as thick; his eyes a more dull blue; his shoulders not quite so broad; his legs not quite so long.

He quite literally paled in comparison to this handsome god in front of her.

Speaking of God, this had to be God's reminder that no matter how handsome Zane Risley was, she wanted absolutely nothing to do with him. She wasn't *that* dumb.

I'm listening, Dios mío. *I won't make that mistake again. I am here for his son, not him, no matter how blue his eyes are.*

He spoke first. "I'm Zane Risley," he said, putting out a hand to shake. Instinctively, she reached out too, and it was this automatic movement that jolted her out of her trance.

"I'm Louisa Vargas," she said, shaking his hand quickly and then dropping her hand back down to her side.

Zane stepped back and swept his arm in a welcoming gesture, letting her walk by him. She instantly felt a wall of stifling perfection wash over her as she stepped through the doorway. This had been decorated by a professional designer, she was absolutely sure of it. There was roughly a zero percent chance or so that the man standing in front of her had picked out the gilt-framed paintings or the dark wood furniture or the oppressively ornate curtains. It looked like the lair of a seriously rich 95-year-old white man, not the 30-something-year-old country music singer standing in front of her in a wife beater, ripped jeans, and bare feet.

Oh, and blond hair down to his shoulders.

No, this house did not fit this man, not at all.

Before Louisa could ask any questions and piece together the mystery, the dark-paneled elevator doors slid open and out wheeled a boy on the cusp of becoming a teenager, his blond hair so light, it looked like ripe wheat just before harvest. He rolled to a stop, expertly maneuvering in his wheelchair without a thought to making it happen.

He's used to the wheelchair now. He isn't wanting out of it. The drive, the desire…it isn't there. He's resigned himself to it.

She'd asked for Skyler's medical records before accepting the job, signing an NDA before receiving it stating that she wouldn't reveal its contents to anyone, and then poured over them, trying to piece together what'd happened, understanding the medical terminology in the records as easily as she understood English. Skyler's T12 vertebra had been crushed in the accident, all of the force of the accident hitting him in that exact spot, like someone had taken aim at his spine. He'd had other damage, of course – a broken arm, contusions, cuts – but all of that had long ago healed. It was only the spinal cord damage that'd had long-lasting effects.

Well, that and losing his mother in a car wreck, but those

were the kinds of wounds to the heart that no nurse could heal.

"Hey, Skyler," Louisa said quietly, smiling just a little, wanting to appear friendly and kind without being overwhelming. "I'm Louisa Vargas, your new nurse." She put her hand out to shake, and with a quick glance at his father, Skyler shook her hand, his fingers delicate and limp and small inside of hers. He jerked his hand back and then stared up at her, not saying anything, just assessing. She stared right back, not saying anything, waiting for him to finish his assessment of her. She wasn't in any rush. She could wait for him to make a move.

"You're a nurse?" he finally asked, his skepticism blazingly obvious. She apparently didn't fit his idea of what a nurse should look like.

"I am. Have been for a while now. I've never had just one patient, though. I usually have a whole floor of patients that I'm in charge of. So you could say that I'm new to being a one-at-a-time nurse."

He took that in and then nodded slowly, abruptly wheeling over to sit by his dad, saying without words that his loyalty laid with him.

Zane looked down at Skyler, the surprise crystal clear on his face.

He isn't used to Skyler siding with him. I wonder how close they really are…

"You…uhhh…you want me to show you up to your room?" Zane asked, stammering a little, still staring down at the top of his son's head as he asked the question.

"Sure, thank you. And I need you to show me where to park. I only saw the open parking area out front – is there parking out back for staff?"

"Yes, although I don't have many here. Staff, that is. You, a chef who comes out once a day to cook dinner, a housekeeper who comes three times a week to clean, and then the gardeners and groundskeepers are all managed by the rental property company. I don't see them at all."

Well, that answered at least part of that question – this was a rental, not a purchase.

Zane headed for the stairs, Louisa right behind him, her overnight bag slung over her shoulder, the rest of her luggage in the car. She'd get oriented in the house and then work on getting settled. Behind her, she could hear Skyler rolling off into the elevator, the doors sliding closed behind him with a quiet ding.

"He seems to be taking this well," Louisa said quietly as they walked, mostly just to fill the silence that was piling on between them, growing thicker by the moment. Did he *have* to look like an upgraded, five-star version of her ex?

This really *isn't fair*.

"Yeah, he is," Zane said, and there was that surprise again. So she hadn't been imagining it – he hadn't expected Skyler to react quietly to getting a new nurse.

And she really didn't want to think how that boded for the rest of her summer.

CHAPTER 4

ZANE

FROM THE MOMENT that Louisa stepped through the front door, he felt like someone had sucked the oxygen from the room. She wasn't what he expected – not at all. She was young. Like, younger than him, and that wasn't right. She was supposed to be old and wrinkled and able to quell Skyler with just one look and be so terrifying, his son would never even dream of being a back-talking asshat again.

He should've realized how young she was based on the dates of her college diploma, which she listed on her resumé, but he'd thought she'd gone back to school after the kids left home. Why had he been so pigheaded about this? Why had he so stubbornly clung to the idea that Louisa was an old woman?

Actually, that was an easy answer: Her name. He didn't know anyone their age with the name of Louisa. It was an old woman's name – something a grandmother would be called.

If it had just been her age, he would've been fine. He met people all of the time his age, obviously. He normally didn't hire them to be his son's nurse, but he'd get over that.

No, it was her looks that'd practically struck him mute.

Dark, stick-straight hair almost to her waist, huge brown eyes, milk chocolate skin that begged to be kissed and licked. She was tall for being a Latina – maybe 5'9" or so, which made her the perfect height to bend over and kiss…

He shook his head like a dog shaking off water after a dip in the river. *She's an employee. You don't get to touch employees any more than you get to turn back time and make your wife and child sit with their seat belts on. That simply isn't an option.*

"Where did your parents get the name Louisa?" he asked casually as he stopped to push the door open to the bedroom she'd be staying in that summer. It was just two rooms down from Skyler's bedroom, and three rooms down from his.

Suddenly, he wished he'd thought to put her in the guest quarters over the garage. That distance seemed much safer for his sanity, but it was too late now.

"My grandmother," Louisa said, shooting him a little smile as she passed by him and into the room. She smelled fresh, like spring after a long, hard winter. He tried not to breathe in too deeply. "My mother is the youngest girl out of four, and somehow, out of all of my cousins, no one had been named after my grandmother, so my mother snatched up the name and used it for me. Americanized it by adding in the O, though. In Spanish, there is no O. Lovely room."

"Oh. Thanks." He looked around quickly, registering the room for the first time. When the housekeeper told him that she'd cleaned a room for Louisa, he'd just said thanks and went back to scrolling through Facebook. It hadn't occurred to him to actually look at the room, but now that he did, he wasn't happy. It was dark and masculine and not at all suited to the woman who was now standing in it. "We can re-decorate if you'd like," he offered. "Since you'll be staying here for 3 months, it—"

"No, no, I'm fine," she assured him. "It's nice, really."

She hated it. He could see it in her eyes. Why hadn't the

housekeeper told him that the room was better suited to a stuffy old grandpa than a gorgeous woman?

Because you never asked. And because you didn't know she was a young gorgeous woman anyway. And—

"Well, okay then," he said lamely. "I'll just leave you to it. Oh, wait! You have other luggage. I'll help you carry it up here." Inwardly, he cursed the fact that he'd passed on taking his security guard, Andrew, with him out to Idaho. Andrew's wife'd just had a baby and Zane hadn't wanted to uproot them and move them to Idaho for the summer, and after all, nothing ever happened in Idaho. He'd be fine without the security out here.

But now, just when he could've pawned this off onto Andrew and gone on with his life, Andrew wasn't there. If Zane let a woman carry her own luggage in, his mother would have a heart attack. She wasn't good for much, but making sure her son had manners was definitely on the short list.

"I'm all right," she said brightly as she moved about the room, opening up the curtains and letting the filtered sunlight in. "I've been sitting for a while – long drive from Pocatello. It's good to stretch my legs. I'm not used to sitting." She flashed him a smile as she brushed past him and back into the hallway, the clean spring smell trailing behind her. He felt his dick tighten at the glimpse of straight, white teeth, her lips a perfect pink bow.

He was well and truly screwed.

CHAPTER 5

LOUISA

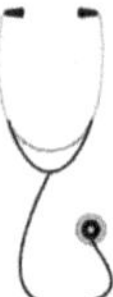

L OUISA SAT IN BED for a while after waking up, enjoying the chance to just lie there and read a book. When was the last time she'd done that? Working 12-hour shifts at the hospital meant she left for work early and came home late, so lounging around in bed for hours was ridiculously decadent. Like swimming through a pool of dark, rich chocolate, but even better.

Finally, around 8:15 or so, she heard some stirrings down the hallway and figured that the Risleys were coming alive for the day. They weren't awake at 5:15 like she was but hey, 8:15 wasn't terrible. She wasn't sure if she'd be able to work for a family who slept in until noon each day. Every day, she'd feel like her whole day had been wasted, and that was nothing short of hell on earth. She liked being busy and productive.

She set her latest book off to the side – *The Pursuit of Happyness* – and headed for the hall where she met a very sleepy and rumpled Zane. His eyes were only open to half mast, and he looked like he'd just rolled out of bed.

He looked delicious.

She sent him a bland smile and said cheerfully, "Is Skyler up already?"

He blinked a couple of times, his brain slowly processing her words, and then eventually said, "Skyler. Right. No, I'm not sure where he's at. Is he awake?"

She decided to ignore his question. He was obviously one of those people who didn't function until he'd had at least a cup of coffee in his system; maybe even a whole pot.

"Let's go downstairs," she said with another bland smile, and they headed for the staircase, her skipping down it as he lumbered after her. They could use the elevator, of course – there was nothing saying they had to always stick to the staircase while Skyler always used the elevator – but Louisa did not want to be inside of a small 4'x4' enclosed space with Zane Risley.

Nope, not even a little bit. The staircase was much, *much* safer.

They walked into the breakfast nook off the kitchen which she'd found during her explorations the night before, and saw Skyler was already there, pulled up to the end of the table, the spot built specifically for people in wheelchairs. He looked up at them as they came in, a weirdly bright smile on his face.

Louisa knew that face. She'd seen it plenty of times during the course of her life. Five younger siblings, and all of them thought that practical jokes were just hilarious, and liked to see what they could get away with.

Skyler thought he was about to pull something over on her, she was willing to bet her next year's paycheck on it.

"Good morning, Skyler," she said, her tone friendly and unsuspecting. It was best if they thought they'd won. It made the loss just that much more painful. "Wow, you made us coffee?" she said, looking at the two mugs sitting on the table, steam rising from them, while Skyler had a glass of milk and piece of white bread toast in front of him. "How sweet."

Skyler's grin grew. "Oh yeah," he said, all but rubbing his hands together with glee. "That mug is yours," he pointed to his right, "and that mug is Dad's," he pointed to his left.

She felt Zane stiffen up behind her and knew without a doubt that he too was sure her coffee had been doctored in some horrendous way. Skyler really needed to up his game if he thought he could pull one over on her like this. Before Zane could say anything, Louisa quickly snagged her cup off the table.

"Thank you so much," she said loudly, drowning out the warning Zane was trying to sputter.

Had Skyler done this before? Probably.

Was this why the last aide decided that Idaho just wasn't for them? Probably.

She took a tiny sip and instantly, the strong taste of salty coffee invaded her mouth.

It was, to put it lightly, absolutely disgusting. Salt and coffee were *not* a good mix. Skyler watched her, the anticipation for the spewing out of her coffee and the yelling about to come, having him on the edge of his seat.

"It seems like there's something wrong with this," she said mildly, pulling the mug away from her lips. "Salt?"

Crestfallen, Skyler nodded. She hadn't screamed or ranted or raved or spit out her coffee. That hadn't been *nearly* the show he'd been hoping for.

"I have five younger siblings," Louisa said bluntly. "If you're going to pull practical jokes on me, you better step up your game."

"Five younger..." Skyler stopped abruptly, the desire to hear more stamped all over his face. He was an only child. Of course he wanted to know more about having five brothers and sisters.

But he was also bound and determined to hate her.

Oh, the quandary...

"Yup. Two brothers and three sisters. Two out of the three

sisters are actually identical twins," she said mildly. "I swear those two were trying to pull pranks on me since the day they were born. It took me years before I could tell them apart. Anyway," she said, waving her hand dismissively, "now that you've made this disgusting cup of coffee, you get to drink it." She sent him a beatific smile as she set it down on the table and pushed it towards him, and then headed for the coffee pot to pour herself a clean, non-spoiled cup.

"Drink…?!" He was practically spluttering at the thought. "I can't drink…Dad!" He turned in his wheelchair and sent his father a look that was a mixture of horror and pleading. "I'm just a kid. Kids can't drink coffee."

"They can if they think that it's okay to ruin someone else's," Louisa put in mildly. "If you thought it was okay for me to drink, then it's certainly okay for you to drink." She didn't even look at Zane for approval. Either he backed her on this, or she was heading home. Screw the contract. She wasn't about to spend the summer having everything she said countermanded by Zane.

Hell no.

"Coffee stunts the growth of kids," Zane said, and at that, Louisa's eyes did shoot up to meet his. Really? Dammit all, she'd had such high hopes for getting her student loans paid off early. "But one cup won't make a difference," he continued smoothly. "You made it, you can drink it."

The silence at that was almost palpable. "You…I… Daaadddddddd!!!" Skyler wailed. Zane sat back in the booth and simply smiled at his son.

Huh. It was going to be a great summer after all.

CHAPTER 6

ZANE

ANE TAPPED THE STEERING WHEEL of the Audi Q7 rental, whistling cheerfully under his breath as he drove. He snuck a peek in the rearview mirror at Skyler in the backseat. Yup, still pissed.

Zane grinned to himself as he refocused on the road. He just had to make it through today so Louisa knew how to get Skyler to the therapy camp, and then after that, he was free. Monday through Friday, 9:00 to 2:00, he would be childfree.

He turned the radio up louder, just barely refraining from bursting into song. He loved his son. He'd die for his son. But he had absolutely *no* idea how to manage him, and somehow, he'd lucked out into hiring someone – sight unseen – who did. In fact, after Skyler had whined and moaned and fought drinking the doctored coffee for far too long, threatening to make them late for therapy camp, Louisa had cheerfully poured it into a thermos, after warming it up, of course – "After all, no one wants to drink cold coffee," she'd said with a perfectly straight face – and then had handed it over with an angelic smile. "Here. This way, when you're thirsty today, you can have something to drink."

In that moment, Zane was quite sure Skyler's dearest desire had been to dump the coffee over her head, but he didn't. Instead, he'd dropped the thermos into his lap and snarled something that Zane was happy he didn't hear, and sped off in his wheelchair. Louisa hadn't batted an eyelash. Apparently, she was used to patients hurling obscenities at her.

Yup, hiring her was the best decision Zane had made all summer. Maybe even all year.

"So, tell me about this therapy camp," Louisa half-shouted over the music, bringing him back to the present. Even as she talked to him, she was watching out of her window at the passing fields of cows and horses, grazing peacefully on the bright green pastures. "How did you find it, first of all? Aren't you from Tennessee?"

She seemed strangely determined to look out the window even as they talked, which he found disconcerting. Did he have something on his face? He discreetly checked the rearview mirror. He looked like he always did.

Weird.

"I am. Born and raised in Nashville," he said, turning the radio back down so they could have a conversation at a decent level. "Almost every kid in my class grew up thinking they were going to be the next Garth Brooks or Reba McEntire. You should've seen our talent shows at school – everybody's talent was either dancing or singing or both. I'm one of the damn lucky few who actually made it in the music world."

Finally, she turned in her seat and was looking at him, and he found a sudden urge to watch the road very, very carefully. Best not get into another car wreck, right?

"Anyway, I ended up here because I found an article about Dr. Whitaker's horse camp online one day. I liked that he only worked with kids – no adults would be attending the camp – and in the video that accompanied the article…I don't know. He seemed like a straight shooter." He shrugged. "Passionate. Some of my friends thought I was nuts for going out to Idaho for an entire summer, but hell, it wasn't like I was doing much back in Tennessee." He tried to laugh cheerfully, as if that was nothing more than a very funny joke, but the laughter came out sarcastic and bitter instead. He hurried on before she could have too much time to contemplate that laugh. "Adam's been great so far – it's a good camp."

"Who's Adam?" Louisa asked, her brows knitted together in confusion.

"Dr. Adam Whitaker. You know, the veterinarian. I thought you were from around here." Now it was his turn to look confused.

"Oh no. I've only been up here a few times myself. My parents were born here; my aunt Carmelita has lived here all her life; my grandparents lived here practically for forever; but when my parents got married, they moved to Pocatello." At his blank look, she clarified, "One of the larger cities in Idaho – on the other side of the state, though. Anyway, my dad got a job with the state transportation department and has been in eastern Idaho ever since. We've come to Sawyer a handful of times for family events and such, but I've never lived here."

"So, do any of your other aunts or uncles still live here, or just Carmelita?"

"Only Carmelita is still here. My aunt María lives outside of Seattle and Aunt Consuelo lives in American Falls, only a few miles from my mom's house. No uncles. Four girls on my mom's side, and my dad was an only child. Carmelita didn't have any kids but my aunt María and Consuelo sure did, so I grew up with lots of cousins, and of course, five younger brothers and sisters. Life was…never boring, let's put it that way." She gave him a rueful smile.

Before Zane could probe more – he was sure more than a few insane stories were hidden behind that smile – he realized they'd already reached the therapy camp. "We're here," he said with a cheerfulness he didn't feel as he pulled to a stop in front of the barn.

He didn't want to stop talking to Louisa. She was simply so damn easy to talk to. She was…

Well, she was…

Before he could come up with just the right word that captured her verve and personality, though, he realized that he was leaving the hardest part of the whole camp experience for Louisa to do by herself. Getting Skyler in and out of the SUV – well, and getting him on and off the horses – was a damn struggle. He'd almost dropped his son on his head last Friday, a fiasco he was sure Skyler was never going to let him forget.

With an inner groan, he forced himself out of the SUV and around to the passenger side to help Louisa get Skyler out of the car. This was–

"What the hell?!" he blurted out. He hadn't meant to say that, of course. He just…

Louisa looked up at him, her expression quizzical, as she helped Skyler arrange his legs on the footrest of the wheelchair and his hated thermos of coffee in his lap, before he took off for the barn like a scalded cat. She'd already gotten him out of the SUV and into the wheelchair in the time it took Zane to walk around the vehicle. How was that even possible? He knew she had a lot of experience transferring patients in and out of places, but still…

"What's wrong?" she asked, but her gaze wasn't on him. Her eyes had followed Skyler and he could tell she was anxious to be closer to him, in case he needed help. Skyler was already disappearing in through the open barn door.

"Nothing," he said quickly. "I didn't mean to keep you from him."

With a brief, professional smile, she took off after Skyler, her J.Lo ass swinging enticingly with every step.

Kids today would call that a Kim Kardashian Ass. You're showing your age, old man.

Whatever. He didn't care. He preferred Jennifer Lopez – who actually had talent and a good heart – over Kim Kardashian any day of the week.

And, more importantly, he really shouldn't be checking out Louisa's ass, no matter how J.Lo-esque it was.

Hands off the help, asshole.

He began to follow after that enticing ass when he stopped. He didn't actually have to go in there and stand amongst all of the other parents and pretend that they weren't staring at him and whispering behind their hands, while they pretended that a huge country music star wasn't standing in their midst. With Louisa there, she'd make sure Skyler was taken care of, and he could…

He looked around the place curiously. Well, he could find something else to do until they were done for the day. Then after today, he'd be free every day. He could finally start creating music again and sing and decide what in the hell he was doing with his life. Really get his head screwed on straight.

With a cheerful refrain from his last album running through his head, he headed for a pen that had the oddest noises coming out of it. His curiosity was almost irresistible, and he could only hope that the Whitakers wouldn't be offended by him poking around into parts of the farm they probably weren't intending him to see.

He folded his arms across the top of a dilapidated fence and looked down over the other side, spotting a small flock of chickens, all scratching in the grass, their butts pointed towards the sky, clucking and talking amongst each other as they worked to catch the worms.

Oh. So that's what chickens sounded like in real life. Somehow, he'd always imagined them more raucous than this. Instead, they were content, at peace with the world, like they knew exactly what needed to be done and were doing it without another thought or concern.

What would it be like to be so sure about what I was doing? What if I was this focused?

He used to be. He used to be driven to be on top. To beat everyone else. And he had been beating everyone else. If only they'd made it to the CMAs, he would've found out while sitting in the audience that he'd won *Male Vocalist of the Year*. He would've gone up to the stage and given the acceptance speech he'd been practicing since he was five years old.

But he hadn't made it to the CMAs and when he'd been told later that he'd won the most prestigious award in country music, it hadn't meant a thing to him. That night, all of his drive, his ambition, had simply disappeared. As he'd tried to explain to Jacob – a close friend and fellow musician – a couple of months ago, it was like his tank had run out of gas and no matter how hard he pushed on the pedal, nothing happened. He was stuck in place, and didn't know how to get out.

Maybe, he thought, the noises of the chickens lulling him into some quiet moments of serenity, he'd actually acted on the horse therapy impulse because there was something or someone here who he needed to meet, or do. Maybe he was supposed to move forward in his life this summer when he hadn't been able to for the last 18 months.

Or maybe he'd gotten literally stuck in place – not moving from Nashville, not touring, not traveling, his grief wearing him down – and this trip across the country was exactly what he needed.

He wasn't much for believing in fate or destiny or God – especially not after Skyler lost his ability to walk *and* his mother at the same time – but maybe it didn't matter if he believed or not.

Maybe it was all true anyway.

A loud squawk jerked him out of his thoughts and he looked up to see one light brown chicken running as fast as her short legs would carry her, a squirming bug grasped tightly in her beak as another chicken, this one a black-and-white striped one, tore after her, clucking and squawking indignantly.

Zane chuckled to himself. Well, there went the theory that chickens led a zen life. God, he was losing it. He'd been starting to feel like chickens had it more together than he did, and just what did that say about his life?

Nothing good?

Shit. He'd once been on top of the world. Unstoppable. Unbeatable. Untouchable. Every kid in rural America had wanted to be him. He'd get that back someday. Now that he had Skyler taken care of, it was time to take care of himself. He—

"Hey, Zane Risley?" a man's voice said behind him, jerking him out of his thoughts. He spun on his heel and saw a man about his age or so striding towards him, his hips loose like every real cowboy Zane had ever seen. He wasn't as tall as Zane, but he was as muscular. He had a presence about him – a sureness of who he was without being cocky – that Zane instinctually liked.

"That's me," he said with an easy smile, holding his hand out to shake. "And you are?"

"Declan Miller." The guy's handshake was firm and strong, his face open and honest. There was an air about him that told Zane he wasn't there to pester him into signing autographs or take pictures or get an unguarded quote that could be used in a tell-all article. Zane prided himself on being an excellent judge of character, and everything in him said that this guy was a-okay. "I heard you were bringing your kid over to Adam's place for his therapy camp and thought I'd welcome you to the valley. Lots of good people here. Everyone been making you feel welcome?"

"Sure," Zane said. Not a lie, but not the truth either. Some of the other parents – specifically, the women – had been trying to walk that awkward line between being too friendly and butting into his life, and being standoffish and pretending he didn't exist. It'd been a while since he'd hung around "normal" people, and found that humanity hadn't changed at all – it was rare to find people who could walk that line and do it well.

"Good, good." Declan looked at the pen full of chickens – they'd calmed down and were back to pecking away in the dirt, their fat butts pointed towards the sky again – and chuckled. "Chickens are some funny creatures. Watchin' them is almost as interesting as watchin' pigs, although pigs are a hell of a lot smarter."

Pigs are smart? This was certainly a revelation to Zane. It was on the tip of his tongue to ask Declan if he was a pig farmer, when Declan continued, "Anyway, just thought that while you were in the area, you might want to go and hang out with the guys. Me and a bunch of my friends go down to the bar some Saturday nights and just shoot the shit. Our wives get together and bitch about how we drop our dirty socks on the floor and never think to pick them up, and the local high schoolers take the kids off our hands and make some extra cash. Works out well for everyone." He shot Zane a friendly grin. "If that sounds like somethin' you'd be interested in, we'd love to have you along."

"I don't have an old woman to complain about my socks," Zane said dryly, "but if you wanted me to send the housekeeper over to hang out with the women, she could probably provide a whole list of things I don't do right."

Declan threw his head back and laughed. "You can skip the old woman part of the equation. And your kid – is he old enough to be on his own, or should he be watched by a babysitter?"

"Oh yeah, he's good. He'll just spend the whole night blowing shit up on the Xbox One if I leave him to his own devices. But, I'd love to get out and do something, especially something that doesn't have anything to do with horses or chickens." Truthfully, he'd love to spend time around other people who weren't either his child or in his employ. He'd been cut off from the world for far too long.

Declan chuckled. "I promise you, O'Malley's doesn't have a single chicken or horse in it, although I think there's some decorations using saddles and horseshoes."

"I'll probably survive that. Saturday night, you say?" At Declan's nod, he asked, "What time?"

"Usually on around 7:30 or so. Late enough that we can eat with our families before going, but not so late that we end up staying all night. We're a bunch of old, married men. We don't party hard."

"Sounds good," Zane said with a smile.

The silence fell between them and they went back to watching the chickens scratch in the dirt, industriously finding every bit of interesting morsels available. Zane was surprised that he was comfortable around a guy he hardly knew, the silence not strained at all. What did Kylie call Carmelita a while back? Good people? That seemed to fit Declan, too.

"Well," Declan said after a while, "I better get a move-on. Lots of piglets just showed up and I best be checking in on them; make sure the moms are feeding well. Pigs are smarter than humans, I'd swear it, but they still need a little help along the way. See you Saturday," and with a tug on the brim of his cowboy hat, Declan turned on his heel and headed toward the row of trucks parked alongside the barn. He hopped into an oversized diesel truck, backed out, and headed back to town.

He doesn't have a kid in the program, or at least he didn't go look in on the kid while he was here. He came all of the way down here just to invite me over to the bar.

If everyone else in his group is as laid-back as Declan, I just might grow to love this town after all.

CHAPTER 7
LOUISA

L OUISA ABSENTMINDEDLY began tugging a brush through her hair, trying to decide what to do that day. It was Saturday, which meant no therapy camp, which meant it was just her and Skyler at the house all day, with Zane around…well, somewhere. After he'd driven her and Skyler to camp on Monday, he'd pretty much disappeared, leaving Skyler completely up to her. But with a whole empty day ahead—

Something was wrong, though. Her brush wasn't easily moving through her hair like it normally did. She tugged harder on it and felt a dull pain shoot through her head.

Ouch! What the hell?

Sleepily, she pulled the brush away from her scalp and watched in the mirror as her hair rose up in the air too, stuck like glue to the brush.

Stuck like glue—

She leaned in close to the mirror and squinted. There was…was that liquid stuff in her hair? She squinted harder. Sure enough, she could see the glint of golden liquid in her dark, straight hair.

Honey. Holy shit, that little terror put honey on my brush!

Carefully, she pulled the brush away, trying to keep as much of her hair intact as possible, wavering between laughing at Skyler's impressive leap forward in practical "jokes," and letting loose a string of swear words.

This morning, he'd played it straight, not sitting outside of her bathroom door and telling her that she really needed to brush her hair while holding the brush out to her. No, he'd poured a little string of honey on the brush, put it back, and walked away.

Well, wheeled away.

It would've been a lot funnier if it'd happened to someone else. As it was, Louisa was the one with a head full of honey, which did tend to severely limit the hilarity factor for her.

With a regretful sigh, she stripped off her bathrobe and stepped into the shower, setting the temperature as high as she could stand it. Her best bet would be to soften the honey and run it down the drain. At least, she hoped that'd work. It wasn't like she had previous experience with this.

She had long hair, almost down to her waist, and it'd been her one point of pride all her life. If she had to chop it all off to get the honey out…

Death and destruction would ensue.

Death and destruction.

As she carefully tried to pull the gooey honey out without taking chunks of hair out too, she managed to push past her shock and started to focus on revenge. Of course, the most obvious revenge of all was not to respond. Just like with the coffee – which it'd taken Skyler two days to finally finish but finish it he did – no reaction at all would put a pin in Skyler's balloon. What was the fun of putting honey on someone's hairbrush if they weren't even going to squeal and yell and run around like a crazy person afterward?

Almost no fun at all.

In fact, he'd probably be tempted to come into her bathroom to check on the hairbrush as soon as he thought he could get away with it, because if she was blasé about the whole thing, that'd make him think she just hadn't brushed her hair that morning, and thus hadn't run into the booby-trapped hairbrush. The curiosity, though, meant he'd have to double check…

The older sister in Louisa instantly kicked into action and she began daydreaming about rigging the door with a bucket of ice cold water to pour down on his head the moment he pushed the door open, but then she caught herself. She was an adult and this was her patient, not her younger brother. She couldn't *actually* make him regret the day he was born, like any decent older sister would.

As she continued to gently tug on her hair – the heat of the water softening the honey but still, she had so much damn hair, she was afraid this was going to take all day – she realized she could hurt him where he'd hate it the most, *and* do it under the guise of helping him.

Well, no, it actually would be helping him. She'd just be gaining revenge at the same time.

Two-fers. They were a brilliant thing.

After getting out what she hoped was all of the honey and carefully combing her hair into a long braid down her back, she hurried down to the walk-out basement, where she'd found that Skyler spent nearly every waking moment when he wasn't being forced to go elsewhere. As far as she could tell, Skyler lived and breathed solely for video games.

Well, that was all about to change.

Sure enough, she found him lounging on the couch in front of the large-screen TV, blasting away and killing something, his pencil-thin legs draped sideways across the leather. He didn't even bother saying hello; he just kept his eyes glued to the TV as blood splattered across the screen, turning it a brilliant red. She shuddered. As a nurse, seeing needless gore and violence like this was hardly a treat, but then again, she didn't figure she was the target demographic for Call of Duty.

Without a word of warning, Louisa walked up to Skyler and snatched the wireless controller out of his hands before he could realize what she was doing. They convulsed reflexively in the air, grabbing at the controller, but Louisa was already holding it above her head.

"What was that for?!" Skyler howled, his face turning red with anger. "Give that back to me – I'm going to—" Just then, the video beeped and then sounds of doom ensued, finishing with a pathetic-sounding beep.

His character was dead.

"You killed me!" Skyler hollered. "Give! That! Back!" He was swiping in the air, trying to reach it, but of course, Louisa had the height advantage on him even if he hadn't been sitting on a couch.

She just stood there, keeping a look of serenity pinned to her face, holding the controller above her head as she waited for the wailing and yelling to calm down. Once she could speak without having to shout to be heard, she said in a pleasant, even tone, "Before you start in on your day of vegging in front of the TV, slowly destroying your brain cells, we need to get your exercises done. Then you can kill off all of the brain cells your heart desires."

"What do you mean, kill off my brain cells?!" he demanded, his face a brilliant red. His arms were crossed across his chest as he stared up at her defiantly, ready to snatch at the controller as soon as she brought it even vaguely within reach.

"Countless – and I do mean countless, as in *too many to be able to count* – studies have shown that too much video game time is bad for your mental capacity, especially as a child. Your brain is developing, and you should be doing more than just jamming your thumbs down on a controller. However," she held up a hand to stop his cascade of protests, "considering that it's summertime, I'll let you destroy your brain all you want, *but*! You have to do your exercises first."

"What exercises?" He had his lower lip stuck so far out, she was surprised he could still talk around it. He had pouting down to a science.

"Physical therapy exercises. I'm not a physical therapist – I went to school to be a nurse, which means I'm rather good at giving you shots and helping you manage your pain, not rehab exercises – but I know enough to get by. Some of the PTs on the floor would get bored and liked to practice on us nurses when we had a slow afternoon, so I know a few things. We're going to start working on getting your legs back into shape, and how best to use your arms to help compensate for your loss of muscle control in your legs. Once you've done your PT for the day, you can kill as many imaginary beings on the Xbox as you want."

He glared at her, practically shaking with anger. "Why'd you have to kill me?" he demanded. "I could've just finished the level I was playing and *then* done the exercises. You didn't need to grab the controller like that."

"And you didn't need to put honey on my hairbrush," she said mildly.

Bam.

The guilt washed over his face and she knew in that moment that he'd completely forgotten about his little prank on her. She guessed he'd probably put the honey on last night, and in kid time, that was years ago. "So, I think we're even," she continued. "For now. But if the practical jokes continue, I'm going to be forced to do something a lot worse than kill off your character in a video game. You've been warned."

He gulped, his face draining of all color. She kept hers impassive. She'd been told by her younger siblings that she was terrifying when she wanted to be, and in that moment, she really, really wanted to be.

"Now, are you ready to do some exercises?" she asked, no hint of anger in her voice. It was like they'd just been discussing the weather, which was exactly how she wanted to play this. The guilt of what he did was enough – she didn't need to yell at him. She could see that plastered all over his face.

"I don't know why I need to," he muttered, looking away and staring at the floor. "It doesn't matter. I'm gonna be a cripple for the rest of my life. Why do a bunch of work just to stay stuck in this stupid chair?"

He wasn't meeting her eyes, and she knew in that moment that they'd finally hit on at least part of Skyler's problem. She was pretty sure his father's distant manner and losing his mother didn't help, of course. But that aside, he'd given up on the hope of ever getting better.

And without hope…

"I've read your file," she said softly, turning and putting the controller down on the top shelf of a built-in bookcase, next to some serious-looking tomes that she was quite sure no one had actually ever read. These were the kinds of books bought by an interior designer to impress, not to read. "I asked your dad for it before I even agreed to this job." She turned back to him and leaned casually against the bookcase, crossing her feet at the ankles, trying to convey a sense of calm and surety. "You *can* walk again. Based on the muscular responses after the accident, and where the damage was done, you could walk again just as easily as any other kid does. It's nothing but your choices that have kept you trapped in this chair."

But his face had gone blank and his eyes were glued to the floor as if he'd found the most interesting of sights down there. He didn't believe her.

No, he *couldn't* believe her. What if he tried, and he failed? Wouldn't it be better if he just didn't try at all?

At least, that's what he'd convinced himself was true.

Now, it was up to her to break through his defenses.

She was being stupid. She knew she was. The number one rule in dealing with patients in rehab was you could never want it more than the patient did. Well, you could, of course, but it wouldn't do you any good. You could want something more than you wanted to breathe, but if the patient didn't give a damn, all of your desires amounted to a hill of beans. How hard the patient was willing to work was what mattered. She'd seen patients overcome impossible odds through sheer dint of will.

Skyler didn't want it, or rather, he was too scared to want it. She'd read his file. He'd been sent home early from rehab because he'd stopped making any progress. He'd been trying in the beginning, but something had happened, and he'd quit. After that, the physical therapists had had to cajole him just to get out of bed. Progress had become a thing of the past, and eventually, they'd just sent him home, ready to move on to a patient who actually wanted to get better.

But Louisa was good at cajoling and prodding and pushing and refusing to take "no" for an answer. She also didn't have to justify her choice to continue to work with Skyler to the insurance company footing the bill. So yeah, she had a few tricks up her sleeve.

Now it was time to see if she could outsmart a 12-year-old boy.

CHAPTER 8

ZANE

"T HIS IS LEVI," Declan said, introducing Zane to a tall, dark-haired man who put out his hand to shake, "and his half-brother, Moose."

Zane was already turning to shake hands with the half-brother when Declan's words registered. "Come again?" he said blankly. He would've sworn he heard the name *Moose*, but that couldn't possibly be right.

"My birth certificate says Dear, but only my mother calls me that, and only when I'm in trouble," Moose said smoothly, shaking Zane's hand.

That didn't clear up a damn thing.

"Your mother named you 'Dear'?" Zane said slowly. "As in, 'Oh dear, I forgot to put the roast in the oven'?"

Small towns are officially strange-ass places.

"No, no," Moose said, laughing. "My father owns a John Deere dealership. I was named Deere after the tractor." He was smiling but there was something dark in his eyes, a shadow that Zane wondered about. No matter how much Moose was laughing about this story, there was something not-so-funny going on there. "But then all of my friends started calling me Moose instead, and the nickname stuck.

Get it? Deere? Moose? I guess I should just be grateful they didn't stick on Elk."

Zane let out a half-snort of laughter at that one.

"Levi and Moose are on the local volunteer fire department," Declan said with a proud smile, slapping Levi good-naturedly on the shoulder. "Last spring, the Muffin Man bakery caught fire, and these guys were the heroes, pulling people out. Compared to them, I live a damn boring life."

"Well, hell," Stetson, Declan's younger brother, put in, "that's 'cause you *are* boring. You think chattin' about pigs is a grand idea. It's a real good thing you talked Iris into falling in love with you back in high school, before she realized how damn boring you are. Now it's too late for her to back out of it!" Everyone busted up laughing as Declan shot his younger brother a disgusted look.

Rolling his eyes, Declan turned back towards Zane and began talking as if his younger brother hadn't said a word. "So, you're here so your son can attend Adam's therapy camp. Are you doing some riding yourself while you're here?"

Stetson, Declan, their older brother Wyatt, and the two firefighters all turned expectantly towards Zane, waiting for his answer. He shot them a pained smile.

"Honestly? Uhhhh…I've never been on a horse."

My publicist would kill me if she heard me admit that in public.

After all, a "real" country music star was supposed to pack concert halls on the weekends and brand cows during the week. Hiding his complete lack of any so-called "country" skills – virtually anything to do with farm animals, hunting, fishing, or ranching – had been a big part of his publicist's job.

Not surprisingly, this group reacted exactly how Zane had expected them to. There was dead silence in their little group for the space of several heartbeats. The thump of the music continued on, as did the drunken hollers of the other guys in the bar and the clink of glasses on tabletops, but amongst the six of them, there was dead silence.

And then like someone had hit play, they all burst out talking at the same time.

"But you're a country music star!"

"But you grew up in Tennessee!"

"How have you *never* ridden a horse?!"

If he'd just announced that he'd actually been born with two heads and the doctors had had to lop one off at birth, he didn't think they could've been more surprised.

He took a small sip of his beer, giving himself time to come up with a decent explanation. "I was born and raised in Nashville, Tennessee. As in, in the city of Nashville itself. Concrete, skyscrapers…I'm what you might call a rhinestone cowboy." He shrugged, trying to downplay it. This was exactly why his publicist had worked so damn hard to hide this information from the public all these years. She'd once said dryly that fans would be more forgiving of him robbing someone on the street than not knowing how to castrate a calf.

He was starting to think she wasn't exaggerating.

"Well," Stetson said after a while, pushing his hat back and scratching his forehead before pulling the brim back into place, "if you ever decide that you want to see a real working ranch in action, you just let me know. I'm not a big horse person, not like Wyatt or Declan here, but they can bring their horses on over and we can tour my place on horseback anytime you want. Hell, then you could meet Carmelita, Louisa's aunt, and have some of the best damn cooking you've ever tasted in your life."

At that, there was a round of, "Amens."

"Oh, her homemade bread," breathed Wyatt, rubbing his stomach.

"Her pies," Declan put in. "All of 'em. There isn't a bad pie amongst them."

"Gravy," Stetson said seriously. "Her gravy is to die for. Anyway, you oughta come on over. Bring Louisa and Skyler. Carmelita would love to have someone new to cluck over."

"Or come on down to the fire station," Moose put in. "We don't have horses there, but we do have a pretty lookin' fire engine that we can take out for a joy ride. Hell, we'll pretend Mrs. Gehring got her cat stuck up in a tree again. We live in a small town and not much happens, so sometimes it's fun to take the engine out for a spin, just to liven things up."

That had to be the most hick thing Zane had ever heard. If his friends back in Nashville heard someone say that, they'd laugh their asses off. But was that really so bad, compared to going down to a high-end bar and getting smashed on $9 beers? At least taking the fire engine out for a spin didn't leave you wishing you were dead the next morning.

The topic drifted from there onto the cost of beef on the hoof – whatever that meant – and how silage was going up in price – whatever the hell that was – but Zane was only half listening. Stetson and Moose had meant what they said, Zane was absolutely sure of it. Neither had said it in that generic way that was socially acceptable but not meant in the slightest, the way that Zane was so used to hearing it said.

"You should come over sometime!"

"Oh, you too. You can come to my place for dinner."

Did either person mean it? Hell no. Would it happen? Never.

But Stetson meant it. Moose meant it. There was a reality to them – a down-to-earth demeanor – that Zane had somehow missed in his adult life. When you were a superstar; when you could fill huge stadiums with screaming fans, people didn't stand around and talk to you about the price of beef on the hoof. Everything revolved around Zane – his thoughts, his next songs, where he was going on tour, how high his album was charting.

Not having anyone ask him what it's *really* like to be

famous; not having anyone elbowing others in the ribs to get closer to him; not having anyone even asking for his autograph…

It was weird. He wasn't going to lie – it was just downright bizarre, really. When was the last time he'd gone to the bar as just a normal Joe Schmoe? Before his first major hit, he'd guess. After *A Honky Tonk Life* went double platinum, everything had changed. He'd gone from being able to run down to the corner store in his sweatpants and ripped t-shirt and not having a soul pay attention to him, to paparazzi following him, hoping to get that unflattering shot that would prove he'd already reached the pinnacle of his career and was sliding down the backside.

Did he miss that limelight? Did he miss being the center of attention?

Yeah, probably.

But on the other hand, it was damn nice just being a normal guy once again. If this was what every trip out into public was like in the Long Valley area, Zane could get damn used to it. Just being himself, not what people expected…

As the evening went on, he tipped back a few more beers, saw a few people take pictures of him discreetly from across the bar, signed a bar napkin for the bartender to frame and hang up on the wall, and listened to a group of guys who were all about his age or so, talking about work and crop rotation and wives with morning sickness and getting the bills paid on time.

Was this what his life could've been like, if he hadn't met Tamara? They'd been toxic for each other, there was no doubt about that, but when they'd first met, it was she who was the rising star, not him. She was making it as a regional star, with real hope of hitting it big, and it was through her connections that Zane had met an agent who was willing to take a chance on him and push him to the top.

But while his star had been rising, hers had begun falling,

and she never did have that breakout hit. She became *just* Zane's wife in all of the news stories. That hurt her in a way that she never really recovered from.

If they hadn't met, if Zane had given up on his dream of making it big and just went to work down at the corner store, would he still have been happy?

Questions I'll never have answers to…

"You ready to head out, Zane?" Wyatt asked, jerking him back to the present. Shit. How long had he just been standing there, holding his empty beer bottle like a dumbass?

"Yeah," he said, and flashed a grin to the group, trying to cover for his wandering mind. "Thanks for letting me hang out with you guys tonight."

"Sure, sure," Wyatt said. "But if you don't mind, my wife will kill me if I come home tonight without a picture with you. She's one of your biggest fans. Can we take a quick shot?"

"Absolutely," Zane said with a genuine grin, and then trotted out his well-worn line. "Just as long as you tell your wife that I'm even more handsome in real life than I am on TV, I'm happy to take all of the pictures with you that you want."

As he knew they would, the group busted up laughing at that one.

Some things never changed.

CHAPTER 9
LOUISA

S KYLER WAS IN HIS WHEELCHAIR as Louisa bent over him, her hands around his hips as they worked together to transfer him to the recliner. She paused, though, deciding on the spur of the moment to deal with a problem that'd been simmering for a while.

"Hold on, Skyler, let's ease back into your chair."

He sat back and looked up at her, surprised. After she'd been there for a couple of weeks, his overt hostility had disappeared for the most part, but he still didn't trust her.

No, they were a long ways from that.

"Turns out, you've been transferring wrong all of this time," she said, hoping her smile would take some of the sting out of her words. No one liked being told they were doing something wrong. "It's been a while since you started transferring yourself from one place to another, so I'm gonna guess it'll take a while for you to unlearn and then relearn the right way, but if you do, you'll find that it's a hell of a lot easier to move from one spot to another all by yourself, and also when someone else is helping you."

"What am I doing wrong?" he asked suspiciously. "I move all of the time by myself, so I can't be bad."

"You're making it work, for sure," Louisa reassured him. "But it's like going uphill in your wheelchair with the handbrake halfway in place. Sure, you can do it, but you're putting in way too much effort for that gain. Here's the trick: You need to start leaning *away* from where you want to move, not *towards* it."

At this bit of instruction, Skyler gave her a clearly skeptical look, and she laughed. "I know, I know, it sounds weird, but it works a hell of a lot better. Let's practice for a minute."

She put her hands down at his hips and together they transferred to the recliner and then back again. It took him several tries, but soon, he was transferring like a pro. She shouldn't have been surprised by how quickly he picked up on it – unlike adults, kids weren't stuck axle deep in how it was always done.

"Wow, Louisa, this is so much easier!" he crowed, his face lighting up with excitement. "Why didn't anyone else show me this?"

Louisa just flashed him a smile but tactfully chose not to answer him. Honestly, chances were damn high that they had shown him the right way when he was in rehab, but when he'd shut down on the physical therapists and had refused to work anymore, she guessed they'd given up trying to rectify mistakes he was making. Why try if he wasn't?

But here was a mark in the win column. This, along with a hundred other tiny wins, would add up, and Skyler would start trusting that she knew what the hell she was doing, and he would start believing when she told him he could walk again.

One baby step at a time.

Once he was actually settled in the recliner where he'd wanted to go, she asked him the question she'd been working on in the background for a while now. "How would you feel about kayaking down at Wolf's Bend Lake?" she asked casually. "Go out, kayak around, get some sun?"

He hesitated. "I…I don't know how to swim without…" He gestured at his legs, thin and knobby and useless as a pair of pick-up sticks. "What if I fall in?"

"Well, a couple of things. First off, you'll have a lifejacket on, so even if you do fall in, you'll be able to bob along until we can fish you back out again. But that's just the back-up plan – I called and made sure that the kayak rental place has outriggers, which are basically these big floaties that stick out from either side of a kayak like airplane wings," she held her arms out to demonstrate, "which makes a kayak super stable. I'm not gonna say that it's impossible to flip a kayak over with outriggers on it because if you want something badly enough, you can almost always make it happen, but you would have to really, really want it, and be trying to do it. Plus," she leaned forward like she was revealing a secret she didn't want anyone else to hear, "I was thinking about asking your dad to come along. What do you think about that?"

The skepticism and doubt disappeared, and a huge flash of excitement took its place. "You think you could make him come?!" Skyler squealed in that high-pitched boy's voice that would disappear all too quickly with the onset of hormones. "I don't know. He doesn't…" As quickly as it appeared, though, the excitement faded away, replaced by pure disbelief. "Well, if you can get my dad to come, I'll come," he said in a bored voice as he picked up the remote from the arm of the recliner and clicked on the TV.

There was a part of her that was irked by his high-handed dismissal of her – she was the adult here, after all – but she smothered that down. She knew what he was doing. She knew that he didn't want to show how much he really wanted his dad there, because if Zane didn't show up, it would hurt all the more. Better to act as if it didn't matter one way or the other to him. He was an old hand in this battle for affections, and was damn used to losing.

"I'll let you know," she promised him as she headed out of the room and back up the stairs. He didn't bother to look away from the TV as she went.

Now, she just had to convince Zane to take more than a passing interest in his own son. Basically, an impossible task, but she liked the challenge.

CHAPTER 10
ZANE

H E SAT IN THE STUDY, the oppressive dark maroon and forest green colors swallowing him whole. It was a study straight out of a Victorian novel – dark wood, dark fabric, too-formal furniture. Not his style, any more than the rest of the house was.

Handicap-accessible houses aren't exactly a dime a dozen, especially in the middle of Nowhere, Idaho.

He ought to just count his blessings that one was available so close to the therapy camp – just the next town over – but after living in his custom-built home in Nashville, this place just felt…

Not like home.

He twirled his whiskey glass in his hand absentmindedly as he stared into the dancing flames of the electric fireplace. No heat – it was too warm in the middle of summer for heat, even up in the mountains of Idaho – but the flames were nice to look at. They made him think, and tonight, his thoughts were certainly drifting.

What did he want out of life? Did he want to start singing again? Touring again?

Yes!

Even through the pleasant haze of alcohol running in his veins, his soul was jumping up and down at the mere thought of getting back on the road again. To tour, to sing for screaming fans…

Yes, that was absolutely what he wanted.

His head thumped against the tall back of the chair and he stared up at the ceiling, groaning. He couldn't go back to touring. He knew that. What if they got into another wreck on the way to another awards ceremony? What if it killed Skyler that time? It was bad enough to lose Tamara, but they'd been headed for divorce anyway. They both knew it. Not that she'd deserved to die or that he'd wanted her to, but he also couldn't pretend that the great love of his life had died that night.

But the only reason they were in that car was because of Zane's career. If Zane were just a salesman or firefighter or computer programmer, Tamara never would've died.

Because of Zane, his son had lost the one person in his life who knew what the hell to do with him, and Zane sure hadn't stepped up his game since then. He knew he was failing his son, but he just felt so damn lost. He'd heard that you often mimic your parents when you become a parent, even if you didn't mean to, and the way Zane figured it, that was damn spot-on. You couldn't find two more worthless people as parents than Zane's had been.

And that was exactly how he was turning out to be as a father – worthless.

When Tamara had been alive, the raising of Skyler had been one of their biggest flash points. Nothing started off a fight faster than discussing their son. Zane had been so damn sure that if it'd been up to him, he'd be doing all of the right things – making completely different choices than Tamara was making.

Well, he got half of that right – he was definitely making different choices than Tamara. She would've died rather than let someone else raise her son. There at the end, being a mother was all she wanted to do. Being a trophy wife rankled her soul, because it was supposed to be her up there. It was supposed to be her making it big. And by God, if she wasn't going to make it big in her own right, then she could at least be a damn good mother.

No, being a trophy wife wasn't for her, although she sure as shit didn't mind spending money like one.

He stared blearily down at his whiskey glass, realizing thickly that it was empty. That wasn't possible – he'd just poured some a minute ago. Hell, maybe he'd only *thought* he'd poured some. Maybe he'd gotten sidetracked and hadn't actually done it.

Comforted by the thought, he sloshed some more into his glass and settled back into his chair, letting the flames mesmerize him.

Louisa...

The thought of her drifted, unbidden, to the forefront of his mind. Now there was someone who knew how to raise a child. She was the kind of person who should have five kids, and who would make the raising of them look effortless. She'd mentioned, several days after it'd happened, about the honey on her hairbrush. Instead of hysterics and demands that he make Skyler pay or else, Louisa had simply laughed about it, and had told him about her "revenge." Getting his son into better shape was her idea of revenge? Not that he was complaining, he was just confused. Revenge to him were live snakes in bed, or turning off the hot water when someone was taking a shower, or switching the contents of the salt and the sugar containers.

And then, as if the mere thought of her had somehow made her appear, she was standing in front of him, talking to him about Skyler.

"When'd you come in?" he asked, talking over whatever she'd been saying, his words coming out weirdly slurred.

That wasn't right. He wasn't drunk – he knew he wasn't. So why was everything so hazy? And why wasn't his tongue working right? He took another sip of whiskey, just to wet his mouth. Maybe that was his problem – dry mouth. Nothing more than that.

She heaved a sigh and then started again, ignoring his question. "I want your permission to take Skyler to Wolf's Bend Lake and go kayaking with him. I think being out in the sun would be a really good idea for him. When we aren't at therapy camp, he's inside, hiding in front of the TV or the game console. I think that—"

But he wasn't listening anymore. His mind was wandering into more…delicious areas of thought as he watched her tits bounce up and down with every exaggerated sweeping movement of her hands. She liked to talk with her hands. He rather thought that if someone tied her hands behind her back, she'd instantly go mute. Incapable of talking without them.

Incapable…

What a funny word. He moved it around and around in his mind, prodding at it like it was some creature about to come to life. Funny words. Was he funny? He felt funny. Hot. Flushed. Blurry around the edge.

It couldn't be the alcohol, though. He'd barely had anything to drink. Maybe he was coming down with something.

Funny, funny, funnnnyyyyy…

"So what do you think?"

His eyes snapped up to hers. Well, more like sloshed their way up to hers. He was moving through liquid, and that was just…*weird*.

"What?" he croaked, and then cleared his throat. "What?" he asked again.

She planted her hands on her hips and glared down at him. "Did you hear *anything* I said?" she demanded.

"Yes. Ummm…boating. You wanted to go out boating. On a lake." He was rather proud of himself for pulling that out of his ass. He toasted himself and took another sip of his whiskey as a reward.

"*Kayaking,*" she corrected, clearly peeved. "On Wolf's Bend Lake. I would like you to come, too."

"Me?" he asked blankly. If she'd asked him to climb onto a rocket and fly to the moon, he couldn't have been more surprised. He didn't go hang out with his son at the lake. Or anywhere else for that matter. This was why he hired Louisa – so she'd take care of Skyler. Leave Zane to…

Well, do something. So far, it was just a lot of thinking, but he had to get his head screwed on straight, and *then* go forward from there.

He realized she was talking again, her arms moving around like she was conducting an orchestra only she could hear. He interrupted her. "You've got beautiful hair, you know that?"

He wasn't quite sure why he said it, other than the words just needed to be said. Straight as a ruler, thick, almost to her waist…it was gorgeous. He wanted to bury his hands in it. He wanted to wrap it around his fist and pull her close and kiss her cupid bow lips.

Lips she was now wetting with her pink tongue.

"I don't think that has anything…" She cleared her throat and continued, "Anything to do with kayaking. Or Sky-Skyler…"

He was reaching up and picking up the end of her heavy braid then, testing its weight in his hand. It was as soft as he'd thought it would be. She pulled it out of his reach and flipped it over her shoulder to fall down her back again.

"I better go to bed now, Mr. Risley," she said quietly, and with that, she slipped from the room, closing the heavy wooden door behind her.

Mr. Risley? She'd never called him that. He'd told her to call him Zane and she had from day one.

He rubbed his fingertips together, the memory of her hair already slipping out of his alcohol-soaked mind. He wanted to feel it again.

He wanted…

He snuggled further down in his chair, letting the warmth of the evening wrap around him.

He wanted…something. He'd remember what it was tomorrow. Tonight, he needed sleep.

CHAPTER II

LOUISA

LOUISA SLAMMED the tea kettle back down on the gas burner a little louder than she meant to, but—

No, screw that. She did mean to. In fact, to prove just how very much she meant to, she picked it up and slammed it back down again. There. That felt nice. Not as nice as slamming the tea kettle against a certain somebody's head, but still, it was nice.

"You okay?" Skyler's thin voice drifted through the air, full of fear and worry, and she spun on her heel, her hand over her heart.

"*Dios mío,*" she muttered, closing her eyes for a moment and then letting them pop back open. "Yes, yes, I'm fine," she said with a small but genuine smile. If anyone deserved to bear the wrath of her at that moment, Skyler was not it.

No, a significantly taller and much more handsome man deserved every bit of it.

She'd lain in bed last night, fuming for what seemed like hours, unable to fall asleep. The jackass, hitting on her like that. He was about 10 cups in, from what she could tell, and drunk as a skunk, but still, that didn't give him the right to touch her – even if it was just her hair – like she was some sort of prostitute. She had half a mind to "accidentally" bang some pots with a wooden spoon right outside of his bedroom door this morning. See how he was feeling the day after a drinking marathon.

"You don't look it," Skyler said, giving her a worried look. She closed her eyes for a moment again, gathering her inner strength – *it's not his fault, it's not his fault* – and then looked at Skyler, making sure that none of her anger was showing in her eyes.

"No, no, everything is fine," she said brightly. "We're going to go kayaking today. Are you excited?"

"We are?!" Skyler practically shouted. His face lit up, as bright as the sun, and he snapped upright in his wheelchair, spine straight. "So Dad said yes, he'll come with us?"

Louisa paused, biting her bottom lip. She couldn't lie to him. Honestly, they ought to go whether or not Zane deigned to "bless" them with his presence, but to Skyler, this was his whole world.

How can Zane not see what a precious gift he has in front of him?

"Well, I talked to your father last night," Louisa started out, still not sure how she was going to end the sentence, when a deep, grumpy voice behind her said, "Talked to me about what?"

Louisa froze – when the hell had he come downstairs?! – and then turned to look at him with an extra-bright smile. Maybe the brightness shining off her face would hurt his pounding head, the bastard—

"About how you're going to go kayaking with us today," she lied smoothly. "Don't you remember?"

His eyebrows shot to his hairline and he ran his fingers through his rumpled hair. "Kayaking?" he mumbled, looking like he'd rather dunk himself into a moat full of snakes. Or crocodiles.

"You're gonna come, you're gonna come!" Skyler yelled,

and then took off like a rocket for the doorway to the breakfast nook, scooting past his father. "I'm gonna put on my swimsuit!" he yelled over his shoulder, and she could hear his wheelchair zoom across the ostentatious living room and over to the elevator.

Louisa sent Zane a blasé smile, as if her deepest desire wasn't to jam her foot down on his instep. Lifting her mug of tea to her lips, she took a sip, and then before the questions bubbling up in Zane's eyes could be spoken out loud, she said blandly, "Well, I'd better go get my own swimsuit on, too. Skyler's pretty excited. Can't keep him waiting."

She swept from the breakfast nook, leaving a gaping Zane behind. She had to work hard to stifle a giggle. Honestly, Zane deserved this, and a whole lot more.

At the last moment, though, she changed directions and headed for the kitchen instead to talk to the chef. He'd be coming in any minute now to do the cooking for the day, and she wanted to have him put together a fun picnic for the three of them.

If nothing else, today should teach Zane Risley not to mess with her. She could lie with the best of them, as long as it was for a good cause, and having Zane actually do something with his son was a very, very good cause.

CHAPTER 12

ZANE

*D*ID *I* AGREE *to go kayaking last night? I don't remember actually agreeing to that.*

He scrubbed at his eyeballs with the palms of his hands. His head was thumping painfully with each beat of his heart, and he felt like someone had filled his head with sludge.

Brain…thinking…painful…

He poured himself a cup of coffee and swallowed too quickly, burning his tongue. "Shit!" he muttered, spitting the coffee into the sink. He blew on his cup, trying to patiently wait for the temperature to drop before trying it again.

He took a tentative sip – *much better* – and leaned back against the counter of the breakfast nook. After a few more tentative sips, he started to feel wakefulness begin to creep in, and with it, a search of his memories of last night. He'd been sitting in the study, staring at the electric fireplace, thinking about Tamara, and then…Louisa had come in and had talked to him about boating.

No, it'd been kayaking – she'd corrected him on that point. He smiled a bit at the thought – some of the top people in the entertainment industry got used to having their every whim obeyed without contradiction, but Louisa…

She wasn't that type. If someone was wrong, they were wrong, and she wasn't about to kowtow to their idiocy.

His hand stilled halfway to his mouth, a memory flitting across his mind. Had he…had he hit on Louisa? He remembered picking up her braid that was cascading over her shoulder and telling her how beautiful her hair was. But had he really done that? Or had that just been part of his fitful dreams of the previous night? He'd fallen asleep in that damn chair and had spent the night dreaming about Louisa and Tamara, talking to one and then they were suddenly morphing into the other, and he'd woken up that morning with a kink in his neck and a hangover only a frat boy could appreciate.

He scrubbed at his eyes again, willing them to feel less like sandpaper and more like functioning eyeballs. If he'd actually hit on Louisa the night before, he owed her an apology. Some guys had the reputation of hitting on any woman with two legs and a heartbeat, but Zane wasn't one of them. No matter how utterly frustrating it'd been at times to be married to Tamara, he'd never cheated on her. That was the one line even he wouldn't cross.

But with Louisa…hitting on an employee was just disgusting on all sorts of levels. He never wanted to be one of *those* guys. Sure, he wasn't married to Tamara any longer, but that didn't change the fact that Louisa was still his employee, and that meant the power balance between them was completely out of whack.

He needed to apologize to her.

Except, what if he hadn't actually hit on her? What if it had only been a dream? Then he'd be apologizing for something he hadn't actually done, *and* creeping her out by letting her know that he'd been dreaming about her.

He rubbed his temples, his blood pounding in them like a

gong repeatedly being hit by an overly enthusiastic two-year-old. He wished there was a way to ascertain if he'd hit on her without creeping her out at the same time, but if there was a way, he sure as hell wasn't coming up with it. The state of his brain wasn't helping things.

"C'mon, Dad," Skyler said, zooming into the breakfast nook with all of the speed and enthusiasm of Superman. "You're still in your PJs! You gotta put on your swim trunks." He pointed down at his own surfboard shorts that were showing off his painfully thin, white legs.

You wouldn't be in a wheelchair if it wasn't for me.

"You're right. Sorry. I'm moving my ass," Zane said, and tossed back the rest of his coffee. Hadn't he just been thinking last night that he needed to be a better dad to Skyler? Kayaking with him wasn't exactly at the top of his list of activities he would've picked, but hell, Louisa knew what she was doing, and Skyler was proof of that. He hadn't looked this excited about doing something in…ever, really.

It wasn't until they were almost to the lake that Zane realized he'd forgotten to ask the important questions. "Skyler isn't a strong swimmer," he said quietly to Louisa, watching Skyler in the rearview mirror, earbuds in, singing along to some dreadful rap song. *As if that's real music…* "Are you sure it's safe to go kayaking with him?"

"Of course," Louisa said, shooting him a confident smile. "The rental place has outriggers, which are basically big floaties for a kayak. Skyler had the same worry, but honestly, you can't flip one of these kayaks over unless you're really trying, and even then, Skyler will have a life jacket on, so he'll just float along until someone can fish him out."

"Oh. Good." He didn't know what else to say. It was becoming obvious even to him that Louisa thought of *everything*, and was thus much more qualified to be a parent than he was, or probably could ever hope to be. "How is it that you don't have kids of your own?"

The words were out of his mouth before he could stop them, and he regretted them immediately. It was absolutely *no* business of his why his employee was or was not married; did or did not have kids.

"That's a funny story I'll have to tell you sometime," she said, but she was looking out of the passenger window again, and her voice all but screamed that it wasn't funny in the slightest.

"Sorry – I don't know why I asked – I don't know what I was think—" He was absolutely mortified, and felt the tips of his ears go pink, something that hadn't happened to him since he was in junior high and asking Heather Zuck to go to the dance with him.

"It's okay," she said lightly. "No worries. Kids are…I love 'em." She turned back towards him and smiled. "You happen to have a particularly wonderful one."

Zane automatically looked in the rearview mirror but Skyler was still bobbing his head, singing some words under his breath that Zane could only be glad he couldn't actually hear. He was pretty sure they probably weren't appropriate for a 12-year-old to sing.

"He sure is something," Zane finally said. And he was. Zane just wished he knew what the hell to do with him.

At the dock of the rental company, Zane watched as Louisa worked with the employees to get Skyler fitted with a life jacket and then transferred into a kayak with the outriggers sticking out on either side. Zane couldn't help being impressed by her knowledge. How did he luck out with her as a hire again? He tried to imagine the last aide doing this with Skyler and almost laughed out loud. That prick's only redeeming quality was that he showed up to work every day, despite how much Skyler hated his guts. Looking back on it, Zane hadn't been nearly as upset about losing the aide over Skyler's little prank as he should have been. Paying him a six-figure check to keep the guy from suing over poor work

conditions, plus a free private plane ride back to Tennessee…
it should've rankled more than it did. Instead, he'd just been
happy to finally get rid of the guy.

Zane thought about Louisa flying off, going back home
again, and felt a clutch of panic in his heart. It had only been a
month but he was already starting to wonder how he'd ever
live without her. Could he convince her to move with them
back to Tennessee? It'd mean leaving her family behind, but
surely she'd be okay. She'd lived in Salt Lake City for years.
Tennessee wasn't so far away when you had a private plane
to fly around as you needed to.

He looked up just in time to see Louisa shuck off her loose
capris and tank top, leaving her in just a one-piece bathing
suit worthy of an 80-year-old woman. It was as boring, as
straitlaced, as non-sexy as bathing suits could possibly get.

And yet…seeing her with only a thin piece of material
covering her body was painfully erotic. She shouldn't look
this good in a bathing suit any great-grandmother would be
happy to wear. He'd seen women in far, far less. He'd had
women literally drape themselves over him wearing far, far
less.

But still, her long, muscular legs, a dark cocoa color,
ending in a solid waist that said she was capable of doing
whatever needed to be done without breaking into a sweat,
including screwing him in bed seven ways to Sunday, never
at risk of being crushed beneath his body…

Oh, and her tits. They were perfect. He could tell they
were natural – they didn't stick out a foot past her sternum
like she'd borrowed them for the weekend. They looked
round and soft, and they wouldn't slip and slide around
underneath her skin like water balloons. Like Tamara's had.
She'd believed that the reason she wasn't getting further in
the music world was because her chest wasn't large enough,
so Zane had paid for the surgery despite liking her tits just
the way they were. Afterwards, she had a chest worthy of a

Hooters waitress that never felt quite right, balloons slipping every which way, the nerve-endings shot to hell.

No, Louisa's looked…perfect.

It was when he found himself wondering exactly what shade of pink her nipples were that he forced himself to stop.

Employee. Bad. Get your ass in your kayak and keep your eyes on your own paper.

He slipped into his kayak and then splashed a little water on his face from the lake to cool down. It was hot here at the dock without any shade, the sun bouncing off the lake and dazzling his eyes. His appreciation for Louisa's figure hadn't helped a bit.

He paused and grinned over at Louisa and Skyler, so innocently readying themselves for this trip around the lake. With one quick stroke of the paddle, he sent a tidal wave of water straight towards them.

"What the hell?!" Louisa sputtered, shoving wet strands of hair out of her face, but she was already grabbing a paddle laying on the dock and shoving a wave of water back at him. "You think you're tough, old man? You think you can pick on a Latina and not pay the price?"

Skyler, already settled into his kayak and waiting for Louisa to get into hers, was slower on the uptake, but after several heartbeats, he joined in. "I'm gonna get you, Dad!" he yelled, swinging his paddle inexpertly and getting almost as much water on himself as he did on Zane. "You can't get me, you can't get me!"

"No fair!" Zane crowed. "Two on one?! What did I do to deserve this?!" He was alternating between trying to splash Skyler and then Louisa, when one of the rental employees came hurrying up to the dock.

"I'm sorry," he called out in his most officious voice that clearly showed he wasn't sorry at all, "but you are going to get other kayakers wet. No horseplay here at the docks." He pointed at a large sign that said just that in large, red block letters.

Zane shot him a look and opened up his mouth to argue with the man – after all, anyone who was going kayaking should damn well expect to get wet – when Louisa straightened up, putting her paddle behind her back as if to hide it. "Sorry, sir," she called, and then looked down at Skyler who was still trying to splash Zane. "Okay, Skyler, that's enough. We can't do that here."

Skyler scowled but began trying to paddle instead, mostly going in circles as he worked to figure out how to maneuver a paddle correctly. Zane just stared at Louisa, open-mouthed. She seemed to actually think that rules were meant to be followed, not challenges to be broken. Did she always follow the rules like this?

The employee headed back to the rental shack while Louisa slipped into her kayak and then began demonstrating how to use a paddle to Skyler, seemingly oblivious to Zane's astonishment. After a few practice strokes, Skyler and Louisa set off, leaving Zane to follow along behind them, also something he never did.

You're kayaking, you're spending time with your kid, you're following rules, and now you're following someone else around. What the hell is happening to you?

That was a question he just didn't have an answer for.

CHAPTER 13

LOUISA

L OUISA STEERED them towards a popular day-use area along the shoreline, at least according to all of the info she could find online, letting the joy of sweeping cleanly through the water flow through her. This was nice.

No, it was more than that. This was *wonderful*. The heat of the sun on her skin, Skyler calling out every little thing he spotted, Zane actually spending time with his son...there wasn't much that could beat an outing like this.

Sure, next time it'd be nice if she could get Zane to come without bald-faced lying to him, but baby steps. From what she could tell, it wasn't that Zane didn't want to spend time with his son, it was just that he didn't know how.

Maybe I should be as bold with him as he was with me. Flat-out ask him how it is that he has no idea how to relate to children, not even his own. What kind of family life did he have growing up? It had to have been bad.

The warmth of the sun, the fun of the day, all worked to wash her anger away about last night. Whatever had caused that drinking binge, she was sure that he hadn't meant to be an asshole, and didn't remember today that he'd even done anything inappropriate.

She was willing to let it go, but only this once. The next time he tried making a pass on her, she'd knee him in the nuts and be gone by morning, Skyler or no Skyler. Sure, she was a Latina while he was a white male, and she was poor while he was so very, very rich, but that didn't mean she'd put up with his shit. There wasn't enough pay in the world to make up for that.

They drew up to the day-use area Louisa had been hoping to use and found it packed to the brim with hoards of screaming children. Skyler watched them longingly, and Louisa knew he was wishing he could run and play tag with them. *I'm so sorry, cariño. But I will do my best to make you better, if you'll just help me along the way.*

"How about if we head down to the next pull-out?" she called out, deliberately playing it cool, as if she couldn't read the haunting disappointments and what-if's etched on Skyler's face. "Then we can pull out our picnic."

"We have a picnic?" Skyler brightened right back up, his pain falling away in the face of the promise of food. "Did you pack dessert?" he asked eagerly.

She mentally patted herself on the back. Skyler had been picking at his food from day one, and she'd been sure it was because he just didn't get enough physical exercise to build up a healthy appetite. Getting sun on his skin and a hunger in his belly was part of his healing process, even if it didn't directly relate to him walking again.

"I had Chef Ralph make up a picnic for us, and I told him I wanted it to be a surprise," she answered. "So your guess is as good as mine."

"Ooohhhh…" Skyler breathed, even more excited at the thought of the spontaneity of it all. "I hope he remembers I don't like bread with the nuts in it." He scrunched up his nose. "He's always trying to get me to eat sandwiches with the yucky bread."

"How about you?" Zane asked, paddling up on her other side as they began working their way down the shoreline. "Do you like the yucky bread with the nuts in it?"

She laughed. "I forget sometimes that bread exists. I usually use tortillas for everything. There aren't any nuts in my tortillas, though, so I don't know if I'd like nuts in my bread."

"Speaking of tortillas," Zane said, his muscled arms pulling the paddle through the water with ease, "guess who invited us to dinner at their house?"

"Who?" she asked blankly. Who did Zane know in Idaho to invite him to dinner?

"Stetson Miller. Your aunt works for him, right?"

"Yeah, she has for years. But how on earth did you meet Stetson in order to be invited over for dinner?"

"Declan came over to the therapy camp several weeks back and invited me out to the bar with the guys. Had some beers with the Miller brothers and two firefighters named Levi and Moose."

"Moose?" she repeated blankly, certain she'd heard him wrong.

"Yup. Hand to God, he introduced himself as Moose. His real name is Deere, as in John Deere, but everyone calls him Moose."

"Someone named their child after a *tractor*?" She wasn't sure if she was more or less surprised to hear that, versus someone naming their child after a large herbivore. "Idahoans sure are weird," she muttered under her breath.

"Hey, you're the one who's from Idaho!" Zane said, laughing.

"I know! That's why I can say that. I know first-hand just how weird Idahoans can be." She shot him a laughing smile, and then called to Skyler who'd paddled far ahead of them, "Sky! Look to your right! You're passing the take-out spot!"

She upped her pace, wanting to catch up to Skyler and make sure that his transfer out of the kayak was safe. He was a pro at getting on and off the couch, and even on and off a horse now, but in and out of a kayak, he still needed her.

She pulled up onto the concrete ramp and hopped out of her kayak, splashing through the cold water to pull her kayak up on shore and out of the way, and then pulled Skyler's kayak up onto the ramp. Working together, they managed to get Skyler out of the kayak and onto the bank with only a minimal amount of splashing. *Not too shabby.*

She looked up to see where Zane had gone off to, and saw that he was floating a little offshore, a weird look in his eyes. She tilted her head to the side, trying to read that expression, and he caught the movement. "I'm coming!" he called, and just like that, the weird look was gone. He pulled up beside Skyler's kayak and climbed out, wading through the water with ease. She had never seen him in shorts, and now that she had a good look at his legs…

Wowsers. They were just as muscular and defined as his arms. *No wonder all of the girls went crazy over him.*

She'd done a little more research since starting the job, wanting to know her employer a little better, and if half of the things she'd read online were true, he'd had no shortage of women throwing themselves at him over the years. More than a few articles had said that this was why he and Tamara were having so many problems – everyone had seemed to think they were on the edge of divorce – but then when she died, every article suddenly started to treat him like a tragic figure mourning for his dead wife. No mention was made again about almost divorcing Tamara.

She still didn't know which of those stories to believe, or if either of them were true, or something else entirely, but this was an itch she wasn't going to be able to scratch. Zane was not about to open up and tell her everything.

You're just the nanny. No matter how great his legs are. Never forget that.

Zane turned to Skyler with a smile. "Where should we eat lunch?" he asked his son, scooping him up into his arms from his perch on the rocky beach. Louisa was surprised – she'd expected she would have to carry him around since they hadn't been able to pack a wheelchair onto the kayaks, and she had not been looking forward to it. Having Zane carry him instead was unexpectedly lovely.

"Let's go over there," Skyler said, pointing to a clump of pine trees.

"Good call," Zane said, and with Louisa following behind with her backpack slung over her shoulder, they wandered over to the trees. Louisa quickly pulled a blanket out and spread it on the ground, and then Zane carefully placed Skyler on it.

Skyler picked up his legs and arranged them on the blanket and then looked up at Louisa with anticipation. "Let's see, let's see!" he said.

"I am going to start calling you *mi gordito*," she said with a laugh as she began unloading the backpack. "Ohhh…it looks like he packed you a sandwich made with the whitest bread you ever did see." She tossed it to him.

He caught it but was still looking at her with a quizzical look on his face. "What does *mi gordito* mean?" he asked as he unwrapped his sandwich.

"Literally, it means *my fatty*, but in Mexican culture, it's a term of endearment."

"Term of endear…what?" he asked around a mouthful of sandwich, spraying her with partially chewed food.

"*Cariño!*" she said, swiping at the bits of food on her swimsuit. She tried not to remember Alex doing just that only a couple of months ago. Oh, how she missed her brother.

"Sorry," he said abashedly after he swallowed the food in his mouth. "What does *cariño* mean?"

She picked out a piece of watermelon from the Tupperware container and took a small bite, making sure *not* to spray him with food while she talked, as much as she was tempted to seek revenge. "First off, 'term of endearment' is a fancy way of saying a nice nickname. Like, sweetie. Or honey. Or dipshit."

Zane choked on his food as Skyler let out a howl of laughter.

"Perhaps it was only my mother who liked that particular term of endearment," Louisa said sweetly. "And *cariño* is Spanish for sweetie. My mother alternated between *cariño* and dipshit."

The two of them let out another howl of laughter while she smiled at them angelically. Nothing was more fun than shocking the hell out of people. They always made the mistake of looking at her sweet face and smile, and never saw it coming.

"What is dipshit in Spanish?" Zane asked, leaning back on one hand as he ate with the other. She focused her gaze on his fingers, spread out against the dark dirt of the forest floor. They were much safer to look at than his mesmerizing blue eyes.

But then, she found herself thinking about what those fingers could do, and switched her gaze to his elbow. Even she couldn't find anything sexy about Zane's elbow.

"I can't tell you that!" she replied in mock horror. "What kind of example would it set to swear in front of your *son*?"

Skyler was laughing so hard, he was rolling around on the ground, holding his sandwich against his stomach as he howled.

"Of course," Zane said solemnly, a tiny quirk of the corner of his mouth giving it away. "I'd hate for my delicate flower of a son to ever hear any swear words."

"Of course," Louisa repeated, but this time, she did it while instinctively meeting his gaze and *wham!* It was like a punch to the stomach. She didn't want to look away. She couldn't look away.

She tore her gaze away.

Employer. Bad. No touchy.

"C'mon," Skyler said, wheedling. "Just one swear word. No one will even know it's a bad word when I say it."

She raised her eyebrows at him, and with that one swift look, he knew she wouldn't budge on the topic. "Now, since you don't have any siblings," she said primly, "I will tell you what it is like to have them. Just in case you ever thought it might be fun to have siblings, you can remember my stories and know that no sane person would ever want them."

"Tell me about the twins!" Skyler exclaimed. "I always wanted a twin. Then no one would ever know who they were talking to."

"That, unfortunately, is a very true statement," Louisa said with an exaggerated sigh. "As soon as their pudgy little hands would let them, they'd swap their colored headbands, the only way my mom had of trying to keep them straight. Then they'd spend all day laughing while she tried to guess who was who. They were naughty, but everyone loved them. You couldn't help it. Big brown eyes, long thick eyelashes, and cute-as-a-button noses." She leaned over and tapped Skyler's nose with the tip of her finger. "They'd bat those big eyes," she fluttered her eyelashes, "and smile so angelically," she put her hands under her chin like she was praying, "that you'd forget that they'd just used a whole stick of butter on the bathroom floor. They claimed it was a science experiment – they wanted to see if it'd make people slip and fall. My youngest brother, Alex, landed right on his butt and started howling. My mother made them scrub the floor on their hands and knees."

"What are their names?" Skyler asked eagerly, like he was trying to soak up every bit of this family knowledge that he could.

"Francesca and Isabel, but everyone calls Isabel Izzy, and then, it just became Frizzy for the two of them. That way, we never have to be able to tell them apart. They're just Frizzy. They go *everywhere* together. The school administration, sick of them playing pranks on the teacher, decided to split them last year. Wouldn't let them in the same classes together anymore. Suddenly, Frizzy were too sick to go to school. You've never seen such sick teenagers in all your life. I think they were sticking their fingers down their throats and swaddling themselves up in blankets with heating pads underneath, because they were puking and sweating...it wasn't pretty. This lasted for a week. Everyone knew they weren't *really* sick, but every time Mom hinted about them going to school, they threw up all over her shoes. Finally, she went to the principal and said," and here, she used her best thick Mexican accent, "'Either you let my daughters back in the same classes again, or I will go stark-raving mad. I cannot keep washing all of my shoes.' Frizzy went back to school the next day, fit as a fiddle. It was *magic*," and she snapped her fingers right in front of Skyler's nose.

He laughed so hard, he snorted. "I want to meet Frizzy," he said plaintively when he finally stopped laughing. "Would they come over here and visit us?"

He looked so eager, so anxious to meet them, that Louisa's heart hurt a little at the look on his face. Here was a kid who'd grown up with only staff to take care of him, and no siblings to tease or torment or love. She wanted to look up at Zane, to ask him with her eyes, *Do you see what your son needs? More than just you and a giant house and servants and the occasional pony ride.* But she didn't, because his eyes would suck her in and she wouldn't be able to look away.

"It's pretty far from Pocatello to here," she said after a moment's pause. "But maybe."

Skyler didn't believe her. She could see it on his face. Her comforting lie – *but maybe* – wouldn't happen, and he'd been disappointed enough in his life to know it. She tore her eyes away from his too-mature gaze and looked at the tip of Zane's nose instead. "What about you?" she asked, trying to lighten the mood. "How many siblings do you have?"

"A baby sister," he said after a moment's hesitation. "She died when she was just a toddler, though. Fell in the pool when no one was watching. I was four years older than her. My…my parents never really got over it."

"Her name was Holly," Skyler announced, and she could tell he wanted to add something to the conversation. Feel older and important.

Louisa nodded, not sure what to say. Her attempt to inject levity certainly hadn't succeeded. She met Zane's eyes and he smiled wanly, reassuring her without words that it was okay.

Still, she tore her eyes away from his and back to Skyler. "Ready to head back?" she asked overly brightly. She was trying too hard; she knew that. But she just didn't know what else to do.

My parents never really got over it.

"But I didn't eat all of the cookies!" Skyler protested, bringing Louisa back into the moment, swiping another two of the delicious snickerdoodles from the container. "We can't go back with leftovers."

"*Mi gordito*," she said, shaking her head at him. "Just wait until Carmelita meets you. She will spend all of her time doing nothing but feeding you cookies and saying that you need to fatten up."

Eyes brilliant as the sun at the thought, Skyler looked pleadingly at his dad. "Can we go visit Carmelita?" he asked without missing a beat. "Please?"

"I've been told she's quite the cook," Zane said, ruffling Skyler's hair, the light blonde strands swirling around the boy's face. "We should probably test this rumor out for ourselves. Just to make sure."

"Yes!" Skyler said, pumping his fist into the air, and Louisa laughed.

No, it wouldn't be hard at all to fall in love with Skyler.

But a much bigger problem was, it wouldn't be hard at all to fall in love with his father either. And *that* was where Louisa would get into trouble.

CHAPTER 14

ZANE

Z ANE LEANED against the arena fencing, watching as the kids rode by in an endless parade, waving to parents or family members while also trying to stay in the saddle as the horse did something Dr. Whitaker had informed him was "trotting."

Personally, Zane thought it looked like a great way to ensure that the males in the group never had children of their own. The way they were bouncing up and down in the saddle with every jarring step made Zane cross his legs protectively. If he did end up riding a horse while here, he was definitely going to skip the trotting stage.

Just then, the oldest Miller boy came up – William? No, Wyatt – and leaned against the arena fencing alongside Zane, watching the kids. "My son's out there," Wyatt said after a quiet moment. "He's sure lookin' good today. Smooth ride, even while the horse is at a trot, and that ain't easy to do."

"Your son, eh?" Zane said, his eyes automatically scanning the group for a dark-haired, blue-eyed miniature version of Wyatt. He couldn't see any who had Wyatt's stubborn tilt to his jaw or his thick eyebrows, but maybe the kid took after Wyatt's wife instead.

"Yup. He's my boy." They stood there for a moment longer, and then Wyatt said with a twinkle in his eye, "So, which one do you think is mine?"

"I was guessing him," Zane said, pointing at a rail-skinny boy with dark brown hair and pale skin. He looked much too skinny, like Skyler, and Zane could tell the kid had spent most of his life indoors, too ill to do much else. Also like Skyler.

"Nope," Wyatt said with a small smile and shake of the head. "I'm not even sure who he is, actually. I think he just started coming recently."

"Huh." Zane scanned the rest of the group, but wasn't finding any boy even remotely close to Wyatt's build and looks. There was a girl with what appeared to be Down Syndrome who looked the closest, but he'd said son, not daughter, so… "All right, I give up," he said finally. "Which one's your son?"

"Him," Wyatt said, pointing at the gangly Mexican boy Skyler had tangled with when he'd first started attending camp. "Juan is his name."

"Oh!" Zane said, and shot Wyatt a laughing smile. "I didn't realize your wife is Mexican."

"Oh, she ain't," Wyatt said, a grin of pure pride spreading across his face. "She's as white as I am. No, we can't have kids, so after I got thrown in jail – Abby was my jailer, by the way – I got assigned a bunch of community service on the way out of the clink. Served it here at this camp. When I first started working here, you shoulda seen it – Juan had a chip on his shoulder the size of Texas. You looked at him sideways and he was liable to punch you, just for looking at him funny. He couldn't walk three steps down the hallway at school without getting into a fight. He was with a foster care family and they did their best, but the system just isn't supported like it needs to be, and…some kids get lost in it."

Wyatt shrugged, his jaw set, looking like he had a lot more he could say on the topic, but was choosing not to.

"I was just like him when I was a kid. Angry at the world. We might not look the same on the outside, but on the inside…I knew what he was going through. After I married Abby, we started in on adopting him. We're in the middle of getting set up to do another kid – a girl this time, we think – so we can foster-adopt her. These kids need someone to know they care."

Skyler bounced by again, holding onto the horn of the saddle for dear life, looking like he'd rather be dropped into a pit of snakes than continue this horse ride. Zane waved cheerfully, trying to give him some encouragement. Skyler didn't seem too impressed.

Zane's eyes sought out Juan again, and as he watched him ride, the gait much smoother than any of the other kids, Zane thought back on what Wyatt'd just said. Thrown in jail, eh? He couldn't help his surprise at the thought. The night they'd all met up at the bar, Wyatt'd been the designated driver for the Miller brothers, and hadn't touched anything stronger than a Coke all night. Was that why he'd ended up in jail – driving drunk?

"People are never what they seem on the outside," Wyatt said quietly, almost as if he could read Zane's every thought. "My wife is a cop; I met her while in jail; and I met my future adopted son while serving out community service. Most everyone around here knows my story, but I imagine if you didn't, it'd come as a real shock to you."

"I have to admit I didn't have a clue," Zane said, his voice just as quiet, keeping it from the prying ears of the others milling around the arena. "You don't look like the convicted criminal type. I—"

But a ruckus broke out on the other end of the arena, cutting off the rest of Zane's sentence. He couldn't hear what Skyler was saying but even from over here, he knew it was his son, hollering about something.

"Shit," he muttered under his breath, and took off at a run for the far end of the arena, Wyatt on his heels.

When he got there, he pulled up short, staring at the disaster in front of him. It was Skyler and Juan again, knocking heads over something. Skyler was perched on a hay bale, his useless legs dangling as he shouted up at Juan to stop bossing him around. Juan was shaking his finger in Skyler's face and shouting back that he wouldn't do it if Skyler didn't need it.

"Dammit," Wyatt muttered under his breath.

Before either of them could figure out what to do, though – pick the two boys up by the scruff of the neck and shake them? Paddle their asses? – Louisa came striding over from where she'd been hanging out with some women. "All right, you two," she said calmly, hands on both of their chests, pushing them apart, "I could hear you hollering from all of the way over there." She jerked her head towards the knot of women who were looking on with interest.

At least, the ones who weren't looking at Zane with interest. He carefully avoided any eye contact with The Herd, as he mentally termed them. It hadn't gone unnoticed that every day, the group of women who were staying at the camp the entire time instead of just dropping their kids off and picking them up later was growing. In fact, Zane was fairly sure that at least a few of them didn't even have kids attending the camp.

Both Juan and Skyler started in on their version of the story, trying to talk over the other one and be heard, when Louisa let out a low whistle. They both shut up.

"I don't care if you guys poured gasoline on each other and then set the other person on fire," she said calmly. "The police might, but I don't. You two need to knock it off. You've been sniping at each other all morning. Juan, I know Skyler is new to this, but you've got to stop hovering over him and critiquing every little thing he does. If someone followed you around and told you that you were screwing something up every 30 seconds, how would you feel about it?" She cocked an eyebrow at him. He glowered but said nothing.

"And Skyler, Juan has been doing this a whale of a lot longer than you have. He's beat the video game, and you just picked up the controllers yesterday. Stop acting like you know how to do every damn thing. You might just learn a thing or two from him." Skyler's glower was a perfect match to Juan's. "Skyler, get back up on your horse. Juan, you too. Then you two can ride around the arena together. Side by side. Do ten laps. I don't want to hear a peep out of you until you're done."

She helped Skyler maneuver his horse over to the mounting block made specifically for paraplegics, and then helped him get on. She waited until he and Juan took off at a sedate walk around the arena before turning back to the crowd and saying with a cheerful smile, "Okay, whose kid did I just boss around?"

A ripple of laughter spread through the group at the question, and then as they all dispersed, Wyatt and Zane came hurrying over. Zane couldn't keep his eyes off Louisa. She was a wonder. A miracle. A gift from the gods.

"Juan is mine," Wyatt said, doffing his hat with one hand and shaking hands with Louisa with the other. "He's a bit of a know-it-all," he admitted with a sheepish grin as he settled his hat back on his head.

"Hey, aren't you the oldest of the Miller brothers?" Louisa asked.

"I am. Damn good memory you got there. I think we only met once, and you were just a kid."

"You just look a lot like Stetson," Louisa said with a shrug and grin. "He was there whenever we came visiting Carmelita."

"Him being the baby and all, he stuck around a lot longer than Declan and me," Wyatt said. "But anyhow, thanks for taking care of Juan and Skyler like that. Juan's got a good heart but he isn't always the best at knowing when to step back and let other people just make a mistake for themselves."

"Eh, he's a kid. He'll learn soon enough. I think him and Skyler could become good friends if they could stop bickering long enough."

They both chuckled that *aren't our kids so cute* chuckle together, leaving Zane just standing there, quiet as he watched the two of them start to chat about their sons, swapping war stories.

Except, Skyler was Zane's son, not Louisa's.

But when shit hit the fan, who knew what to do with him? Louisa.

Why was it again that she didn't have kids? Oh, that's right. She wasn't sharing.

His gem-of-a-find was hiding more than a few secrets, and unlike that herd of women all standing together and tittering at God knows what, he actually wanted to learn all of Louisa's secrets.

And that was a very, very, very bad sign.

"What do you think, Zane?" Louisa asked him, yanking him out of his thoughts.

He blinked and then plastered a smile on his face. "Sorry, you caught me daydreaming," he admitted with a sheepish grin. "What was the question?"

"You said the other day that Stetson had invited us over for dinner," Louisa said with barely concealed annoyance, "and Wyatt here was just seconding the invitation. He was thinking my aunt can cook for us and we can have a big get-together with the Miller clan. Get to work on fattening up Skyler."

"The kid could stand to have a little meat on him," Zane said with a sigh. When he was Skyler's age, he had a hollow leg. He could eat anything and everything in a ten-mile radius and still be hungry when he was done. Skyler only picking at his food was a foreign concept to him, that was for damn sure.

"He's eating a little more lately," Louisa reminded him. "It's his activity levels. Just sitting around, playing video games doesn't work up an appetite. Kayaking, horseback riding, our exercises…he's starting to eat more, and get more color into his cheeks. Anyway," she waved a hand dismissively, "what about Wyatt's offer? Dinner at Stetson's place?"

"We'd love to," Zane said, shaking Wyatt's hand with appreciation. "After everything I've heard about Carmelita's cooking, I think I just might show up with sweatpants on, though. Just so I'm prepared."

Wyatt let out a belly laugh at the idea. "Carmelita is not one of those people who approves of a body wearing sweatpants outside of their bedroom, but I bet if you told her why you were, she just might forgive you *and* give you an extra helping of dessert."

"She does sound like my kind of woman," Zane said with a naughty grin. "My publicist would kill me if I came back to Tennessee this fall twenty pounds heavier, but ooohhhh, the memories would be worth it."

Louisa rolled her eyes. "I don't even want to hear about it," she said primly. "Guys get a little potbelly, and they're just 'getting a little stocky.' Women gain three pounds in their thighs, and suddenly, they're letting themselves go and need to survive on celery sticks for the next month to lose it all."

"You sound like my wife, Abby. If I had a dollar for every time she pointed out the discrepancies between how men and women were treated…well, I'd have a lot of dollars."

But Zane had stopped paying attention again. He was busy mentally drooling over Louisa's thighs. They were delicious-looking in her short shorts – long and caramel and smooth, with lots of muscle and thighs that'd wrap around his head as he was down between her thighs, taking her on a ride to heaven…

She could say what she wanted, but in Zane's mind, she was as perfect as they came.

And that was a really, really, *really* big problem.

CHAPTER 15

LOUISA

THEY PILED out of the Audi and into the bright summer sunshine, Skyler quickly transferring himself to his wheelchair and zipping up to the front porch of the farmhouse where he came to an abrupt stop. He stared at the two steps that led up to the front porch, so innocent. So benign.

So unattainable.

"Dammit," Louisa muttered under her breath. The Miller family farmhouse had been built over a hundred years ago, long before anyone had any concept about ADA and wheelchair access. "Coming," she called out, hurrying over to his side before he could spend too much time contemplating the unfairness of the world. He had enough chances to think about things like that; he didn't need to do it here, in the home of her *tia*.

As if her thoughts had summoned her, Carmelita opened up the front door with a wide smile. *"Mi sobrina,"* she said. "Oh, it is so good to see you again. You look just like your mother." Louisa chuckled under her breath as she maneuvered the wheelchair up the steps, trying not to jostle Skyler too much. Carmelita said that every time she saw

Louisa. It was true that Louisa was a spitting image of her mother, but 24 years younger. If anyone ever wanted to know what Louisa would look like when she was older, they just had to take one look at her mother.

Finally, Skyler was firmly on the front porch and Louisa could turn to give her *tia* a long hug. She was a short, round woman who always wore her graying hair up in a bun, her mouth curved into a permanent smile. Louisa had inherited her height from her father, and found with a bit of shock that her beloved aunt only came up to about her shoulder or so. Had Carmelita shrunk? Or had Louisa just grown a lot since they'd last seen each other?

"You are so tall," Carmelita clucked. "Just like your father. Now, who is this handsome young man?"

"*Tia* Carmelita," Louisa said, "this is Skyler Risley, and his father, Zane Risley." She stepped out of the way so Zane could shake her hand too, but Carmelita only had eyes for Skyler.

"Oh, it looks like you have not been eating enough *pan dulce*," Carmelita said with a sad shake of her head. "Come inside, come inside. I do not have any *pan dulce* made right now, but I do have cookies. Peanut butter – do you like peanut butter?"

"I do," Skyler said eagerly, popping his front tires up over the doorstep and then waiting impatiently for Zane to lift up the back part of his wheelchair and get him over the hump. Once he was in there, he was off, Carmelita leading the way to the kitchen, chatting about the different cookies they could make together that afternoon.

Stetson, who'd apparently been hanging off to the side to allow Skyler through, stepped forward, shaking Louisa and then Zane's hand. "Good to see you both again," he said with an easy smile. Louisa waited for the storm of butterflies to swarm through her stomach as they always did when Stetson was around. She must've harbored a secret crush on him for a dozen years by this point.

But even his calloused hand in hers didn't do a thing. No butterflies – hell, not even a solitary moth – took up fluttering.

Interesting…

Was she immune to married men? That must be it.

"Have you two met my wife, Jennifer?" he asked, stepping back and bringing his wife forward. She was just a tiny thing, dwarfed by her tall husband, and holding a sturdy-looking toddler on her hip. "And this is our baby, Flint." The pride was so obvious in his voice, he sounded like he'd just won the national rodeo championship. Jennifer lifted Flint's chubby arm and waved it at them.

"Oh my goodness," Louisa said, "he is such an adorable baby!" She heard Stetson and Zane move off to the living room to chat, but she only had eyes for Flint. "How old is he?" she asked, looking up into Jennifer's startling green eyes. She stifled a sigh of jealousy – her eyes were an ordinary brown that no one would pay a bit of attention to, not the color of spring like Jennifer's.

"He's a little over two – two years and three months, if you count such things," Jennifer said, just as much pride in her voice as Stetson had had. "I'm quite afraid with Carmelita as a grandmother, he's going to be spoiled rotten, but at least he'll be the cutest kid on the block, too. It'll help him weasel his way out of trouble a little easier."

"I have five younger brothers and sisters, including a pair of twin girls, and unfortunately, every word of that is true." She wrinkled her nose at Jennifer. "My mother let my younger siblings get away with *murder*. She always told me that she was becoming a better mother as time went on because she was learning patience, but to me…" She shook her head mournfully. "I always told her that we just needed to make one of them disappear, and the other ones would shape right up. It only takes one."

Jennifer threw her head back and laughed, and then let the squirming Flint down onto the floor where he gripped her finger and began pulling her towards the kitchen. "Carma, Carma, Carma," Flint chanted, tugging his mom's finger.

"You should talk to Stetson's older brothers," Jennifer told Louisa as they began following her son. "According to them, Stetson was the most spoiled child on the face of the planet."

"Who was the most spoiled child?" Declan asked as they came through the kitchen doorway. He was tossing a fresh-from-the-oven cookie back and forth, trying to get it to cool down so he could eat it.

"My husband," Jennifer said dryly.

"Oh, that's true," Declan affirmed fervently. "Spoiled *rotten*. It was terrible. I kept telling Mom that she was creating a monster, but she wouldn't listen to me. Damn good—" Carmelita cleared her throat loudly, "darn good thing you showed up, Jennifer," he corrected quickly. "Straightened him out."

"Stetson has a good heart," Carmelita said, sliding a plate of gooey-looking cookies onto the kitchen table shoved against the wall. "He just has to be reminded sometimes to make good choices, too." She sent Declan a meaningful look. "Like not swearing."

Declan's ears turned pink.

"Best go see that Stetson is taking care of our guest," he said loudly to the room, and scooted out past Louisa and Jennifer and back into the living room.

Skyler was pulled up to a long counter, cutting cookies out of sugar cookie dough. "Look at the pumpkin!" he said, proudly pulling a pumpkin-shaped cookie off the counter for Louisa to inspect. "Carmelita says she has a ghost in here too."

"You can't make Halloween cookies already," Louisa protested, scooting up beside him and tearing a small corner of the cookie dough off and popping it into her mouth. "It's only July!"

"No eating the dough!" Carmelita reprimanded, smacking Louisa's hand lightly. Skyler laughed uproariously at the idea of his nanny getting into trouble. Louisa glared down at him. He grinned unrepentantly.

"Don't you have something else to do?" Louisa asked pointedly. "Where's Juan at?"

Jennifer, sitting at the kitchen table and doing her best to feed Flint a cookie without having most of it end up in his hair, said, "In the backyard. Actually, Skyler, you should go check it out. Juan has this huge area where he uses bulldozers and trucks to create racetracks for cars."

"Real bulldozers?" Skyler asked, his eyes round as quarters.

"Oh heavens no," Jennifer said, laughing. "Toy ones. But very realistic. I bet if you asked, he'd let you help."

Skyler's mouth screwed up at the corner and Louisa was sure he was thinking, "Don't be so sure about that," but the idea of playing with bulldozers – even if they were toy ones – won out.

"Thank you, *Tia* Carmelita," he said sincerely, grabbed two cookies, put them on his lap, and raced out the back door. Louisa followed right behind him, but saw that Skyler was going to be able to easily get over to the sandbox where Juan was playing, and came back into the kitchen. It was best to always have him do whatever he could by himself whenever he could, and getting out of his wheelchair and down to the ground was absolutely something he could do on his own.

"*Tia* Carmelita?" Louisa asked, snagging a delicious-looking peanut butter cookie from the platter on the table. "So you adopted him, too?"

"That boy needs someone to fatten him up," Carmelita said, sliding a tray of cookies into the oven and setting a timer. "He is only skin and bones. He needs to be outside more."

"If you think he's bad now," Louisa said dryly, "you should've seen him when I first took over. He was white as a sheet all of the time – no color in his cheeks. Hardly any appetite. Only ever wanted to play video games downstairs in the basement. I think he'd decided that he was only going to be in that wheelchair for the rest of his life, so why even try at anything at all? But now he's riding at Dr. Whitaker's camp, and you should've seen him kayaking. He took right to it. He's starting to realize that you can do a lot with your arms that have nothing to do with a game controller, and not only that, but he actually has more control in his legs than I think even he realizes."

"Really?" Jennifer said, surprised. She'd given up on trying to hand-feed Flint and was letting him do the job now. He looked like he'd taken a bath in crumbled cookies…and was completely delighted about it. She was sitting back in the kitchen chair, watching Louisa closely. "So what do you think that means for Skyler?"

"Not much at all if I can't convince him it's true," Louisa said with a dispirited shrug. "Nothing matters more than how much a patient wants something, and Skyler gave up way back when he was still in the hospital. He didn't think he'd get any better, therefore, he didn't get any better. We've started doing exercises together every day before going to camp – I hold the controller for the console hostage until he does them with me – but he's only half-hearted at best. If I can just get him to believe…"

Carmelita hugged her tightly. "*Mi sobrina*," she said quietly into Louisa's hair, and then pulled back. "You have always cared so much about other people – it is one of your biggest strengths. You are in Skyler's life for a reason. Do not question *Dios*. He knows what He's doing. Now," she said in a happier tone of voice, "let us carry some of this food outside. I am sure everyone is ready to eat, eh?"

With a woebegone look at the platter of cookies, Louisa picked up a hot bowl of green beans with bacon bits, plopped a serving spoon in it, and carried it outside to the buffet table set up off to the side. It was a bright summer's day, which also meant a hot summer's day, and Louisa was glad to see that the Millers had thought to set up canopies to shade them from the sun. There were a few pine trees at the edge of the lawn but with the sun coming straight down on them, there wasn't any way to scoot under them to find some shade.

With reluctant groans, Skyler and Juan left the sandbox behind, covered almost head to toe in sand and grit, and went inside to clean up. Louisa looked at her aunt and noticed the tight corners of her mouth, and grinned to herself. She was probably counting down the minutes until everyone would leave and she could clean up her doubtlessly dirty floor.

After all of the food had been carried out of the house and placed on the groaning buffet tables, everyone began serving up. Louisa spotted a petite woman with fiery red hair maneuvering around with a cane in her hand, which brought Louisa up short. She was much too young to be using a cane, and Louisa wondered what her story was, and which Miller brother she was married to. She also saw a larger woman – not fat, but lots of work muscle on her – juggling two plates. One was Declan's wife and one was Wyatt's wife, and Louisa entertained herself while waiting in line by guessing who was paired up with whom.

After she filled up her plate to the brim with only a small portion of the food her *tia* had laid out, Louisa carefully carried it back to a table and slipped in beside Jennifer. Skyler and Juan were at a table by themselves, eating and making what appeared to be farting noises to each other, laughing uproariously together. She pretended deafness. As long as they weren't fighting, Louisa could put up with almost anything.

"Louisa," Jennifer said while carefully guiding a spoonful of mashed potatoes into Flint's mouth, "this is Abby," the dark-haired woman raised her hand in greeting, "and this is Iris." The redhead farther down the table next to Declan raised her hand in greeting. *Well, that answers that question.* "Abby and Iris, this is Louisa. She's helping take care of Skyler this summer. Abby is married to my oldest brother-in-law, Wyatt, and Iris is married to Declan. None of us women have killed our husbands yet, and thus we consider ourselves to be highly successful in our marriages."

"Hear, hear," said Declan, raising his glass in a mock toast. "As one of the men in question, I appreciate my wife's tolerance, and the fact that I'm on the green side of the grass. Thanks, sweetie." He popped Iris a kiss on the lips as everyone roared with laughter.

Louisa sat back and listened as the talking flowed around them, enjoying the food and the company and the warmth of the summer day. It would be back to snow soon enough. For right now, she was happy to revel in the high 80s.

She caught eyes with Zane who was sitting further down the table next to Carmelita, and he gave her a silent toast with his beer bottle, a happy grin on his face. Instead of being overwhelmed by the sheer number of new people who were there, he was in his element. He was clearly such an extrovert that it made her wonder again why he was spending so much of his time out of the spotlight and away from people. This was where he was happiest – why torture himself by secluding himself far away from everyone and everything?

You, Zane Risley, are one big mystery, and I absolutely cannot unwrap all of your protective layers to 'solve' you, no matter how much I'd love to…

And that was something she could not let herself forget.

CHAPTER 16

LOUISA

S HE PICKED UP the baby bib from the craft market display and laughed to herself. *I'm the world's cutest tax deduction* was embroidered across the front of it. This would be *perfect* for Jennifer's baby, Flint, considering she was an accountant for small business owners. Louisa was debating between that one and *My fingers may be small, but I still have my grandma wrapped around them* when a small ruckus broke out behind her. She looked around and saw Zane being piled on by a ton of tourists, squeals and high-pitched laughter ringing out from the aggressive group.

Dammit.

They'd been having such a lovely morning down at the Franklin crafts fair, just browsing, Skyler trying to find the perfect present for Carmelita's upcoming 70th birthday party, but now…

Zane was signing a few autographs and posing for pictures, but she knew him well enough by now to know that he wasn't happy. He looked up and caught her eye and mouthed, *Sorry,* as if it were his fault that he was being mugged by people who had no concept of personal space.

Impulsively, Louisa put the two bibs down – she'd pick something out later – and strode over to the group.

"Okay, okay, that's enough," she said, trying to put a happy face on while still being blunt about the reality of the situation. "Mr. Risley here needs his privacy. Let's give him some space."

She made shooing motions with her hands, trying to brush them off, when a male voice behind her muttered, "What's with the spic thinking she can boss us around?"

Louisa spun on her heel, her cheeks flushing red with anger, trying to find the person who made the comment but whoever he was, he was too much of a coward to meet her eye and own up to what he said.

Bastard.

She looked at Zane and the thunderous look on his face… she knew he'd heard it too. Zane finished his signature on the piece of paper a woman was thrusting at him and then pushed his way out of the crowd even as people surged forward, trying to get closer.

"Skyler," he barked, and then took off at a trot for the Audi. Louisa swept in behind Skyler, grabbed the handles of his wheelchair, and began following on Zane's heels, running over one person who'd gotten too close and refused to back off.

"Hey!" the woman yelled. "That was my foot!"

"And that *was* my peaceful Saturday morning!" Louisa yelled back. "So we're even."

Skyler lifted himself into his seat in the Audi, Louisa collapsed the wheelchair down into the carrying position, slid it inside, and hurried around to the driver's seat as the woman yelled back, "You can't talk to me like that! I wasn't doing anything wrong!"

Louisa slid inside the SUV and slammed the driver's side door shut, blocking out all sound before she could be tempted to do something that'd make the headlines of every gossip rag in the country. She threw the vehicle into reverse and tore out of the parking lot.

She gripped the steering wheel like her life depended upon it, feeling the anger grow larger with each passing moment instead of subsiding. *Spic? Spic?! How dare they*—

"How are you, Skyler, are you okay?" she asked, her voice deliberately calm, as if they were out for nothing more than a Sunday afternoon drive. Nothing was wrong. Nothing bad was happening. Everything was fine.

"What happened?" Skyler asked, his voice high and reedy like it always was when he was scared. Louisa blew out a breath. She was causing him to panic. That wasn't okay.

She purposefully relaxed her shoulders and the grip on the steering wheel. "Someone—" she said at the same time that Zane started, "There was—"

They both stopped.

Zane sent her a sideways glance. "It was you they were calling names," he said quietly. "Would you like to explain? Or would you prefer I do it?"

"Someone back there called me…called me a…a *spic*." She couldn't believe she'd just said that word. She'd take the Lord's name in vain before she said something so foul, and that was really saying something.

"A spi—"

"Don't say that word," Louisa said savagely, and she realized that the world was watery and dammit all, she was *crying*. She pulled over onto the shoulder of the road, flipped on the emergency blinkers, and took a few shuddering breaths. Why was it that she cried when she wasn't sad? She was pissed. She was angry. She had a ball of fire and anger boiling inside of her.

She was *not* sad.

"Sorry," she said into the silence. She unbuckled her seat

belt and turned in the driver's seat to look back at Skyler. He looked horrified. Crushed. Even when he'd put salt in her coffee and honey in her hairbrush, she'd never yelled at him. "I'm sorry," she said again, softer this time. "I'm not mad at you. I want you to know that. You haven't done a damn thing wrong. That…*word* is a very, very bad word. It's a really awful way of saying that I'm Mexican. There's a similar word for black people that starts with an N – if I ever catch you saying that word, I'll paddle your ass so hard, you won't be able to sit for a week. You hear me?"

Skyler nodded, his brilliant blue eyes, just like his father's, were huge. Distraught.

"When people call a Mexican person a…*that* word, they're saying that I am less than them. I am less important. I don't matter, not really. In their small little brains, this makes them feel better, because I feel worse. But truthfully, I probably have more years of education than that bastard back there. I'm sure I make more than him. Hell, I probably made more than him when I worked down at the hospital. We had people transfer in from all over the nation just to get our specialized care in our hospital, the kind of care they couldn't get anywhere else, because we were damn good at what we did." The anger was rising again, threatening to boil out of control. "I'm smart, dammit," she yelled, pounding her fist on the steering wheel. "No one gets to call me a—"

She stopped herself. She was breathing hard, like she'd just run a mile. She wanted to scream at the injustice of it all. A little bit of extra melatonin in her skin, and she was somehow sub-human?

"I'm sorry, *cariño*," she said softly. "I have a lot of pride in my heritage. People who look at me or *Tia* Carmelita and only see the color of our skin are not people I want to ever be around. I guess it's better if they say terrible things about me so I know who they *really* are, and can avoid them, right? Makes it easier to spot 'em."

"I wish I'd heard him," Skyler said savagely. "I woulda punched him in the nuts."

Zane let out a choked laugh. Even Louisa felt herself smile just a bit. "Although I appreciate your willingness to punch a full-grown man in the nuts for me," she said dryly, "my mom would say that violence never helped anything. There are days when it's awfully tempting, though."

She felt a little calmer, a little more capable of driving, and so she put the SUV into gear and pulled back out onto the road. "The truth is, Sky, most all of us face discrimination in one form or another. Me, because I am a woman and Mexican. You, because you're in a wheelchair. You're going to have people who can't look past the wheels and will think that you're stupid or deaf or something, because your legs don't work. Be prepared to explain to people that just because your legs don't do what you want them to doesn't mean your ears don't work." She could tell he wanted to interrupt – probably to talk more about punching people in the nuts – and so she hurried on to the important part, before they could get sidetracked into when it was appropriate to hit people and when it wasn't.

"You want to know what the best revenge is, Skyler?" she asked, and then plunged on before he could answer. "Living your best life. You are worthy, just the way you are. Live a happy, contented life doing what *you* care about, and let those judgmental assholes go elsewhere. Don't you ever let anyone tell you what you can or cannot do. The only boundaries you have in life are the ones you set on yourself."

She felt like a football coach in one of those dramatic sports movies, right before the team runs out onto the field and makes a comeback to win the game, but she couldn't help herself. She wanted Skyler to know this – no, *needed* him to know this, for himself.

She pulled into the garage of the mansion, the lights turning on automatically, the garage door closing behind them, but still, it was quiet inside of the SUV. After her rah-rah-rah speech, Louisa wasn't really sure what else to say. Skyler didn't move for a little while, just thinking, and then finally he said, "Okay."

She smiled at him in the rearview mirror. "You ready to go inside?" she asked, more than ready herself to lighten the mood.

He pushed the button on the sliding side door, waited for it to open silently, shook open the wheelchair and placed it just outside of the door, eased himself into it, and then looked up at Louisa with a taunting grin. "Beat you inside!" he crowed, and sped off through the mudroom door and into the house.

"You cheater!" she called out after him, fumbling with her seat belt and finally flinging it off. She tore off after him but of course, he'd already made it to the kitchen by the time she got inside.

"Since I beat you inside, can I go play on the Xbox?" he asked hopefully. Those gorgeous blue eyes were trained on her again, and she knew she was a goner. She couldn't believe how susceptible she was to them. Where was her tough-stuff exterior that she'd always used with her brothers and sisters?

"Yes," she said with a sigh, and he whooped with delight, tearing off for the elevator before she could change her mind.

"You did good," Zane said quietly behind her, and she clutched at her heart as she spun in a half-circle.

"*Dios mío*," she muttered under her breath. Somehow, just for a moment or two, she'd forgotten about Zane, which considering how he normally set her nerve-endings on fire whenever he was in the same zip code as her, was really saying something.

"You want something to drink?" Zane asked, heading for the fridge and pulling out a longneck for himself.

"No, I'm okay," she said, waving off the offer. It was only

11:30 in the morning – a little early to start drinking in her opinion – but then again, what they'd just gone through would probably drive the pope to drink.

"Why did you quit the hospital?"

The question fell like a bomb in the quiet between them.

CHAPTER 17
ZANE

E KNEW he was kind of a bastard for pushing Louisa like this, especially after such a rough morning – *screw that, I am a bastard* – but after listening to her passionate speech about all that she did at the hospital, and it being the finest in the nation…

There was something there, something huge, and he wanted to know what it was. As her employer, maybe it wasn't any of his business, but as her friend…

He needed to know.

"I wanted to spend more time with my family," Louisa said, her gaze slipping away from him like a soap bubble sliding over the surface of the water.

"Bullshit," he said bluntly. Her eyes snapped up to his and her temper – a side of her that she'd kept hidden so well before today – came swinging into action.

"Are you calling me a liar?" she demanded. She looked like she was ready to dish out Skyler's idea of revenge and kick Zane in the nuts. He took a step back just in case, but continued on.

"I am," he said calmly. "At least about this. I looked it up on Google Maps – Salt Lake City is *way* closer to your hometown of Pocatello than Sawyer is. If you really quit the hospital to be closer to your family, why would you then agree to move to Sawyer a week after that? And don't even try to give me any bullshit about how Carmelita is family also. She is, but you sure as hell didn't quit your job at the hospital with the expectation that I would hire you and move you over to this side of the state. *I* didn't even know that I needed to hire you, considering I came here with an aide on the plane sitting next to me. I didn't expect to hire anyone at all. So tell me again: Why did you quit the hospital?"

She ground her teeth furiously, her brown eyes brilliant with anger and some emotion he couldn't identify. The "nut punch" was looking more and more likely by the moment.

But still, he kept eye contact with her, refusing to look away, refusing to back down.

"Dr. Matthew Funk," she finally spit out, pronouncing each word like she'd pronounced *spic*. "He was my boss…and my boyfriend. I was that stupid, naïve nurse who fell in love with the doctor." She shook her head disdainfully. "You two look a lot alike, by the way," she said in an off-hand tone of voice, as if mentioning that day's weather to him. Zane's eyebrows snapped together. He did *not* want to look like this douchebag. He knew virtually nothing about the man, but he did know that. "I almost didn't take this job because of it. Freaked me out a little. But I'd signed a contract, and…" She waved the thought away. "We weren't supposed to be dating, of course. He was my boss, for heaven's sakes. It breaks every rule in the book. But I made him into a better man and completed him and la-di-da. You know the bullshit line you feed a woman when you want to get into her panties."

Zane opened his mouth to defend himself – he didn't feed women bullshit lines to get into their beds – but she continued, oblivious to the insults she was indiscriminately lobbing his direction.

"Another nurse was retiring and I was going to be

promoted and because of the hierarchy of the hospital, this would've technically taken me out of Matthew's line of leadership. Once that happened, we'd go public with our relationship and get married. Finally start having those kids I've always wanted." She sent him a wry smile. "Yes, I've always wanted to have children and yes, it's been a huge disappointment in my life that I'm 28 years old and still don't have any. Thanks for asking that question, by the way."

Zane wanted to shrink down inside of himself at her sarcastic words. He was a bastard. He didn't deserve her putting up with him as a boss, that was for damn sure.

"Except he came home one day with a CNA in tow. They'd met at the hospital and fallen in love, right under my nose. I'd thought they'd seemed awfully chummy, but I told myself to stop being a jealous woman and to trust Matthew. Turns out, trusting Matthew was a very, very bad idea. She was pregnant, and unlike me, completely willing to drop her virtually nonexistent career in order to be Matthew's wife. You see, I was holding out for the big promotion before we made our relationship public. I wanted the career *and* the family. This…*woman* only wanted the ring on her finger. And God, what a big ring it was. I'm surprised she could lift her hand, it was so huge and gaudy. Matt told me that I needed to move out and find a new place to live, since his place obviously wouldn't work any longer since he needed a home to raise his new baby in, but that of course, I should stay on at the hospital. This wouldn't change a thing between us there."

She laughed bitterly, her brown eyes flashing. "You can imagine how I felt about *that* idea. I packed up, quit the hospital with no notice, and moved back to Pocatello and into my mother's house. I completely screwed over my career by doing that, of course – the hospital won't give me a good recommendation after I quit without notice, and Matt certainly isn't going to help me out, not after the names I called him." She sent him a painful smile. "I went from being on the cusp of having it all, to having nothing at all."

"I'm sorry you hurt your career because of what that douchebag did," he said quietly. "Somehow, it seems like the people who cause the problems rarely have to be the ones to deal with the consequences."

"I'll be honest, I was starting to get worn down by the pace," she admitted. "Nurses work 12-hour shifts. I was bone-deep tired after a while. I rarely took a day off because time-and-a-half was a great way to make some extra cash to pay down student loans, and the hospital always seemed to be in crisis mode, needing someone to take on extra shifts to keep everything covered. I didn't want to say no. I never wanted to be the one who let down the hospital in any way. And then, I just quit on them without any notice at all, soooo…yeah. I'm pretty sure my name was a swear word there for a while. No one knew about Matthew and I, and he sure wasn't going to tell anyone, so I'm sure everyone just thinks I'm a flake."

"But here, I make you work 24-hour shifts without a day off," he said teasingly, trying to lighten the mood. "How are you even surviving that grueling pace?"

"Oh, even worse," she said, leaning forward and whispering as if sharing a secret with him, "you should meet my boss. You've never met a bigger bastard in all your life."

He bursted out laughing at that one and she shot a grin at him, her perfect cupid's bow lips stretching to show her perfect white teeth.

There was something about the angle, about the tilt of her head, about the sound of her laughter, and instantly, it washed over him. "That wasn't a dream," he murmured.

"What?" she asked, startled.

"I hit on you one night. When I was drunk. I'd thought maybe it was a dream but it wasn't, was it." It was a statement, not a question. The horror began to bloom inside of him at what he'd done.

She shook her head slowly. "No, that was real," she whispered.

"I'm sorry. I don't normally do that kind of thing. I was seven flags to the wind and I didn't know what I was doing. That isn't an excuse because it isn't okay. I shouldn't have—"

She put her soft hand on his arm, stopping him. "It's all right. You haven't done it since. You haven't made a habit of it. And twice was all of the chances that you would've gotten, by the way. If you'd done it again, I would've taken Skyler's advice, kneed you in the nuts, and walked out." He grimaced in pain at just the thought of it, crossing his legs instinctively. She laughed. "But you haven't. Your balls are safe, I promise."

They both laughed for a moment and then fell silent as Zane thought through what she'd just said.

I look just like him, but even worse, I've wanted to act like him. Not the CNA part, of course, but the dating of a coworker – no, worse, a boss. I still do. Right at this very moment, I do, and dear God, what kind of an ass would that make me? She's already been down this road with Matt. She's already been screwed over by a boss. I can't do that again to her.

His fingers itched to follow the curve of her cheek but he balled them into fists instead.

Absolutely not, asshole.

He pitched his beer bottle into the trash and snagged another one from the fridge. "I better go do..." and finished the sentence with a mumble that even he didn't understand. *Go anywhere but here and keep my hands off you* was how he wanted to finish the sentence but he couldn't. He wouldn't. He popped the top off the beer, swigged some back, and headed out to the den in his workshop. Some time spent watching TV and not staring at Louisa's lips would be time well spent.

He left her in the kitchen, staring after him, and he let himself wonder, just for a moment, what she was thinking.

Did she want him as much as he wanted her? Surely this couldn't be one-sided. Surely…

But he'd never know, would he? Because the one thing in life he could not have was Louisa Vargas.

CHAPTER 18

LOUISA

LOUISA SNUCK a peek at Zane as they headed for Dr. Whitaker's place. Over the course of the summer, he'd started coming occasionally to the therapy lessons, and her first instinct had been to tell him he didn't have to. After all, he was paying her obscene amounts of money to take care of Skyler, and surely driving Skyler back and forth to the lessons was part of that deal.

But then, she'd taken one look at Skyler's thrilled face and had shut her mouth. More than learning how to balance on a horse, more than learning how to transfer correctly, more than the exercises they continued to do together each morning, Skyler building a relationship with his father was the most important thing Louisa could help facilitate that summer. After she was gone, Skyler would still need his dad – would need his dad even more than ever, actually – and she wouldn't be doing him any favors by telling Zane not to worry about going with them to the lessons.

Not to mention that Skyler would probably never forgive her for it.

After she was gone…

There was a stab of pain in her chest, sharp and hard and

cold, at the thought. It'd only been a couple of months but already, she had a hard time imagining life without them. Skyler was getting better every day – stronger, more control over his legs, more meat on his bones, more color in his face – and Zane…

Well, how did one improve on perfection?

No, scratch that. He hadn't been perfect, at least not when it came to his relationship with Skyler, that was for damn sure. But the two of them were getting along better now than ever before, and she could actually see a real connection building between them, one day at a time. Zane coming to therapy camp with them each day was just one more sign of that. By the time she left, would their relationship be strong enough to survive without her help?

If she'd done her job right, it would.

That's one hell of an if, *Louisa.*

She tried not to let the weight of her task overwhelm her.

They pulled into the open parking lot of the Whitaker place, Juan there waiting for them, hopping from foot to foot, impatiently gesturing for Skyler to get out and get to work with him. Skyler unloaded himself from the SUV – there was no longer any mention of anyone else helping him; he was doing it all himself, another big change from when Louisa had first started – and together, Sky and Juan zipped off for the barn, talking a million miles an hour to each other like they hadn't seen each other in years, instead of just over the weekend.

Louisa sent Zane a small smile and got out to follow after them. After their…discussion in the kitchen on Saturday, when Louisa had finally told Zane the truth about her stupidity, she'd wanted to hide under the couch and not come out for the rest of the day. Preferably the rest of the month. He must've thought she was so dumb, having a secret affair with her boss, believing her boss, living with her boss. *Stupid Louisa. Ignorant Louisa.*

She was grateful that he'd seemed to understand just what she'd wanted, because he'd headed into the depths of the mansion and she hadn't seen him for the rest of the day.

Perfect.

Except now they were back to interacting with each other and she wasn't sure how to navigate this new world. Did they talk about the whole disaster more? Or just pretend like nothing happened?

Ignoring it all seemed like a stand-up idea to her.

She heard Zane's boots crunching on the gravel behind her as they headed for the barn, but she didn't slow down to let him walk beside her, and he didn't hurry up to walk beside her. Good. They were in agreement then. Another handful of weeks just like this and then she'd go back to Pocatello and find a *real* job and get on with her life.

She could make it that long. She could do almost anything for only a handful of weeks.

They stepped inside the cool of the barn where they found a flustered Dr. Whitaker, trying to herd the kids all in the right direction and failing miserably. Louisa knew almost nothing about horses – her experience was limited to the few times her family had come to Sawyer to visit *Tia* Carmelita and one of the Miller brothers would saddle up the horses for her and her younger siblings to ride around the farm a bit – but she did know about getting kids to all move in the right direction. That, she could do blindfolded.

Leaving Zane behind to do whatever it was that he did best – probably schmoozing and flirting with the gaggle of women who'd all started coming to the lessons, dressed to the 9's and hair sprayed to perfection – she hurried over to Dr. Whitaker. "Need help?" she asked.

"Yes, please," he said, his deep voice strained with trying to keep it together in the face of chaos. "I need to start turning people away. I just hate to do that because I want every kid to have a chance to ride, but once word got around that Zane

Risley was here…Well, let's just say that this is the most popular my therapy camp has ever been." He flashed her a quick smile. "If you can just wander around and break up the arguments between kids over who gets what horse and which bridle, that'd be great." A pair of heated voices rose above the general roar of human speech, and they both turned to look at the disturbance and then back to each other.

Louisa laughed. "Well, I'm off."

It was a blur after that of children and horses and oats and leather, a sort of general pandemonium that others would find exhausting but Louisa found exhilarating. This was her in her element. This was what she was good at. Maybe she wasn't busy dispensing pain killers or discussing treatment options with patients, but still, directing traffic and breaking up arguments and prioritizing who got what and went where…it kept her on her toes. It wasn't boring, and if there was one thing Louisa could not stand, it was being bored.

Finally, all of the kids had somehow managed to find their way onto a saddled *and* bridled horse – there'd been a few who'd tried to skip the bridles, much to the dismay of the horse that was getting its mane yanked out by its roots, so Louisa'd had to put a stop to that – and out the door and into the arena. With a happy sigh of relief, she walked out and leaned against the fence to watch the parade of riders, some holding on for dear life while others were comfortably riding, moving smoothly with the horse. It wasn't hard to tell who was new to the program, or at least to riding in general.

She heard the crunch of Zane's boots on the gravel behind her and knew who it was before she even saw him out of the corner of her eye. He just lit up the world around her like a beacon of lust and attraction.

No big surprise that he made it to the top. His magnetic personality…there was no way he wouldn't *thrive.*

"You were a marvel to watch back there," he said, his deep, husky voice sending chills up her spine as he leaned against the fence next to her. "You're like a one-woman tornado of order and discipline. Instead of creating chaos everywhere you go, you make everything work right."

She rolled her eyes at his over-the-top praise. "It's not hard to work with kids. They're straightforward. They haven't learned how to lie yet, or at least aren't very good at it. It's the adults who make life difficult. They always have a hidden agenda that doesn't match the side that they show everyone else." She realized how bitter she sounded and snapped her mouth shut. She needed to put the brakes on her whining. No one wanted to listen to her whine, least of all herself.

"So," she said brightly, bluntly changing the subject, "how are your legions of fans?" She subtly tilted her head towards the gaggle of women all clustered together off to the side, laughing too loudly, sneaking glances at Zane whenever they thought he wasn't looking.

And sometimes when he was, in a bold attempt to catch his eye.

"Oh, the herd?" he said, no interest at all in his voice. Louisa snort-laughed at the term and he sent her a sly grin. "You'd never catch me saying that within earshot of 'em, but yeah, that's what I've nicknamed them."

"I call them the gaggle," she whispered in a confidential voice, leaning close to him so no one could overhear them.

He threw back his head and laughed uproariously. "I'm not sure which I like better," he said after finally drawing in a breath. "You're doing good, Skyler!" he called out as Skyler bounced by, Juan on the next horse over, his ride a little smoother.

Skyler nodded his head in acknowledgement but didn't say anything. Juan hollered, "Hi, Mr. Risley!" and added in a wave as he went. Skyler looked as if he took his hands off the horn in front of him, he'd end up in the dirt.

"Not to put too fine a point on it, but I don't think Skyler's going to grow up to train horses for a living," Louisa said dryly as the pair passed and began curving into the corner of the track.

"No, I don't think he will," Zane agreed. "If it wasn't for you, Juan, and the Miller family in general, we would've headed back to Tennessee a long time ago."

Louisa felt a blush start in her toes and wash over her body in an instant. More so than even his compliment about creating order out of chaos, the idea that they'd stayed in Idaho because of her was…

She was busy trying to figure out exactly what that meant, actually, when Dr. Whitaker walked up.

"Thanks for the help, Louisa," he said gratefully, doffing his hat as he shook her hand in gratitude. "I probably ought to break down and hire someone else to help out but I keep thinking that as the kids get used to the routine, things will calm down. Plus, the summer is almost done, so…" He shrugged. "As my thank-you, would you guys enjoy a ride of your own? *Not* in the riding ring with the kids?"

"Ooohhhh…that'd be fun," Louisa said happily, and then stopped and looked at Zane. He was the boss. She was the hired help. Just because she lived with him and his son and they went a lot of places together didn't mean he wanted to go somewhere with just her. They'd always gone places together with Skyler.

Get a grip on yourself. No one wants to go out for a Monday afternoon horse ride with the nanny.

Except Zane's face was lit up with excitement and he looked like he wanted to do nothing more than just that. "Do you have horses left for us to take?"

"Just barely," Dr. Whitaker admitted. "Once the enrollments started rolling in, I asked some friends of mine around the valley if I could stable and feed their horses for the summer in exchange for using them in this program. Only the gentlest of horses, of course. I have just two left after getting all of the kids out the door today."

"Where would we go ride?" Louisa asked, stalling for time, trying to figure out if she should agree to this insane idea or not. *What happened to the no-interaction-let's-pretend-nothing-happened Louisa of just an hour ago?* She searched frantically inside of herself for that version of her.

Completely and totally gone.

Great. All of that self-discipline that you're normally infamous for has just disappeared in the face of a certain country music star. Nice time for it to go AWOL.

"If you follow that trail," Dr. Whitaker pointed to a faint dusty trail leading away from the riding ring, "it'll lead you out into the trees and down by a little stream. It's gorgeous. After I get all of the kids able to ride in circles without falling off or running into each other, I was going to try taking them down there for an afternoon picnic or something. We'll see. It just depends on how well they start listening to instructions."

Just then, a small argument broke out amongst the riders and all three of them looked up. Thankfully, it wasn't Juan and Skyler, who were at the other end of the arena, working on their cantering. Dr. Whitaker let out a sigh. "Better go see what's going on," he said over his shoulder as he headed for the squabbling children.

Zane looked at Louisa with hope in his eyes. "Do you want to go out riding?" he asked. "You don't have to if you don't want to but…I've never ridden before and have wanted to ever since we got here."

"You've never ridden a horse before?" Louisa just gaped at him, her mind blown. "But you're a country music star!" she protested. "Isn't that some sort of prerequisite?"

"You and my publicist would have a mighty fun discussion together," Zane grumbled. "She told me once that I'd have an easier time explaining away robbing someone at gun point than I would not knowing how to ride a horse."

Louisa paused for a fraction of a second as that sunk in, and then let out a howl of laughter. "I would *love* to meet your publicist," Louisa gasped, wiping away the tears in the corners of her eyes. "She sounds like my kind of gal."

"She really is," Zane said, and then headed briskly for the barn. "C'mon, before the herd descends."

They walked into the cool of the barn – oh, that was *nice* – and began saddling up the two remaining horses, both swaybacked and a bit long in the tooth. "At least we know the horses won't run away with us," Louisa said dryly. She rather doubted either of them could run, let alone with a rider on their backs. Louisa only knew marginally more about how to saddle and bridle a horse than Zane did but luckily, their horses appeared perfectly content to munch on hay and never move again, so they didn't get pissy about being saddled backwards.

When Louisa spotted the mistake, she helped Zane turn his saddle around with only a minimal amount of smirking. The way she figured it, she was operating at saint level and about to move into angel territory.

Finally, they were both on their horses and headed for the barn door. They stopped by the arena for a moment, watching Skyler and Juan trotting together, Juan clearly in his element and Skyler clearly not, and then headed out for their ride, Dr. Whitaker calling out a few last-minute tips as they rode away.

Skyler would be fine without them. She didn't need to worry about him.

But, would she be okay without Skyler's buffer between her and Zane? That was the bigger question, because at the moment, she was quite sure the answer was no.

CHAPTER 19

ZANE

Z ANE CLUNG to his saddle horn, trying to move with the sway of the horse. *Become one with the horse,* Adam had called out to them as they'd started to ride away from the arena.

Zane wasn't sure he wanted to be one with a swaybacked ancient mare, but he was also sure that he presently looked as ridiculous as he felt. Somewhere in the back of his mind, he remembered how part of his impetus for coming to Idaho instead of just sending Skyler with his aide to the camp like he had the music camp and art camp, was that he would finally be able to learn how to ride a horse. He'd had vague visions of becoming an expert horseman and wowing the journalists with his comeback story in the riding arena *and* music arena.

As he gripped the saddle horn tightly, absolutely sure that he looked just as comfortable in the saddle as his son had, he could only count his lucky stars that in a fit of hubris, he hadn't invited a whole gaggle of reporters along for the ride. Not even the kindest of reporters could fail to note his complete lack of mastery in this department, and reporters weren't exactly known for being kind.

Zane made a mental note to never ride a horse in front of a reporter. Ever.

With a disgruntled look, Zane noticed how comfortable Louisa appeared in the saddle. She looked like she was born in one and had never moved again. Actually, now that he thought about it, maybe she was an accomplished horsewoman. God only knew she was accomplished at everything else that she did.

"Can you sing?" he called out to her, the words slipping out before he'd quite realized it. He hadn't meant to ask her that. He just…

He had to be better than her at *something*.

"Not a note," she called over her shoulder cheerfully. "My whole family is tone-deaf. Not a drop of musical talent among us."

Zane admitted, if only to himself of course, that this piece of information cheered him right up. Maybe he was only good at one thing, but he was at least *damn* good at it.

Finally, they got into the cool shade of the pine trees and he heard Louisa let out a sigh of happiness. He could only imagine how hot she got during the summer with her dark, long, thick hair.

Her dark, long, thick hair that he'd had visions of unraveling from the braid she'd worked it into, and running his fingers through it…a vision that he promptly and ruthlessly squashed flat. No matter how much his fingers itched for it, there was no getting around it: Louisa was the one woman he never got to touch.

And wasn't that just the shittiest pickle to find himself in.

CHAPTER 20
LOUISA

"Want to take a little break?" Louisa asked over her shoulder as she spied the stream Dr. Whitaker had said would be there. Although Zane was behind her, making it difficult for her to keep an eye on him, he kept making little grunts and groans under his breath. She didn't figure he was enjoying this ride one little bit, and thus, a break might be useful right about now.

"Sure," Zane called back, sounding a little happier about the suggestion than could strictly be considered normal, and Louisa grinned to herself. So, Skyler took after his father when it came to riding, eh? She wondered for a moment how his former wife had fared in the saddle. She knew so little about Tamara, now that she thought about it. Was it a verboten topic? Or had she just never happened to come up? Was it healthy for Skyler to never reminisce about his own mother?

She swung down from her horse and tied it up to the lowest tree branch, and then turned back to see Zane sort of half-fall, half-slide off the horse. She stifled a laugh. Somehow, she didn't think Zane would appreciate her laughing at him. He walked stiff-legged over to the branch and tied his horse next to hers. Not that they really needed tying up – they didn't look like they were liable to run off, or even work themselves up into a canter any time soon.

"It's beautiful here," Zane said, looking around appreciatively. "And to think that all of this is just in Adam's backyard."

Louisa slipped off her socks and shoes and then began wading into the cold mountain stream, sucking in a sharp breath at the water's icy temperature, and then began to feel her feet get used to the cold and knew her brain could start working again. "What's it like in Tennessee?" she asked, sitting on the bank of the stream, wiggling her toes in the clear water, watching how the water distorted them as it flowed ceaselessly forward.

"Lots of people. Concrete. Horns. Tourists. Live music all of the time. Even a few skyscrapers."

"In *Tennessee*?!" Louisa asked, astonished.

"In Nashville? Yes. I was born and raised in Nashville proper." He toed off his boots and then peeled off his socks as he talked. He began rolling up his jeans. "People don't realize that it's bigger than Memphis. Bigger than Atlanta. It's no New York City, of course, but when you grow up in the middle of it, it's just concrete and stoplights and blaring horns as far as you can see. My parents weren't much for getting out into nature, so..." He shrugged as he sat down gracefully on a smooth rock next to her and slid his feet into the water. He sucked in a quick breath. "Damn, that's cold."

"I keep waiting for miniature icebergs to float by," Louisa admitted cheerfully. "But, at least I can say truthfully that my feet don't hurt at all. They don't feel anything at all, but that includes pain."

Zane laughed. "I know it's better to be an optimist than a pessimist, at least according to the headlines I see at the magazine rack, but I think you're taking this a little too far."

She shrugged. "It isn't any harder to look at things

positively than it is to look at them negatively, so why not choose the positive, right? So, what was your wife like as a mom for Skyler?"

She could've died.

Right there, she could've just sunk into the ground, pulled the dirt over her head, and never no *never* come out again.

She hadn't meant to ask the question. They'd been talking about being positive and icebergs and then, the topic she'd been wondering about for ages was just rolling off her tongue like she actually had any right – any right at all – to ask a question like that.

Zane froze mid-splash, his hand hovering over the stream, an almost comically surprised look on his face. "Tamara?" he asked blankly. "How was she with Skyler?"

Automatically, Louisa nodded but internally, she was trying to figure out how to best extricate herself from the situation. She could jump onto the back of her horse, thump her heels into the flanks, and ride like the devil back to Dr. Whitaker's place.

Okay, fine, she could trot painfully back to Dr. Whitaker's place, if her horse even got up to that speed.

Or she could put her shoes back on and just run back. And then, she could…

She sputtered to a mental stop. Nothing intelligent was coming to her – as if sprinting back to the Whitaker's place itself were an intelligent idea – when Zane started speaking, yanking her attention back to him. He spoke quietly, deliberately, as if carefully thinking through everything he was saying as he said it, maybe for the first time in his life.

"Tamara loved Skyler more than she loved life itself. I didn't really get it at the time. This marks me as the worst father on the planet, I'm sure, but I didn't want Skyler. Not really. I was busy with my career – touring, recording sessions, creating, parties, rehearsals…it never stopped.

Tamara was the big star when we first met. Did you know that?"

Louisa shook her head mutely, just listening. A part of her – a very large part of her – still wanted to make a run for it, but she'd started him talking and it seemed awfully rude to run now, when he was only partway through the story. She'd let him finish and *then* run for it.

"We were just kids. I met this gorgeous girl; she was a country music star, at least regionally, and at first, we couldn't get enough of each other. We had so much in common. I understood her drive to win at all costs, because that was me, too. It took me years to realize that we had so much in common, and almost all of it was shitty personality traits. We were toxic for each other. But there in the beginning, we just didn't know…

"Then *A Honky Tonk Life* blew up the charts and I'd made it big-time. But she still hadn't, and it drove her crazy. She was no longer Tamara, an up-and-coming star. She was Tamara, wife to Zane, who *was* a star. It killed her. We fought endlessly. She was never meant to be the person in the background, working to make sure the other person succeeded. That just wasn't her. She was supposed to be in the spotlight, but…it never happened. Then she starts talking about wanting to have a kid, and I agree to shut her up, basically. Maybe, I figure, if she has a kid she can mother, she'll be more balanced. It'll give her purpose in her life and she can stop driving herself crazy. So Skyler was all hers, from the very beginning. I was always gone, and she refused to bring a child along and raise him on the road. It became just one more thing that we fought about. I felt like she was keeping my kid from me by refusing to let him travel with me, and she felt like I wasn't putting Skyler first by being a stay-at-home dad like she wanted me to be. But how can you be a stay-at-home dad *and* a country music star at the same time? Oh God, how we fought."

His lips curled up at the corners in a rueful smile. "But to answer your question," he said, clearly embarrassed by his digression, "she was a good mom to Skyler. She loved him more than she ever loved me. She only wanted the best for him. But at the same time…she could be an absolute bitch. The more popular I became, the more success I had, the more she hated me. She would make these biting remarks about me to Skyler, and that was in *front* of me. I have no idea what she said behind my back, and I'm probably better off not knowing. I always thought that I could do *such* a better job of raising Skyler than she did, and then when she died and I actually had to raise Skyler, I realized I had no damn clue of what I was doing. None. Poor kid. I turned him over to staff to raise. You're the first time where that's ever worked out."

He flashed her a grin that faded away as quickly as it appeared.

"I always thought that if I imposed consequences on Skyler, he'd hate me. If I just gave him everything he wanted, he'd be happy. Getting everything you want always makes you happy, right? But he turned into this horrific brat, and I didn't have a clue of what to do with him. You know why I hired you?"

She froze, surprised by the turn in conversation. She shook her head, keeping her eyes pinned on him as he spoke.

"Because the high-priced agency back in Nashville that had been providing aides for me ever since the accident had no one else to send. Every person even vaguely qualified had either already been chewed up and spit out by Skyler, or had been warned away from him by someone who'd taken him on. The salt-in-your-coffee thing was a favorite of his. As were live spiders, letting air out of tires, and tripwires in the hallway. Although," he said thoughtfully, tapping his chin as he spoke, "honey on the hairbrush was a new one. He must've been getting bored with all of his other go-to's. When you didn't scream or yell or throw tantrums or cry, he was absolutely crushed. You took all of the fun out of it."

"Of course," she said with a chuckle. "If I'd reacted that way, he would've kept it up. Hell, he would've gotten worse. You can't give him that kind of satisfaction."

He shook his head in disbelief. "You make it seem so simple, but no one else understood that. Skyler was conducting this holy reign of terror under my roof, and I didn't have the slightest clue of what to do with him, and neither did anyone else."

"You know he's a good kid, right?" Suddenly, Louisa was afraid. What if Zane didn't change and they went back to Tennessee and everything went back to the way it was before? What if all of the progress they'd made that summer was for naught?

"Because of you," Zane said simply. "He's a good kid because of *you*."

CHAPTER 21

ZANE

E REALLY DIDN'T KNOW what the hell was possessing him to talk like this – so bluntly, so truthfully. He normally couldn't – *wouldn't* – dare because what if the person he was talking to turned around and sold the story to the tabloids? He'd seen it again and again. Childhood friends turning on their newly famous pal and selling tell-all interviews to magazines for the money, or their 15 minutes of fame, or both. Only a flaming idiot spoke to the damn *nanny* like this.

But Louisa wouldn't tell a soul. He knew that as surely as he knew the sun would rise in the east tomorrow. There was a steadiness about Louisa, a stability and grounding to her that so few people had. The old saying, *It's lonely at the top*, was spot-on because the higher you climbed, the less people you could trust.

But Louisa was one of those few trustworthy people.

She was looking at him, biting her lower lip, deep in thought about how to best argue that Skyler was a good kid whether or not she was in his life, her every thought showing on her face as clearly as if it'd been written there with a Sharpie marker.

He didn't want to hear it, though. He'd had the benefit of watching Skyler devolve for 18 months without Tamara or Louisa there to guide him, and perhaps they'd do better on their own now that Louisa had showed Zane a few tricks, but Zane also knew that eventually, they'd slide back into old habits without her guidance. A guy just couldn't learn how to be a perfect dad in only one summer, after a lifetime of being shown exactly the opposite. He needed more than a few month's example to make sure he did this right.

He didn't want to hear anything about Skyler in that moment, not only because he knew he was right, but because there was something else that he was wanting even more. He wanted to feel Louisa's soft lips under his. He wanted to know the taste of her mouth, her lips, her tongue. What her hair looked like spread around her in a cascade of black water.

He wanted to know *her*.

He shouldn't do what every cell in his body was screaming for him to do, but he couldn't seem to bring himself to care.

Watching her closely, waiting for the slightest sign of hesitation or stalling, he began inching closer to her lips, giving her enough time to say no if she wanted to. She could say no and he'd walk away and pretend this never happened but please, dear God, don't let her say no. He couldn't bear it if she did.

And still, she didn't pull away. Her lips parted, revealing her straight white teeth, as her eyes went liquid. She wanted him as much as he wanted her, he was sure of it. Her eyes began to flutter shut, her chin tilting just a bit up to his, and that broke him. Broke the last of his restraint, and then his mouth was on hers, sucking that bottom lip in, nibbling on it just as he'd watched her do so many times, her fingers digging into his shoulders, whimpers escaping her as he worked his fingers into her hair at the nape of her neck, tilting her head for better access, wanting all of her. He couldn't move away from her if his life depended upon it. All of the desire that had been building up inside of him since that first day she showed up on his front doorstep, a tantalizing temptation, the one person he absolutely couldn't have, but now he was, and oh God, it was better than he'd imagined and how was that even possible?

She was whimpering, these tiny noises in the back of her throat that were driving him wild and if she didn't stop making them, he couldn't be held responsible for what happened. She was everything he'd ever wanted. He eased her back on the ground, lifting up the hem of her shirt, sucking and nibbling at her taut, tanned stomach, working his way up towards her breasts, wanting to finally know what color her nipples were, a question that had been driving him crazy since he first laid eyes on her—

He stopped.

He pulled back and looked around. What in the bloody hell was he doing? There they were on the floor of the *forest*, making out like a pair of randy teenagers where anyone could come along and find them. He jerked back and scooted away from Louisa like she had some contagious disease he was afraid to catch – *lust-itis?* – and gulped in air, trying to get oxygen back into his body. He couldn't do this to her. He couldn't use his position of power against her.

Stupid, stupid, stupid Zane.

CHAPTER 22

LOUISA

OUISA LAY ON THE GROUND, trying to bring herself back to reality. One moment, she was on cloud nine, feeling like she'd never felt before, and the next, she was… being rejected?

The thought hurt so damn bad, she felt like someone was tearing at her heart, destroying it. After months of keeping her hands to herself, of being a good girl, of not touching this Greek god she'd somehow found herself living with, he *finally* made the moves on her, and then, turned away from her in disgust.

She didn't know she was *that* ugly, that she could turn the stomach of someone to the point of them not even being able to look at her any longer. And make no mistake, that was exactly what Zane was doing. He was staring off into the trees, refusing to meet her eyes, his breaths ragged.

And still he didn't speak, or look at her. The silence was getting thick. Painful. Insurmountable.

She scrambled to her feet, straightening her bra, yanking at her t-shirt, running fingers through her hair, trying to get any leaves or twigs or other evidence of what they'd done out of it. She didn't have a mirror and she wasn't about to ask

Zane for help, so she did the best she could and then quickly rebraided it, her fingers flying down the braid, as automatic as breathing.

"I'm sorry," Zane said formally after he pushed himself to his feet. "I shouldn't have done that."

Still, he wasn't meeting her eyes, and she wanted to take him by the shoulders and shake him and ask him if she was really *that* ugly that he could not bear to look at her but she didn't. She refused to. No self-respecting Latina would prostrate herself like that. She was going to get back on her horse, ride back to the therapy camp, and pretend this never happened.

Her pride refused to let her do anything else. She would *never* let him know how much his rejection hurt.

Stupid, stupid, stupid Louisa.

CHAPTER 23

ZANE

"WHAT'S WRONG?"

Skyler's eyes were flitting between him and Louisa as he sat in the backseat of the Audi, watching them both closely. He'd always been so good at watching the moods shift between him and Tamara, monitoring their relationship for the slightest change, and apparently, he hadn't lost that ability.

My very own mood detector.

Why couldn't his son be oblivious to everything around him like most 12-year-old boys were?

"Nothing," Louisa said reassuringly, shooting Skyler a bright smile over her shoulder.

It was as believable as those *trompe l'oeil* paintings. From far away, you just might be fooled, but up close, you could tell it wasn't real.

Skyler raised his eyebrows skeptically.

Nope, not fooled one bit.

Despite how awkward it was currently making his life, Zane found himself a little proud of his son for being so observant. It would be ever so much easier if he'd turn that observant streak somewhere else, but Zane had to hand it to him – Skyler wasn't about to fall for someone's bullshit.

The quiet in the car stretched out, and Zane began wishing quite desperately that they'd been able to find a house to rent that was closer to Sawyer. When his agent had first found him a handicap-accessible home outside of Franklin, Zane had been so grateful, he hadn't paid a lot of attention to the distance between that home and…well, anything else. It was way up in the mountains – not even close to Franklin, let alone Sawyer, where the therapy camp was actually taking place.

How many handicap-accessible houses do you think there are up in the Goldfork Mountains? Stop your bitching.

But still, he was counting the miles until they got home and he could escape to his studio. Maybe reworking a song would help him clear his head. Get it screwed on straight.

Clearly deciding that he wasn't going to get a straight answer out of either of them, Skyler changed subjects. "Juan wants to go kayaking with us. Can we go kayaking together? All of us?"

"We'll have to ask his parents, but I don't see why not," Zane said with a quick smile over his shoulder. He'd loved going kayaking with Louisa and Skyler. Turned out, he was a hell of a lot better in a kayak than he was on the back of a horse.

Something he was definitely going to keep between him and the fence post. If his publicist heard him saying that out loud…

"Louisa, I want to be stronger," Skyler said seriously, as they finally turned down the bumpy dirt road that led back to the house. Zane had kept meaning to get someone out there to fix the damn thing but there they were, nearing the end of summer, and he still hadn't called anyone. "Can you help me?"

"That's an excellent idea!" she replied, genuine excitement

in her voice this time. "If we added lifting weights into your routine every morning, you could use your arms more efficiently to compensate for your lack of muscle control in your legs. Not to say that you shouldn't continue to do your leg exercises, of course, but—" She paused and then shrugged. "It's a fact of life that your arms are always going to be stronger than your legs."

Zane winced at that, but Skyler wasn't paying attention, for once.

"I can be a bodybuilder!" he crowed, flexing his arms in the typical bodybuilder pose, showing off his string-bean limbs.

"Although I like your enthusiasm," Louisa said, holding up her hand to slow his gush of excitement, "it's actually not good for someone your age to try to bulk up by lifting weights. You can do real damage to your body."

"Oh," Skyler said, sinking down in his seat, deflating like a balloon.

"But just because you don't end up looking like a bodybuilder when you're done *doesn't* mean that you shouldn't do it," Louisa hurried on. "Like I said, your arms are always going to be stronger than your legs. It's a damn good idea to strengthen them as much as possible. Were you thinking about how hard it is to paddle a kayak for a long time?"

"Yeah," he said, his voice still flat. "I want to be able to kayak longer, and also push my wheelchair around more without getting tired. Am I ever going to walk?"

The question landed in the quiet of the car just as Zane had turned off the engine, the garage door sliding closed behind them. He froze, his mind racing, his hand hovering in midair, stopped in the act of pulling back from the ignition button.

Skyler had only asked that question once before, and the

nurse in the hospital had brushed him off, saying that whether someone walked or not wasn't a big deal.

It was a statement that Zane had thought was patently stupid. Of *course* it was a big deal. Who was she trying to kid?

Skyler had taken the nurse's words to mean that he wasn't going to because otherwise, she would've said so, right? Zane had seen it in his son's eyes as he sunk back against the pillow. He was giving up right in front of them.

Zane'd frozen up then. He wasn't a nurse. Hell, he barely knew how to apply a bandaid. *Was* his son ever going to walk again? He didn't know. The doctors didn't know. Was it better to lie and say that he absolutely would? Was it better to say nothing at all?

A therapist had come into the room then and life had moved on and Zane never really had to make a choice. He had just let it go and Skyler hadn't asked again and Zane had forgotten the question had even been asked in the haze of guilt and grief and anger and flat-out terror after the accident.

But although Zane had been willing to let the question go, Skyler hadn't. All these months later, and it was still haunting him.

I am a terrible father. My son…I haven't been there for him. Just like I'd been so damn worried that I would, I screwed everything up.

Louisa began talking then, and even before he knew what Louisa's answer was going to be, a large part of him was just so damn grateful that she *was* talking. She didn't seem to suffer from performance anxiety and freeze up in the face of tough questions.

Thank God.

"I told you before that I read over your charts, right?" Louisa said carefully, turning in her seat to look back at Skyler. He nodded slowly. "I was a nurse for a long time. Reading medical charts is just one of my *many* talents." Skyler laughed a little at that as she'd intended, but grew serious again immediately. He did not want to be sidetracked. He wanted a straight answer, and he knew Louisa would give it to him.

Smart kid.

"There's nothing in your charts that told me you couldn't walk again. There was also nothing in your charts that said it would be easy. We've been doing exercises every morning together, and you've been doing all right, but I know you've got more to you than what you've been giving me. You do those exercises because you want the remote back for your Xbox, *not* so you can walk again, and that makes all of the difference in the world. Do you know what the number one indicator is of whether someone will walk again or not?" Zane watched in the rearview mirror as Skyler slowly shook his head.

Zane was still frozen, not wanting to disturb the moment. This was it; this was a turning point for his son. He knew it like he knew Tamara was dead that night in the limo. He knew it in his gut – an unshakeable knowledge.

"Whether they believe that they can," Louisa said simply. "There are limitations, of course. Modern medicine is damn good, but not perfect. Not yet. If the spinal cord is severed, it's like cutting the power line going into a house. No information is going to make it through and there isn't a damn thing we can do about that. Yet. But in cases like yours, your spinal cord wasn't severed. It was heavily bruised, but it wasn't crushed and it wasn't cut. The one thing keeping you from getting out of the car and walking into the house is that you haven't worked hard enough for it. *Cariño*, you cannot give 80%. You can't even give 90%. You have to give it *all* when we're doing your exercises, and you have to want it so badly, you can taste it."

There was silence in the SUV then, and a small part of Zane wondered how it was that they always seemed to end up having life-changing discussions while sitting in the damn garage. Couldn't they talk about this while he was sitting in a recliner, beer in hand?

But much more importantly than that was the fact that Louisa had been asked The Question, and she hadn't frozen up like he had. She'd known what to say.

What if Louisa had been there in the hospital after the accident? What if she'd been the one talking to the doctors and nurses and therapists instead of me? What if she'd been the one talking to Skyler? He would probably be walking right now. My failure as a parent is why Skyler is trapped in that damn chair. It isn't his fault; it's mine.

He realized he had his hands gripped into fists, the anger at himself pulsing through his veins. *Failure. Failure. Failure.* The voice was mocking him and he deserved every bit of it.

He realized then that Louisa and Skyler were heading into the house, Louisa walking beside Skyler as he rolled along, chatting about how hard he was going to work and how someday, he was going to beat Juan in a footrace, and–

The door to the house shut behind them, cutting off their voices, leaving Zane behind in the SUV to wrestle with his guilt. He had so much more to learn. So much more growth ahead of him.

But if he could convince Louisa to stay with them; if he could just convince Louisa to move back to Tennessee, he might have a chance. He could become the dad he should've been from day one.

You also have to keep your hands to yourself, asshole. Mauling Louisa while rolling around on the forest floor ain't an option. You do that again, and you'll lose her for sure. She was hurt once before by dating her boss, and she won't repeat that mistake. For Skyler's sake, you can't touch Louisa ever again.

He thought, as he climbed out of the Audi to head into the house, that the simple fact that he was willing to give up Louisa's kisses for the rest of his life, the kind of touch that most men only dreamed about, was proof that he was already becoming a better father. That afternoon, as he'd held Louisa in his arms, he would've sworn he wouldn't give her up for anything in the world.

But now look at him. He was giving her up for his son.

He ignored the slicing pain that lanced through him at the thought. It was about damn time that he become a real father, and if that meant him keeping it in his pants, then that's just what he'd do.

CHAPTER 24

LOUISA

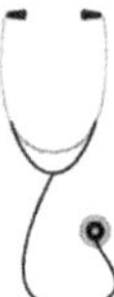

T HEY PULLED UP to the Miller family farm, happiness bubbling up inside of Louisa. It was her *tia's* 70th birthday, which of course Carmelita insisted on celebrating by cooking for three days and inviting everyone to come over and eat. Louisa never understood her *tia's* obsession with cooking, much preferring to eat the hard labor of others than to cook it all herself.

Which, she figured, made her and Carmelita a match made in heaven.

Skyler was talking a million miles an hour, telling her and Zane everything that he and Juan were going to do that day, which mostly seemed to involve a lot of toy backhoes and dirt. It was a damn good thing that Carmelita didn't expect – or even want – the kids to show up in button-up shirts and ties, hair carefully slicked back. She wanted them to be happy, and that meant playing in the dirt. And lots and lots of cookies.

Louisa was sure Carmelita would come through on both accounts.

As she stepped out of the Audi, carefully balancing an elaborate fruit plate that Chef Ralph had put together for the occasion, she spotted her mom's van. She stopped dead in her tracks, shaking her head like a dog after getting out of the canal. That couldn't be right. She blinked rapidly and then looked again.

That was most *definitely* her mom's van. Its side panels were a different color than the hood, the result of an accident in high school, and despite Louisa's pleas for another vehicle – *any* other vehicle – her mother continued to have Louisa drive the van to school every day. It had been *soooo* embarrassing to teenage Louisa, and she'd grown to hate it.

Of course, the damn thing was unbreakable – it would've been much too convenient on teenage Louisa for it to have died somewhere, forcing her mom to replace it – and so here it was, all these years later, still their family's primary mode of transportation.

But her mom wasn't going to be able to come today. She'd said she had too much to do at home that she needed to catch up on. They'd discussed it via text just a couple of nights before.

What changed?

Skyler tugged on her elbow, pulling her out of her thoughts. "C'mon," he said anxiously. "I think everyone's out back. I can't see Juan."

"Right." She started forward, feeling Zane's eyes trained on her back as they walked. Ever since that day by that gorgeous mountain stream when she'd completely grossed him out with her non-starlet body, Zane had been distant with her. She'd spent what felt like days, thinking it over and trying to figure out where they went wrong, and finally decided that it had to have been her body. She wasn't a hefty girl but she also wasn't a stick. He probably took one look at her thighs and realized that she weighed more than 97 pounds and every bit of lust for her had disappeared on the spot.

Well, screw him. She wasn't going to develop an eating

disorder just to please some stupid fantasy men had about banging a bag of bones. If that's what he wanted, then she wanted no part of him.

"Remember me telling you about Frizzy?" she asked Skyler as they neared the front steps. He nodded eagerly as she put the platter on his lap and then began carefully pulling him backwards up the two steps and onto the porch. "Well, you're about to meet them for yourself."

"I am?!" His voice broke, his excitement contagious, and she grinned at him.

"Yup. Prepare yourself. I have like 19 younger siblings, and they're all about to descend."

"You have five," Skyler corrected her, giving her a don't-bullshit-me look.

"Close enough," she said with a laughing grumble, and then knocked on the front door as she opened it. "*¿Tia? ¿Mamá?* We're here."

"Oh, *cariño*," her mom said, hurrying to the front door from the kitchen, her face wreathed in smiles, a younger version of the smile on Carmelita's face, who was trailing in behind her. "We wanted to surprise you," she said conspiratorially, pulling Louisa close for a long hug. Louisa felt herself melting into her mother's arms, the world right again, even if just for a moment.

"And you must be Skyler," she said, pulling back and looking down at him. He'd suddenly gone bashful and Louisa was sure that if he could stand on his own two legs, he'd be hiding behind her or Zane. As it was, it was rather hard to hide while in a wheelchair, much to his chagrin. "Oh, you are just as handsome as *mi hermana* said you were. I am so glad to have you in my family. And you are Zane?"

Her mother was looking at Zane evenly, openly sizing him up, trying to decide whether she liked him or not. Zane didn't seem to be intimidated in the slightest, though, and stepped forward, holding out his hand to shake. "It's nice to finally meet you," he rumbled, his deep voice difficult to hear among the babble of the family. "I have heard so much about you. Now I know where your daughter gets her beauty."

Which was when Louisa's mother *blushed*. Louisa stared at her mother, open-mouthed. All her life, she'd *never* seen her mother blush. And now she seemed to be falling for the charms of Zane.

She wasn't sure if she should glare at Zane for flirting with her mother, or glare at her mother for appreciating it. Really. After he'd practically run away from her in the meadow, he certainly hadn't looked at *her* that way.

Am I jealous of my own mother?

She decided not to spend too much time dwelling on that thought.

"*Feliz cumpleaños, Tia* Carmelita," Skyler said, slaughtering the words even more than he had when he'd been practicing them earlier with Louisa. He'd begged her that morning to learn how to say *Happy Birthday* in Spanish so he could say it to Carmelita, and she'd done her best to teach him, but his light southern twang combined with Spanish words…Louisa wasn't sure if she wanted to laugh or to cringe in pain.

Carmelita did neither. Instead, her eyes filled with tears and she leaned over to hug him in his chair, snuffling as she did so. "Thank you, *cariño*," she said softly into his hair, and then turned her back on them to dab at her eyes with her apron, clearly embarrassed to be seen crying.

His birthday surprise having been delivered, Skyler tugged on Louisa's hand. "Where's Juan?" Skyler asked in a loud whisper, his one-track mind on full display.

And to think they fought like cats and dogs when they first met.

"Probably out back in the sandbox. Here, I'll take the platter," she said, grabbing it out of Skyler's lap before he could take off for the backyard and dump dirt on it or something. And then he was gone, zipping through the house, thrilled to go hang out with his new best friend.

The women began talking then, moving towards the kitchen as Mom told her all about planning this surprise and Carmelita talking about how good Skyler was looking. Louisa felt a piece of her soul slide into place, as if something had been missing and now it was there, a joy that came from seeing her favorite people in the world all under one roof.

What would it have been like to have Matt here?

The idea set her back on her heels a little. Matt was supposed to come home and "meet the family" a couple of times, but something had always come up at the hospital and he hadn't been able to make it. Louisa had been fine with it, of course – she understood better than anyone the pressures of working in a premiere spinal-cord unit – except, now she realized that she hadn't been fine with it.

Had he *actually* needed to stay at the hospital? Or had he just been looking for an excuse to get out of meeting her family?

Or, even worse, had he just been looking for an excuse to bang the CNA while Louisa was out of town?

All of the truths she'd never let herself really think about. No wonder Matt had stuck with her for so long. She'd proven to be a damn easy mark.

She knew she shouldn't allow herself the luxury of the thought, but still, her eyes sought out Zane in the crowd, watching how he chatted so easily with everyone, continuing to charm her mother with the worst Spanish accent she'd ever heard – well, other than the one his son just used – clearly trotting out his high-school Spanish in an attempt to win Mom over.

Why is he trying so hard with her? It isn't like he and I have a future together. Why does he care?

He shouldn't, and the fact that she couldn't think of a good reason for what he was doing scared the bejeezus out of her. People always had an agenda. Always. Not knowing what his was made small slivers of panic run down her spine.

As the flow of people and laughter and chatter continued, Flint doing some charming of his own by producing enough drool for three kids, Louisa realized that another important question she needed an answer for was why Zane wasn't on stage anymore. Why wasn't he touring?

He was the very definition of an extrovert. Right then, among the kids and adults, he was telling an apparently hilarious story about how one time, a stage manager forgot to turn off his mic and so his barked orders to the stage hands were loudly broadcast throughout the stadium, right along with Zane's opening song for the concert. Abby and Jennifer were gasping with delight; Stetson and Declan were laughing uproariously.

Zane was where he wanted to be – where he deserved to be. Why was he stopping himself from doing something that he so clearly loved?

He looked up from the group just then and caught Louisa's eye. They both froze, unable to blink or look away or even breathe and it was then that Louisa asked herself the most important question of all:

Why was he stopping himself from touching her again? He liked her. She couldn't believe otherwise. Not after she saw *that* look blazed on his face.

So why was he staying away?

CHAPTER 25

ZANE

Z ANE FELT LIKE he'd been gut-punched. The world was
narrowing to just Louisa, everything else falling
away. She was nibbling on her bottom lip and he felt
his groin tighten with need. His fingers were itching to reach
out to her, his palms sweating with lust and desire, and if he
could just pull her into his arms and kiss her again, he could
make the world right. He wanted—

"Louisa," Carmelita said, tugging on her niece's arm,
severing the connection between them. With a bright smile,
Louisa turned toward her aunt. "Come. Your mother misses
you. I know she will want you in the kitchen with us."

Louisa moved away, not looking back over her shoulder
as she went, and Zane let a sigh of disappointment escape his
lips. God almighty, just *looking* at Louisa made him feel more
alive than he'd felt in years.

*Hands off, asshole. You. Can't. Have. Louisa. Get over her
already.*

Maybe he should drive over to Boise some weekend and
hit a few clubs. He could pick up a girl – or three – and take
'em back to a hotel room in Boise. Work Louisa out of his
system. She wasn't the only woman in the world, for hell's

sakes. There were plenty more fish in the sea. He just had to go looking for them.

Even as he thought that, he re-adjusted his position on his chair to better see what Louisa was doing. She was in the kitchen, talking a mile a minute in Spanish with Carmelita and her mom as they all chopped and prepped food. He scooted the chair a bit and found that by sitting *just right*, he could see the back of her as she worked. He was forced to put his foot out to brace himself, though, and he could already tell his leg was going to tire of this position pretty quickly. He sipped his beer nonchalantly, his thoughts swirling as he listened to Louisa's laugh spill out of her over something she and her mom were chatting about.

What if he'd met Louisa when he was 19, instead of Tamara? What if he'd had her steadiness and kind outlook and love for others from the get-go?

He closed his eyes and groaned to himself. Who was he kidding? The 19-year-old Zane would've overlooked Louisa. She wasn't flashy. She didn't wear a lot of makeup, and he wasn't even sure she knew what hairspray was, and as for her taste in clothing…he thought back to the kayaking trip to the lake, and Louisa's one-piece bathing suit. She'd looked spectacular, of course, because she had a body most women would give their right arms for, but Tamara never would've worn a one-piece bathing suit to the lake. She would've been in a string bikini and jewel-encrusted flip-flops, reapplying her lipstick every 30 minutes.

No, 19-year-old Zane wouldn't have noticed Louisa; wouldn't have given her the time of day. He wouldn't have hated her; that would've required him even paying attention to her existence. He just would've been so involved, so wrapped up in the stylized, primped, fashion model Tamara that nothing else would've penetrated the bubble of lust he'd operated in back then.

He used to equate lust with love, and had thought that the

wild sex between him and Tamara had meant their love would last forever. No one could possibly feel like he had and not be happy for forever.

Except now, he knew none of that was true. Lust always fades. Without the basis of a friendship, without the basis of love for each other, it all falls apart.

His relationship with Tamara was a poster child for that reality.

"You're going to hurt yourself, craning your neck like that," a deep voice said, scaring Zane, his chair falling back down to the floor with a thud. He jerked his head up to see that it was one of Louisa's siblings, although Zane didn't know which one. She had two brothers but dammit all, he couldn't remember either of their names at the moment.

He quickly stood. "Zane Risley," he said, putting his hand out to shake. This brother was almost as tall as Zane's 6'2" frame, which took Zane a little off-guard. He thought of most Mexican guys as being pretty short.

Is that a racist thought? God, please don't let me be a racist.

"Tomás Vargas," he said, his handshake firm. "Louisa's younger brother."

Zane thought he detected a note of warning in Tomás' voice, and couldn't say he blamed the guy. If his younger sister had lived, he could only imagine how he would've felt if he'd caught some guy drooling over her.

I wasn't drooling. I was just…appreciating. Totally different.

"You're the older of the two brothers, right?" he asked, mostly for something to say. Tomás was a serious person – it was clear to Zane that even when he wasn't trying to intimidate the men in Louisa's life, he didn't smile much.

"Yeah. Alex is the younger one, and the *baby* of the family."

"I take it he's spoiled?" Zane asked, his lips quirking at the corner. Tomás may be serious but he wasn't good at hiding his feelings.

"Rotten," Tomás confirmed, and for the first time, a ghost of a smile passed his lips before fading away immediately. "How long are you planning on staying in Long Valley, you think?"

"Just a few more weeks, and then we head back to Tennessee. School starts up after Labor Day, so I need to get Skyler back in time for that." Why did he feel defensive?

"And Louisa?"

And there it was. Tomás wasn't even pretending to dance around the subject. Zane had to appreciate the guy's ballsiness, even if he didn't appreciate it being directed towards him.

"Louisa signed a contract that ends on August 31st," Zane said smoothly.

"That doesn't answer my question."

Zane stared at him evenly, one eyebrow cocked, not blinking, not answering. If Tomás thought he could intimidate Zane, he was sorely mistaken. He'd picked the wrong guy to try to push around.

Of course, he had picked the guy who he'd caught drooling over his sister.

That didn't mean Zane was about to open up and spill his guts to the guy, though.

"I love my sister," Tomás finally said in a low voice. "I would do anything to keep her from being hurt."

With one last meaningful look, Tomás turned and headed for the cooler, snagging a Tecate beer and popping the top off before joining the group around Flint, Jennifer's toddler, who was entertaining the group by blowing raspberries and giggling. He was a damn adorable kid. Zane tried to remember back to when Skyler was his age, but dug up precious few memories. He'd been on the road so much at that point, always trying to hit that new sales record, that new concert level, that Skyler's childhood was only a few scattered snapshots in time.

His mind drifted back to Tomás' warning without him even realizing it, settling back into his chair as he thought. Did he deserve that heavy-handed warning? There was nothing to warn him about. He wasn't falling in love with his nanny. He was...

He heard Louisa's shout of laughter in the kitchen and he found himself balancing on his chair again, craning his neck to see what she was laughing about. The flow of Spanish washed over him as she worked side by side with her mom and aunt, the three of them clearly reliving a hilarious story. Dammit, why hadn't he paid more attention in high school Spanish class? He wanted to know what made Louisa that light and happy. He wanted to know what made her laugh like that, so he could make her laugh, too.

Make her laugh? Why would you want to make her laugh? She's just...

She's just...

The air was sucked from the room and black spots swirled on the edges of his vision as his brain finally grasped what his heart had known from the get-go.

You dumbass. You went and fell in love with the one woman you can't have.

How had he done it? How had he made such a stupid mistake? Even as he berated himself, he found the air was easing back into his lungs and he was feeling a lightness, a buoyancy he hadn't felt in a very long time.

He loved Louisa. Dear God, *he loved Louisa*. The strife, the confusion, the push and pull that he'd been battling with for what, weeks? Months? The very beginning? It was all gone, washed away.

He loved Louisa. Now, all he had to do was make her love him back.

Well, go throw up in the bathroom from nerves. *Then* get her to love him back.

CHAPTER 26

LOUISA

"YOU NEED TO flirt with your Mr. Risley," Mom said bluntly as Louisa chopped up carrots for the vegetable tray. Her knife slipped and she only narrowly avoided slicing off her finger in the process.

"Mom!" Louisa exclaimed, horrified, and then switched over to rapid-fire Spanish. "If you're going to say things like that to me," she hissed, "you could at least say it in Spanish."

"What?" her mom said innocently. "You think your Mr. Risley does not recognize his name, even in another language?" Thank God she at least said it in Spanish this time.

Louisa glared at her mother. "It would help if you would stop saying his name every other sentence," she said dryly.

"He's in love with you, you know," her mom said airily, as if announcing nothing more important than a quick trip to the store. "Poor man. He's fallen hard." She shook her head sorrowfully. "This is why I came, you know. Carmelita is an old woman and getting older all of the time—"

"I am always going to be older *and* wiser than you," Carmelita called out from across the kitchen as she slid a casserole dish into the oven.

"—but more important than a birthday is to meet my future son-in-law," her mom continued, as if her older sister hadn't said a thing.

"I cannot believe this is happening," Louisa groaned, burying her face in her hands.

"That was my reaction, too," her mom said cheerfully. "Really? My daughter and a famous country music singer?!"

"You didn't even know who he was before this summer. Don't pretend to be impressed by his stardom." Louisa planted her hands on her hips and threw in a good glare for emphasis.

"No, but I do know how to operate Google," her mom said with a smile of self-satisfaction, "and know all about him now. His former wife…" She shook her head and let out a low whistle. "She was beautiful. Her boobs were out to here," she said, holding her hands about two feet in front of her petite frame.

"I cannot *believe* this is happening," Louisa groaned again, dropping her knife this time and burying her face in her hands again. Could a person die of mortification? She was surely about to find out.

"But my daughter is prettier," her mother went on. Louisa peeked out from between her fingers, trying to gauge if her mother was being serious.

She was.

Oh, Mamá, you are so sweet. Delusional, but sweet. I'm nowhere near as beautiful as Tamara Risley had been. Tamara had the kind of flashy beauty that could stop men in their tracks. Louisa was not ugly, but she was not Tamara-Risley beautiful, either.

"Zane agrees with me, too."

Louisa let out a squeak of horror. "Don't tell me you asked him. *Please* don't tell me you asked him."

It was official – a body *could* die from mortification. The world was already fading away, the black swirling in on the sides of her vision as she tried to keep upright. This had to be the worst thing she'd ever lived through, and that included the time that her father started showing her prom date baby pictures, including the requisite naked-in-the-kitchen-sink pic.

"No, no, I did not ask him," her mother said, waving the suggestion away, crumbs from the bread she was cutting flying everywhere. "I did not need to ask him. I just needed to look in his eyes. He loves you. So, you should flirt with him. He needs a little encouragement, is all."

It was one of those moments in Louisa's life when she was overwhelmed with gratitude that she spoke a second language. If she knew that Zane could walk into the kitchen at any moment and understand what her mother was saying, she might be tempted to bind and gag her until dinner was over. As it was, she just had to keep focused on not turning fire-engine red from embarrassment.

"I'll keep that in mind," she finally got out, picking up the knife and carrot again, trying to hold onto at least a shred of dignity. "Hold on, what is that?" Music from the living room caught her attention, and she headed into it, carrot and knife still in hand, as she tried to find the source of the sound.

It was Zane. From somewhere, he'd pulled out a guitar – *has there been a guitar in the Audi all of this time? How did I miss that?* – and had begun singing a soulful country song. She'd never heard it before, but it was about love and loss and a lifetime of knowing someone and as he sang, he looked straight into her eyes. He was singing this song to her. She felt herself sagging against the wide doorway leading into the kitchen, using the pillar to keep herself upright.

Zane was singing a love song.

To her.

The sound faded away, the last strum of the guitar blending into silence, and then the room erupted into applause and cheers. "Again, again!" Flint demanded, waving his chubby fist in the air, and everyone laughed. The corners of Zane's mouth curled into a smile at the toddler's antics, but still, he didn't look away. Didn't break their gaze.

"I want to hear *A Honky Tonk Life*," Abby said. "Oh my God, no one at the jail is gonna believe that I got an in-person concert like this in Stetson's living room."

Everyone was laughing even as Zane broke out into song, finally pulling his gaze away from Louisa's. Like she was finally released from chains she hadn't even realized were there, she shook her head, trying to clear it. Zane *couldn't* be in love with h—

"See?" her mom whispered in her ear, raising on her tiptoes. "I told you so." She pulled back, winked, and carried the platter of veggies outside.

She had indeed.

CHAPTER 27

ZANE

H E BEGAN planning it out with all of the precision and strategy of a general going to war. It took him several days of putting a plan together but finally by Friday, he was ready to go.

Step One: He begged off from going to therapy camp that morning, telling Louisa and Skyler that he had a headache. Skyler looked crestfallen – he'd gotten used to his father attending every day with him, and didn't seem to believe that a mere headache was a valid reason for missing.

It's okay, Sky. Just you wait. I'm going to get you a new mother. You'll forgive me for all of my shortcomings once I pull this off.

Step Two: After they left, Zane headed down the hallway and into Louisa's room, looking through her closet and dresser to see what her clothing sizes were. He felt like a peeping Tom and sincerely hoped the housekeeper wouldn't catch him in there. He could only imagine what she would think.

He entered every size of every possible item he could think of into a text message, doing his best not to stare too longingly at the merest wisp of lace he found in her panties drawer, and then hurried back to his room before he could get caught.

Step Three: He hit send on the text and then immediately dialed the same number.

"Hey, Buttons," he said cheerfully, using his nickname for Alice Branston, one of his closest friends in the music business and one of the few whom he trusted. "It's Zane."

"Zane! God, how are you?" Her voice, raspy from decades of smoking, made him smile. It was damn good to hear her voice. "Shit, I'm so glad to hear from you. Hold on." There was a rustling noise and then she was shouting at someone to be more careful before coming back on the line. "Imbeciles, the lot of 'em," she grumbled. "Anyway, so, you're alive. That's good to know. Last I heard, you were holed up in Idaho of all places, and no one's heard from you all summer. I was beginning to have visions of the Aryan Nation kidnapping you and holding you ransom or something. Wait. Isn't it Idaho where the Aryan Nation is headquartered? Or is that Iowa?"

"I think that's northern Idaho, and you'll be glad to know that a) I'm nowhere near there; and b) I always cross the street when I see a skinhead coming, just as a precaution," he said dryly. "Now," he continued on before Buttons could start in again on whatever thought was flitting through her mind at that very moment, "I have a favor to ask of you. I have a girl I want to impress."

"A girl—" The rustling of movement in the background stopped; he was sure even her breathing had stopped. "A girl?!" she finally exclaimed. "You've fallen in love? You've fallen in love. Oh my God, Zane Risley has fallen in love. I can't—"

"Buttons!" he bellowed.

She shut up.

"I have a girl I want to impress," he repeated, unable to say the words *I've fallen in love with*. The feeling was too new.

Too raw. He hadn't told Louisa yet. He couldn't tell someone else before he told her. Not even Buttons. "I texted you all of her clothing sizes right before I called you."

"Yeah, I saw that come through on my iWatch as we were talking. I wondered why you were texting me a bunch of women's clothing sizes. I thought maybe you had another announcement you wanted to make," she said slyly, laughter in her voice.

"No, I'm not becoming a cross-dresser," he said dryly. "After we hang up, I'm gonna text you some pics that I've managed to snag without her noticing. I want you to fly to Idaho – I'll keep you safe from any skinheads lurking around the airport, I promise – with dresses that would work for her. Really show off her figure. Oh, and shoes. Lots of shoes. Give her lots of choices so she can choose what she likes. But no tennis shoes or scrubs. Or jeans."

"I was pretty sure you didn't want me to fly across the country to bring your girlfriend some scrubs," Buttons said, and he could tell she was laughing at him. "Hold on, *is* she your girlfriend? And why don't you fly her here? It'd be a hell of a lot cheaper than me flying everything I need for a dress-fitting plus staff to—"

"No. I want it done here. I want her to be in her element *and* dressed up at the same time." He ignored the girlfriend question. He was *not* about to admit to Buttons that he was willing to spend an arm and a leg on a woman he hadn't gone on a single date with. "How soon can you do it?"

"Dammit, Zane. Fine. Send me the pics while we're on the phone. I want to know what I'm working with first."

"Hold on." He pulled his phone away from his ear and scrolled through his pics app, choosing the pictures he'd managed to take of her during the party at the Miller house. They weren't glamor shots by any stretch of the imagination but he knew how Buttons worked. She needed more than a woman's cup size and jean size to pick out just the right dress. She needed it all. "There, I sent some over. Sorry...I was trying not to let her see that I was taking her picture so they're not the best—"

"Oh, nice Kardashian ass," Buttons said, ignoring his apology. "Wow. That hair. Okay. Good. Let me see what I have here. I can't do custom, of course – no matter how much I love you, even I can't take my entire shop across the country – but I have some dresses that'll set your hair on fire. I've got some fittings here this afternoon that I can't move but I can —" she pulled her phone away from her ear and yelled some obscenities at someone and then her voice was back as if nothing had happened, "rearrange everything else, and leave first thing in the morning. Just send the bill to Nina?"

The question made it clear: She was willing to rearrange her life to make this happen, but it *would* come at a dear price.

"Perfect," he said. Money was one thing he had enough of. She was probably going to charge him three times her usual fee, and he was gladly going to pay it. "I'm going to call Nina and have her call your assistant. They can work out the details. See you tomorrow around noon?"

"Lovely. Bye. Love you," and then she was gone, off to yell at someone else, no doubt.

It was one of her most lovable traits – there was never any doubt about where a person stood with Buttons. Loved you, hated you, or somewhere in between, she'd say it bluntly. It was what made her trustworthy.

Step Four: He dialed his assistant, Nina. The older woman sounded sleepy but quickly snapped to attention when he told her what he needed. When he'd left Tennessee at the beginning of the summer, he'd left her behind just like he had his bodyguard. He didn't need a whole flotilla of staff around to get his son to therapy camp and back every day, and he hadn't planned on doing anything else that summer...except get his head screwed on straight, and he didn't need a flotilla of staff for that either.

He worked Nina hard enough most of the year. One summer off every decade wasn't going to land him on the list of the World's Best Bosses, and he knew that.

One of the reasons he'd kept her on all these years wasn't just her willingness to take one vacation a decade, though; it was her organizational skills, her sharp mind, and her ability to do more in one afternoon than most people could accomplish in a week.

He got to the end of his explanation and exactly what he needed to be done, and there was a long pause as she finished writing it all down. "Got it," she finally said. "And Mr. Risley?"

After all these years, she still refused to call him Zane.

"Yeah?"

"Good luck." And with that, she hung up.

Lady luck. He hated to rely on it but this was one time where he had no choice. He could work as hard as he wanted to, but he couldn't force Louisa to fall in love with him.

No, that was one thing he could not do.

CHAPTER 28
LOUISA

L OUISA WATCHED as Skyler loaded himself into the Audi, talking a mile a minute about everything that Juan had said and done and thought that day, and Louisa just listened, the door sliding closed and cutting off his words, but he simply stopped mid-sentence, waited until she opened up the driver's side door, and started right back up again.

He was nothing if not persistent.

Once he'd told her every word and action and thought of Juan's for the day, he rattled to a stop.

She looked at him in the rearview mirror, but he was staring out the window, his brow creased as he thought.

"A penny for your thoughts, *cariño*," she said quietly.

He shot her a confused look and she knew he wanted to ask her why a penny because after all, a penny was practically worthless, but then, his mind zipped right back to the important question at hand, refusing to get sidetracked.

"Do I have to move back to Nashville with Dad?"

Louisa paused, trying to think of how to answer this. The obvious response was yes, of course. Skyler was more independent now than he was when the summer had started, but he was twelve years old, for hell's sakes. He certainly wasn't old enough to live on his own, no matter how adept he'd become at transferring in and out of his wheelchair.

"I don't want to leave Juan. He's the bestest friend I've ever had. He doesn't care that I'm in a wheelchair."

Louisa wanted to close her eyes and cry.

Dios mío, *my heart hurts for Skyler. How can I help him?*

"He is a good friend," she agreed, fighting to keep the warble out of her voice. She cleared her throat. "But don't you think your father will be sad without you?"

"Maybe." He still wasn't meeting her gaze in the rearview mirror. "He likes me more now than he did before. You made him like me."

"I helped him realize what a great person you are," she corrected him gently. "Your father has always loved you. I think he just needed a little bit of help in getting to know you. But now that he does, I think he'd be really sad if you weren't there with him all of the time."

Skyler nodded slowly at that, still thinking. "Maybe you shouldn't have helped him to like me. He didn't used to care if I was there or not. I could've stayed behind. But now, he won't let me."

Louisa opened her mouth to argue that assertion but then remembered that Zane had sent Skyler to two therapy camps previous to this one all by himself, and the one – the music camp – had been in Sedona, Arizona, for heaven's sakes. Zane didn't used to have any qualms about sending his kid across the country with nothing more than an aide to accompany him.

Would he have let Skyler live in Idaho with only staff to take care of him?

Maybe.

Not exactly a ringing endorsement of Past Zane, although Louisa was happy to know that Current Zane would never allow it. No matter what Skyler thought, having a loving, caring dad in his life was much more important than having a friend, even if that friend was as great as Juan.

She decided to take a different tact. "Wouldn't you miss your dad if you stayed behind?" She flipped on her blinker and turned onto the Road From Hell, as she personally thought of the rutted two-track potholed road that led back to the house. For the millionth time, she wondered why Zane didn't get it fixed.

Skyler's face became a bouncy, blurry vision in the rearview mirror as the SUV bounced along, and so Louisa gave up trying to read Sky's face in it, and instead focused on avoiding as many potholes as possible.

"Yeah," Skyler finally said grudgingly. "I want Dad *and* Juan."

Louisa couldn't argue against that one. Even as an adult, it was hard not to desperately cling to the cake-and-eat-it-too mentality. Knowing it wasn't realistic was a far cry from then turning off all feeling and simply not wanting it. They were people, not robots.

She knew she certainly was. She wanted Zane – God, how she wanted Zane – but dating her boss? *Again?* Once was bad enough. Once could be written off as temporary stupidity.

But twice?

She couldn't be that stupid twice.

They pulled into the garage, the door closing silently behind them, and Louisa waited for Skyler to say something else. He seemed like he had more to get off his chest. But instead, he transferred himself out of the vehicle and zipped inside, his face a study of thought and worry and conflict.

He's too young to be this serious. He is just a child but yet, he is not. He is so much more.

She pushed herself out of the SUV and walked sedately behind him, trying to keep the thought and worry and conflict off her own face. Zane would want to know what was wrong, and she couldn't break Skyler's confidences by telling him. He hadn't made her promise not to say anything, but she knew it was what he expected. If he wanted to talk to his dad about Juan, then he could. Zane shouldn't hear it from her.

Zane must've heard them come in because he came hurrying down the stairs, beaming from ear to ear. "I just got off the phone with Wyatt Miller, Skyler, and guess who wants you to come over and spend the weekend with them?"

"Really?!" Skyler shot up so fast in his wheelchair, he rocked it back slightly onto its back wheels. "Oh, *cool!*"

He raced for the elevator to go pack his bags, and Louisa called after him, "Don't forget to pack your toothbrush and toothpaste!" Man, she was *such* a mother some days. She looked back at Zane who had a strangely self-satisfied look on his face. "What's going on?" she asked suspiciously. "Is your headache better?"

"My headac—? Oh yeah," he said quickly. "Feeling much better. Advil is a miracle drug."

She lifted her eyebrows and stared at him skeptically. "What's going on?" she asked again. Damn, he was just like Skyler. She could tell where he got it from. Zane was about to play a trick on her. He was *just* short of holding out a doctored cup of coffee and telling her innocently that he'd made her coffee for her that morning.

Well, maybe he hadn't actually poured salt into her coffee, but *something* was going on. She'd bet her career on it.

"I'm just happy that my son gets to spend more time with his best friend," Zane said smoothly.

She stared at him, not buying that for a second.

"What, you don't think I want my son to be happy?" he finally said, breaking under the weight of that stare.

"Oh, I know you do. You'd do anything for your son's happiness. But that isn't why you look like it's Christmas morning, your birthday, and Easter all wrapped up into one."

The elevator dinged open and Skyler came zooming out, a

backpack sitting in his lap. "Let me see what you packed," Louisa said, holding up a hand and stopping him in his tracks. She'd sent enough younger brothers off to overnighters to know that their idea of "packing a bag" could include simply grabbing a t-shirt and a mismatched pair of socks. Alex had tried one time to pack for a week-long trip by only packing seven pairs of underwear. He hadn't thought he would need to change anything else, not even his socks.

Yeah, Louisa knew better than to trust a 12-year-old boy's packing abilities.

She riffled through his bag and found that he'd packed his Gameboy, two packs of Pokémon cards, and a toothbrush and toothpaste. She looked at him, caught between laughter and despair. "Skyler," she said, trying not to show him how hilarious she thought he was. He might be upset that she was laughing at him, or try this trick again in the future because he liked making her laugh. You never knew with 12-year-olds. "Skyler, *mi gordito*, you need clothes to wear tomorrow. And the day after that. And PJs to wear to bed. And new underwear. And new socks. What were you planning on wearing tomorrow morning?"

"My clothes," he said, pulling at the t-shirt he was wearing and looking at her like she'd just lost her mind. She could almost see the word *#duh* flash above his head.

"If the Millers show up, tell them we'll be right down," Louisa said with a grimacing smile at Zane and then turned Skyler's chair around and pushed him back towards the elevator. "First things first: Always pack *clean* clothes to wear when you go on a sleepover to someone's house. You don't wake up in the morning and pull on the clothes that you wore the day before, right?"

"No. Well, not if the housekeeper has done the laundry," he added, really thinking about it. "One time, last year, our housekeeper got sick and I didn't have clean clothes for a week. Dad just took me shopping and we bought all new clothes for me to wear until the housekeeper could come back."

"That's one way of solving the problem," Louisa muttered under her breath, heavily leaning towards breaking out into laughter. Every time she forgot how different their backgrounds were, things like this came up and she remembered all over again what different planets they lived on. "Well, either way, the important thing is, you put on clean clothes every morning. And that still holds true if you go on a sleepover."

The discussion lasted all of the way through the repacking of his bag – somehow, it seemed perfectly logical to Skyler to skip putting on clean clothes as long as he was at his best friend's house – and back down the elevator. As soon as Skyler saw Juan, though, he went racing across the formal living room, his much fuller bag on his lap. They fell to chatting and headed outside, the two of them not even acknowledging anyone else in the room.

"Well, at least they're getting along now," Zane said with a laugh. "I wonder if they even remember bickering like an old married couple when they first met."

"They've certainly come a long ways since then," Abby said with a small chuckle, and then turned to Louisa. "So good to see you again," she said warmly. "Thanks for suggesting this. The boys are just going to love it. I know y'all have to head back to Tennessee soon for the start of school, so every last bit of time they can spend together, I'm happy to make happen."

"Yes, me too," Louisa said automatically, giving Wyatt's wife a bright smile. "I love it when I come up with these *great* ideas." She felt Zane wince slightly next to her in the face of her sarcasm but Wyatt and Abby didn't seem to catch it.

"We're off," Wyatt said, tugging on Abby's hand and pulling her towards the door. "I can hear Maggie Mae getting all riled up – the boys are probably wrestling with her or something. We better get her out of here before she shits on the lawn and Zane's groundskeeper throws a pair of shears at my head."

Sure enough, Juan was on one end of the stick and a nondescript cow dog was on the other, playing tug-of-war with a tree branch. Skyler was sitting to the side, cheering them on. Juan lost his grip on the branch and went tumbling backwards into the grass as the dog went running around the yard, holding the branch up in her mouth triumphantly, obviously very pleased with herself.

"Good job, Maggie Mae," Wyatt said affectionately as the dog came running up to his side, her tail wagging a million miles an hour. "C'mon, Juan and Skyler, let's get going. I heard we just might have watermelon for a watermelon-seed-spitting contest back at the house."

They piled into Abby's mini-van, Skyler adeptly folding up his wheelchair and storing it off to the side. He waved energetically at Louisa and Zane as they pulled away and then was focused on Juan again, all thought of the adults in his life completely gone. He was with Juan, and that was what mattered.

"So," Louisa said after they walked back into the house together, turning and cocking an eyebrow at Zane. "Good to hear how this was my idea. I thought that part was particularly fascinating, actually. Any thoughts you want to share with the class?"

He coughed, and the tips of his ears went pink.

Zane Risley blushes. Holy shit, the country music god blushes. It's kind of adorable, really.

She didn't tell him this. Because she wasn't going to tell him something that personal. She was going to pin him to the ground and make him explain exactly how this whole spend-the-weekend-at-Juan's-house idea came about.

"Want a glass of wine?" Zane asked, oh-so-innocently.

"No, I'm okay," she said blithely. *Two can play this game.*

"Well, if that's all then, I guess I'll head up to my room now that Skyler isn't here to watch over. Have a goodn—"

"I asked Wyatt and Abby to take Skyler for the weekend," he said quickly. She turned at the base of the stairs and looked back at him, one eyebrow cocked. She was waiting for the rest of the explanation. He sighed. "It just sort of slipped out that it'd actually been your idea. I didn't–I don't know why I said that." She put her hand on the knob of the bannister and continued to wait. She could hear the grandfather clock in the formal living room ticking away.

He looked like he was being tortured. A part of her reveled in that. It was only fair, after all of the shit he'd put her through. *Let's make out! Let's not talk to each other. Let's just be friends. Let's hang out all weekend without Skyler.*

Yeah, he deserved a little torture.

"I like you," he said in a rush. "And I wanted to spend a weekend, just you and I, and see if you like me, too."

CHAPTER 29
ZANE

ELL, if he hadn't driven her off with his drunken pawing of her or their roll in the grass up in the mountains, he was surely going to do it with this.

Nothing said "Smooth Operator" like blurting out that you *liked* someone, as if you were both in junior high and hadn't held hands with the opposite sex before.

Louisa stood stock still, not breathing, not blinking, not moving an inch, as she stared at him.

Tamara would've laughed at him. Tamara would've told him that he was so immature to say something so gauche, and what was he, 14?

But Louisa wasn't laughing.

"I...when?"

"When?" he repeated blankly.

"When did you start liking me?"

"I..." He trailed off. "It sort of snuck up on me," he finally said. There wasn't that one moment in time, when she'd smiled just right or tossed her hair that caught a ray of sunshine. It was a million little moments of her being her. Bringing order and laughter and enjoyment back into his life.

"Ahhhh..." she said seriously, like a scientist who'd just

solved a great mystery. "So about the same time that I started liking you."

He burst out laughing and she grinned impishly at him, clearly pleased with herself that she'd made him laugh.

"So, Mr. I Like You, what're you gonna do about it?" She cocked an eyebrow at him challengingly. He liked that eyebrow cock – the way that she pushed back. Gave as good as she got. She didn't kowtow to him, scared of him because of how famous he was or how much money he made. He was pretty sure she wasn't scared of anything at all.

"Well…" He scooted a little closer and picked up her hand. "First, I thought I'd send my precocious and way-too-observant son," he picked up her other hand, "off to his best friend's house." He tugged her hands, pulling her towards him. "It is hard to make a move on a beautiful woman when your son is there, asking you a million questions in a row. 'Dad, why are you staring at Louisa like that?' 'Dad, why is your mouth on Louisa's mouth?' 'Dad, where do babies come from?'" A giggle erupted out of her like a volcano of laughter and happiness. "Not to mention that he might start critiquing my performance. I just don't think I could take it if my son started saying things like, 'A little more tongue in it next time, Dad.'" Louisa was laughing so hard, she was wiping the tears off her cheeks, helpless in the clutches of the laughter. It was his turn to grin, pleased as punch with himself.

When he'd seen her in the kitchen, laughing with her family, he'd wanted to be the one to make her shout with laughter.

And now he had, and damn if it didn't feel just as good as he'd thought it would.

Finally, wiping the last of her tears away, she straightened up, using the elaborately carved newel post for support. "I can see why you'd come to that conclusion," she said seriously, and then wiped a stray tear off, ruining the effect. "What step comes next, though?"

"We have a whole weekend of fun ahead of us, but tonight, we're going to ease into it. I wouldn't want to scare you off by showing you all of my awesomeness at once."

"Of course. That would be too much for a mere mortal like me to take in, for sure."

"Tonight, we're going to start out with dinner and a movie."

"We're going out to the movies?" she asked, surprised. "Is there a movie theater in Franklin? Or do we have to drive to Boise?"

"No, no. We're going to watch a movie, rich-man style. You don't go out to the movies. You watch them in your home theater."

Her eyes popped open with shock. "Don't tell me there's a home theater in this monstrosity that I just haven't discovered yet. No way." She was shaking her head in disbelief. "I know this place is big, but c'moonnn…"

He laughed. "I'm half convinced that there's a secret room to launch rockets to the moon somewhere in here, and I just haven't found it yet," he said conspiratorially. "But seriously, you've been right outside the door to it a hundred times." He snagged her hand and pulled her over to the elevator. He pushed the button for the walk-out basement and then pulled Louisa into his arms, the floor beginning to drop below them. "Let's see how much kissing I can get in before the—" *Ding!* "Dammit," he groaned. "That was the shortest elevator ride *ever*."

She giggled again, a sound that he was quickly determining was his favorite sound in the world. He tugged her through the open door and into the game room where Skyler always hid from the world to play his video games.

"There's a movie screen in here somewhere?" she asked, looking around for the hidden projector.

He looked at her quickly, trying to decide if she was being serious or not.

She was.

She really was adorable.

"Not in here," he said, keeping his voice light. "Can you even imagine if you were throwing a party and one group of friends wanted to have a face-off on the Xbox and another group of friends wanted to watch a movie? You couldn't *possibly* have the same room serve *both* functions."

"Obviously," she said dryly. "I don't know what I was thinking."

He was already pulling her forward, though, towards a nondescript door to the left of the big-screen TV. He swung the heavy door open, creaking on its hinges, and Louisa's eyebrows hit her hairline. "This looks more like a bank vault than a regular door," she said, trying to take a closer look at the door, but he was already tugging her forward again.

"It's sound proofing," he said over his shoulder. "So that you aren't disturbed by the cheering people having a face-off on the Xbox."

"Right. Of course." Her words were all but dripping with sarcasm.

"You're not much for spending money on frivolities, are you?" he said, pulling them fully into the room so she could appreciate it in all its glory. There was the huge screen that took up all of one wall; speakers everywhere; dimmable lights; a row of tables with finger foods and drinks galore so they didn't have to worry about sitting down at a proper table to eat dinner; and then the comfortable couches that you could sink into and never want to get out of again. It looked like the chef had done a bang-up job with the food; all of the kinds of foods that you could eat while sprawled on a couch and not having to worry about spilling any of it.

Just then, his stomach let out a loud rumble, reminding him that he'd skipped breakfast and lunch, trying to get all of this done by this evening.

"It sounds like we better eat sooner rather than later,"

Louisa said with a pointed look at his stomach. "I'd hate for you to starve to death just when we were starting to get to the good stuff."

"The good stuff?" he echoed, confused.

"Yeah. This is the part of the love story where I'm stupid enough to date you, even though I've dated my boss before and ended up homeless and jobless as a result. So, if you let me stand around and think about it too long, I might come to my senses and realize that I'm an idiot for making the same mistake twice, and go running back to Pocatello where I'm safe from all blue-eyed country music stars."

"Wait just a minute! How many other blue-eyed country music stars are after you?" he asked, even as he let her tug him towards the buffet table. He wasn't about to resist the allure of food too hard.

"Wanting to keep an eye on your competition?" Louisa teased him as she began loading up her fine china plate. She wasn't handling it roughly, but he could also tell she was just as impressed by it as she would've been with paper plates.

Note to self: Fine china does not impress Louisa.

"Of course," he said as he began loading his own plate with finger foods.

"Well, I'll tell you if you have anyone to worry about. Right now, the only other blue-eyed boy I'm falling in love with, I've never heard him sing. Both of his parents have talent coming out of their toenails, though, so I'm going to guess this boy can sing, too."

Zane felt his grip relax on his plate as the realization that she was talking about Skyler penetrated through his haze of jealousy.

"Sky can sing," he said lightly, as if he'd been in on the joke the whole time. "Tamara and him used to sing *Raindrops Keep Falling on My Head* together, and the harmonies..." He could hear their voices even now, blending together, haunting him. "Skyler quit singing after his mom died," he said quietly. "I think it was his way of getting back at me."

Louisa paused, her hands full with the plate and a wine spritzer that she'd chosen. "What was he getting back at you for?"

He found that he couldn't meet her eyes. He tried, but his gaze slid away of its own accord, refusing to stay put.

"For letting his mom die."

He'd never known that silences could hurt, but he knew it now. They had sharp edges that cut at your soul, that left you bleeding. Louisa had stilled, her hands gripping her food like a lifeline she was fighting to keep a hold of, and she wasn't saying a word.

"He loves you," she finally said into the stillness, breaking it, releasing its hold on him. He looked at her bleakly, wishing that what she was saying was true. Wishing that his son could have actually forgiven him. Knowing he hadn't. "You're the only parent he has left. He *wants* you to be his dad, even if neither of you really knows what that means."

He gave her a rueful smile. "At least I know that you know what you're getting yourself into. You're certainly not suffering under any delusions about me or Skyler."

She smiled back, chuckling a little. "No, I'm definitely not." She began moving again, picking a leather couch and settling into its comforting folds. "You're right – this is much better than a movie theater," she called out to him over her shoulder as she settled her plate onto her lap. "I don't have to sit upright or make sure that I'm not hogging too much of the armrest that I'm sharing with the stranger sitting next to me."

He finished filling his plate, grabbed a dark brown bottle of beer, and settled down next to Louisa. He opened the beer, stalling for time, hoping that Louisa would be willing to let the topic of Tamara and Skyler and his many screw-ups as a father go, at least for the time being. This was supposed to be his weekend to woo Louisa, not to rehash every single mistake he'd made as a father.

God only knew, that'd take a lot longer than just one weekend.

"So, what movie are we watching tonight?" she asked brightly.

He fought the urge to close his eyes with relief. Yup, there was definitely a reason he was falling fast and hard for Louisa. Her innate ability to sense when to leave a topic the hell alone was just one of her many redeeming qualities.

"I was thinking a suspense movie. That way, every time you were surprised by what just happened on the screen and you jumped, you'd want to throw yourself into my arms."

She threw back her head and laughed, her long braid falling off her shoulder and swinging free behind her.

"But first…" he said, and set his food down on the table, and then tugged on her hairband on the end of her braid, letting it slip free of her hair. "There's something I've been wanting to do for a while," he said, slowly unraveling the braid, watching the slick hair slide and fall straight as an arrow to her waist. Once the braid was undone, her hair shone darkly under the dim lighting, a black waterfall of silky soft hair, not a wrinkle or curl in it, despite it just having come out of a braid. "Your hair doesn't take curl, does it?" he murmured, running his fingers through it, reveling in it. His own hair had a mind of its own, curling and wavy and frizzy, depending on the day and the humidity percentage outside. More than a few hairdressers had told him that they'd kill for hair like his, but he'd always privately thought they were welcome to it, jealous of the people with stick-straight hair, who weren't likely to take a look in the mirror and find out that their hair had formed a halo of frizz around their heads when they weren't looking.

"Nope," she said, and he could tell she was striving for cheerfulness, nonchalance, but instead it came out breathless.

"You can spend an hour on my hair with a curling iron and a whole can of hairspray, and at the end, my hair will be just as straight as when you started. Drove my mother crazy. She really wanted a girl with curls and ribbons in her hair, and instead, she got me. Emilia, the next child in line after me, inherited my dad's curly hair, so she was the lucky duck who was forced to spend hours with my mother, making her hair look just right." She was slowly melding into him, her eyes drifting closed as he pulled her into his arms and partially into his lap, his fingers drifting through her hair as he listened to her. "Once my mom had Em, she stopped even messing with mine. Gave me up as a lost cause. I learned how to braid my own hair, and that's," she sighed a little, her eyes fluttering closed, "what I've done with it ever since."

Her family. Always, it came back to her family. Would she be willing to leave her family behind and move to Tennessee with him? But of course, he wasn't asking her to abandon her family. He was just asking her to take a plane ride home whenever she wanted to see them. And a ride on a private plane wasn't a real hard ask, right?

She was lying there, sprawled across him, loose limbed as a baby kitten fast asleep, her trust in him complete. They were supposed to be down here watching a movie, but he didn't want the distraction of one, not even one that promised to have Louisa clinging close to him every time the hero had to make a daring dive out of an airplane. He just wanted to stay with her forever, right there on that couch, her belief in him absolute.

Louisa stirred a little, her eyes fluttering open, their brown depths promising love and affection and laughter. He felt his dick begin to harden in response to her close vicinity to it. He was only a man, after all, and hadn't found relief with anyone but his own hand since landing in Idaho. Having her mouth that close…if she just turned a bit and unzipped his jeans and opened her mouth…

He squeezed his eyes shut, almost groaning with pain. He had to take this slow. He had to show Louisa what it was like to be in love with Zane Risley, the country music star, and that *didn't* include a weekend of nothing but hot, passionate sex.

He gritted his teeth. He could *not* think the words *hot, passionate sex* while Louisa was a mere hair's breadth away from his dick. *Bad idea, Risley.*

"Why don't you tour anymore?"

And with that, his dick shrunk right back up, as quickly as if she'd doused him with ice-cold water. His eyes popped back open and he stared at her in disbelief. Everyone knew not to ask that question. Hell, he'd finally even made his manager understand that it was completely out of bounds to even *discuss* touring with him until such time that he decided it was okay to talk about it again, and he sure as hell hadn't said that it was time to talk about it again.

But his very best glower did nothing at all when he pinned it on her. Wasn't he just appreciating how she wasn't one to be intimidated by him? He realized the flaw in that particular characteristic. There were times when she needed to know to leave something the hell alone, and touring was *definitely* that topic.

Still, she just lay there, her hair a mass of silk around her head as she looked up at him expectantly, waiting for an answer. He glared at her, the kind of shut-the-hell-up look that could stop a stage hand in his tracks.

She just blinked.

Fine. He'd tell her the same bullshit story he told everyone else. If she was going to pry like this, she deserved to be lied to.

"After Tamara died, I decided to take some time off. Take care of Skyler. He'd lost a parent; he needed me to be there for him."

She laughed.

Not in a you're-so-funny way, like she had been earlier, but in a you're-not-fooling-me sort of way.

"I imagine that excuse probably worked on most people, didn't it?" she asked rhetorically, swooping her hair out from underneath her head and letting it cascade off the side of the couch in one smooth movement that he doubted she even realized she did. It was the kind of movement that had been done millions of times before by someone who'd dealt with the reality of long hair all of her life. "It is a very sweet excuse, after all. Your son's lost his mom – of course you're going to spend time with him. But you forget – I was here at the beginning of the summer, when I'm quite sure you had absolutely no idea that your son hated bread with nuts in it. You knew almost nothing about him, because you have *not* been spending time with him since Tamara died."

He got pissed then. "How dare you say that," he hissed. "I've been doing nothing *but* spending time with him since Tamara died. I've been here, not back in Nashville, all summer long. I—"

It was her turn to get angry, and she sat up, her black hair swinging around her, getting in her way, and he could tell that she wanted her hair tie back. She wanted to hide that gorgeous hair away again. He balled it up in his fist, refusing to let her see it.

"You sent your son to Sedona, Arizona – which is across the country from Tennessee, in case you fell asleep during geography class – with only an aide by his side, to attend a music therapy camp. Now, the art therapy camp was closer to home – at least it was in the same state as you – but still, he was sent to it without you. You could've toured either time. Your son didn't need you waiting at home in Nashville when the camps ended. I asked him – both of those camps were supposed to be eight weeks long. The kinds of camps that rich parents send their kids to during summer break because

God forbid they actually spend time with their own children."

He flinched.

He hated that she said that. He hated that she was right. He hated that they were discussing this at all, instead of snuggling together and making out like two horny teenagers like he'd planned that night.

"And let's not even touch boarding school. That's where the rich parents *really* shine – they hand their kids over to a private school and let them do the raising. You've been handing Skyler over to anyone and everyone who'd take him because you didn't want to raise him yourself."

He shrunk into himself. Here was every awful thought he'd ever had about himself coming out of someone else's mouth, and it sounded just as awful being said out loud as it had rattling around in his brain.

She didn't give an inch, though. She didn't soften her words. She was intent on drawing blood, and she was succeeding.

"You know what? Here's the God's honest truth: I lied to you. *That's* how I first got you to spend time with your own child – by lying. Through. My. Teeth." She punctuated every word with a stab to his chest with her finger, her eyes flashing.

He stared at her, bewildered. Louisa wasn't someone who would lie. She had an innate honesty about her that was so interwoven into her soul and who she was, this was akin to her announcing that she actually ate small children for breakfast.

It *couldn't* be true.

"The night you got drunk in your den and hit on me, I asked you to go out kayaking with Skyler and me. You didn't answer me. You were too busy pawing at me. The next day, I told you straight to your face that you'd promised that you'd go kayaking with us because I knew you wouldn't remember well enough to call me out on my lie. And after Skyler was so damn thrilled that you'd said yes, you couldn't back out of it. I'm going to have to confess my sins the next time I get into a confession booth with a priest, but it was worth it. That day on the lake was the first time that you saw your son as someone you could not only love, but also *like*. So don't give me no bullshit about how you're not touring because you're taking care of your son. You let your wallet take care of your son."

"You don't get it!" he roared, a wounded animal, wanting to come out and defend himself. Fight back. Make her hurt like she was hurting him. "I don't *get* to tour. At least, not for a while. Maybe not ever. I. Don't. Get. To." He bit off each word as if spitting them out like that would force Louisa to leave him the hell alone. Leave this whole topic alone.

"You are an extrovert," she said softly. Placatingly. She put her hand on his arm, and he could tell she wanted him to calm down, but he didn't want to calm down. He wanted to roar with anger. He wanted to make her regret ever bringing this question up. "You *thrive* when you go up on stage. You come alive. I've watched some videos online. I've seen a few of your concerts. Even on the screen, I can see the light switch flip inside of you as you go up on that stage and make your fans forget, if only for a little while, that they have any worries or problems in their lives. You were born to be on stage, Zane, and *not* touring is slowly killing you."

"Exactly."

CHAPTER 30

LOUISA

"**E**XACTLY?"

She stared at him, completely bewildered.

"Don't you see? This is the price I have to pay. I screwed up in *so* many ways. I am the reason that Skyler is in that godforsaken chair. I don't get to tour anymore. I don't get to sing in front of audiences. I don't get any of that ever again. This is my penance." He tilted his head back, gulping down the last of his beer and then standing up to grab another from the bucket of ice next to the buffet table.

It all clicked together then. She'd been so stupid not to see it before. How had she missed it?

She closed her eyes, shaking her head at her stupidity. She heard the pop of the lid on the bottle and then him swallowing, practically chugging the beer down like a frat boy at the induction party.

The sound spurred her to action and she sprung to her feet before she could think through what she was doing. Before she could carefully reason it out.

"No more beer for you," she cried, yanking the bottle out of his hand and dumping it into the trash. He gaped at her, quieted for the moment into stunned disbelief. "You are drinking your life away, feeling sorry for yourself, your own little pity party in your den, your own little pity party every day. Poor Zane. His wife died. His son is in a wheelchair. Now he is trying to drink himself to death. But not on my watch." She folded her arms across her chest and glared at him, blockading the ice bucket.

"I don't – I'm not—" he sputtered. "I drink to take the edge off things. So sue me! Everyone I know does that. Hell, at least I don't snort shit up my nose or stick a needle in a vein. Compared to most major music stars, I'm practically a priest."

She shook her head. "It does not matter what other people do," she said softly. "It only matters what *you* do, and why you do it. You are drinking because you don't know how to deal with the life you've been handed. You have more money than everyone else I know combined together, but that doesn't matter. Money does not make you happy, any more than it's made anyone else happy. You are an alcoholic, and I will not love an alcoholic. My father used to be one. I will never live with a drunk again."

All of those nights, lying in bed, trying not to breathe too loudly, hoping that night would be the night her dad simply fell into bed and went to sleep. That it wouldn't be the night when he hit her mother or broke dishes or smashed up furniture.

It was almost losing his wife after she gave birth to Alex that finally turned Louisa's dad straight. He'd come so close to losing his wife, and ironically, it hadn't been his drinking that had caused the childbirth complications.

Her mom had simply been worn out from having too many kids and shouldn't have gotten pregnant in the first place, but she'd been a good Catholic and hadn't used birth control. After she almost bled out, her doctor removed her uterus during emergency surgery to stop the bleeding. She'd been so angry with the doctor for taking that choice away from her, but Louisa had always been grateful.

Another pregnancy would've killed her mom as surely as a bullet through her brain, but even knowing that, her mom would've refused all forms of birth control.

But that wake-up call of almost losing his wife in that hospital had scared her father straight, and he never touched alcohol again. It was one of the reasons why Louisa could actually come home to her parents' house after Matt threw her out of his home. If her dad had still been drinking…

She didn't know where she would've ended up, actually, but definitely not her parents' home.

Which all of this made her blindness to Zane's drinking problem even more surprising. She should've known. She should've realized. More than anyone else, she should've seen the signs, but she hadn't.

"God," he said bitterly, jamming his fingers into his curls, and even as she watched him, she saw his eyes flick towards the bucket of alcoholic drinks and then back to her face. "I don't know why you're making such a big deal out of me having a few beers. It's not like I'm hanging out over the porcelain throne every morning."

"When was the last day you did not drink? Name the last day you made it through without a single beer." She crossed her arms and glared at him, waiting.

She could tell the moment that he realized he couldn't remember, because his shoulders went back and he looked ready to pounce, ready to fight her for daring to ask such a question.

"I haven't been stumbling drunk in a while," he snarled. "I really don't see how a single beer in a day means that I'm an alcoholic." Again, his eyes flicked, ever so quickly, to the bucket and then back again. He wanted a beer in his hand so badly in that moment, she rather thought he was going to lose his shit if he didn't get one.

Stupid, Louisa. Stupid. You missed this. How could you have missed this?

"You're not in the final stages of alcoholism," she said calmly. "If we were to run tests on you, I bet your liver would still come back as mostly functioning. But it is the direction you are heading. It is not a straight path. You can wander and wind your way through for quite a while before firmly ending up in the alcoholic camp. But it *is* the way that you're headed. Think about it, Zane. Right now: What do you want right now? You want a beer in your hand. Your eyes keep darting over to the bucket."

His eyes jerked back to hers, his face flushing red.

"Don't try to tell me that it isn't true," she said mildly. "You'd just embarrass yourself. You know it's true. It's written all over your face."

He staggered back, shaking his head, wanting to deny it even as he kept his mouth shut, unwilling to be caught in such an obvious lie. He sat down with a hard thump on the couch and stared at the far wall of the theater, not talking, just thinking. Was he slowly coming to realize that she'd been telling the truth?

She could only hope so.

She kept quiet, waiting for him to think through it all. Whatever realizations he was finally having, she didn't want to get in the way of them. She was absolutely sure that the knowledge he was becoming an alcoholic was just as much of a shock to him as it had been to her. No one sat down with the plan to become addicted to alcohol. It snuck up on a body, stealing away your independence and self-respect when you weren't looking.

"I didn't think I was drinking that much," he rasped, and when he looked up, his eyes were pleading with her to believe him. "I just thought I was having one or two occasionally. How could I have become a drunk without noticing?"

"Because no bottle of beer ever comes out of the fridge with a warning label on it. *This is the beer that will turn you into an alcoholic. Proceed with caution.*"

His lips twisted with humor at that. "It would sure be helpful if it did," he mused.

"No doubt," she agreed dryly. "Look." She settled down on the couch next to him, picking up his hand and looking him straight in the eye. "When you were touring full-time, were you also drinking? Not a few beers or a few shots of tequila occasionally, but were you drinking every single day, even if it was just a little bit?"

He closed his eyes for a moment, searching back. "I...no." His eyes popped open. "I drank here and there to celebrate and whatever, but I didn't drink every day. Not like I do now." The admission was humbling to him and she knew that he would've given anything to not say those words. He was so embarrassed to admit that out loud.

She squeezed his hand, proud of him for saying it anyway. God, how she was hurting his pride, and yet, he wasn't lashing out at her – at least, not anymore – and refusing to look the truth in the eye.

Yeah, she was *damn* proud of him.

"I am not an alcohol or drug dependency expert," she said slowly. "I learned about it in medical school, of course, but my unit's specialty was spinal cords, not detoxing people after years of hard drinking. Here's what I understand to be true, though: You can become what is called a *situational alcoholic*. In other words, you begin to rely on a substance to get you through tough times. If the tough times go away, then your desire to drink goes away."

"Uh-huh," he said absentmindedly, only half-listening as he stood up and headed for the ice bucket. She watched, open mouthed, as he popped the top on a bottle and brought the beer up to his mouth, so frozen with shock that she couldn't speak or move or yell at him and then he froze too, the beer bottle pressed to his lips but not drinking.

Slowly, ever so slowly, he lowered the bottle, his eyes wide as he stared at her. "I didn't even notice what I was doing," he whispered. "It was like scratching an itch. I didn't even know. How many bottles of beer have I drunk without even knowing I was doing it?"

She stood up and gently pulled the bottle from his hand, pitching it into the trash. She picked up the heavy ice bucket, grunting with the weight of it, and carried it over to the door, wrestling it out into the game room and out of sight before coming back to Zane. "Automatic responses," she said. "It's how you can eat through a whole bag of potato chips without even realizing you were doing it. If you put the bag away in the next room over and only give yourself a small bowl to eat from, you'll eat a lot less. The same thing is true of anything else. When you have beer right there, you can drink a bottle, or a six-pack, without thinking about it."

She pulled him back to the couch, sitting next to him, holding his hand in hers, willing him to understand that what she was about to say was oh-so-important.

"Not touring is driving you to drink."

He gaped at her. "Wh-what?" he finally got out.

"You are an extrovert. You were made for that stage. You were made to share your gift with the world. By punishing yourself and refusing to let yourself tour, you're slowly driving yourself insane. And so you're dealing with that pain by drinking it into oblivion."

His lips formed a perfect circle as he stared at her. She wished quite desperately that she could read minds, because she knew he was replaying scenes in his mind at the moment, rehashing the last 18 months of his life at least.

"Oh. Oh, my God. That…"

He was back to staring at her again.

"I *was* punishing myself," he finally said. "It's what I thought I deserved after screwing up so royally. I still believe...I screwed up, Louisa. I made a mess of everything. My drive to always come out on top, to be the best...it killed my wife. Crippled my son. If I wasn't a country music singer, we wouldn't have been in that limo that night. My kid would still be walking around. My wife would...well, she wouldn't be my wife anymore," he flashed a small, wry smile at that admission that disappeared just as quickly, "but she would be alive. Maybe she was a bitch. Maybe she was an awful wife. But she didn't deserve to *die*."

"No, she didn't," Louisa agreed mildly, and he flinched at her raw honesty. "I never met her, but it sounds like she loved Skyler a lot, and that alone makes her something special. But Zane, she could've died any other way. Did you know Wyatt Miller was married before?" Surprise registered in Zane's eyes, and he shook his head. "She died on the way to the store to buy milk. Their daughter was in the backseat. They both died *driving to the store to get milk*. Tamara could've died ten thousand ways before Sunday. Drunk driver. Brain aneurysm. Cut gets infected. Food poisoning. Plane crash. I should probably stop before I freak you out so much, you never leave the house again." He chuckled just a bit at that and she knew she hadn't lost him. Not yet.

Please, let him stay with me.

"The only reason," she said, intentionally softening her voice, "that we don't curl up in the corner and refuse to move an inch is because we humans are good at convincing ourselves that it'll 'happen to someone else.' Except, it has to happen to *someone*. We can't all die in our sleep of old age. Life doesn't work like that. Your wife didn't die because you were a country music star, Zane. She died because sometimes, life is shitty. Refusing to tour and share your gift with the world doesn't change a damn thing, except make you crazy to the point that you're willing to numb yourself with alcohol."

He stared at her for a long while, clearly processing everything she just said.

"How is it that you know me so well after only a few months?" he finally asked. "I went to the most expensive therapists money could buy after Tamara died, and all they ever wanted to do was talk about my childhood. I mean, my childhood was as screwed up as you can get," Louisa cocked an eyebrow at that, her curiosity piqued, but he ignored it and continued on, "but that wasn't what was haunting me. How did you know?"

"I'm gonna guess your therapists didn't watch concert footage of you," she pointed out. "That's how I realized how important touring is for you. Stupidly, though, I didn't put that together with your drinking until tonight. So you can stop thinking I'm a genius right now. If anyone should've put two and two together, it was me, but I still missed the signs."

"Why you?" She quirked an eyebrow at him, confused. "Why should you have been able to put two and two together?" he clarified.

"You met my dad at the Miller's house at Carmelita's birthday party." It was a statement, not a question, but he nodded anyway. "Tall, big bear of a man. Quiet, but he'll give you the shirt off his back if you need it. Good heart." She sucked in a breath. *Talk about childhood traumas.* "But an alcoholic. I grew up worried my dad was going to beat one of us. Beat my mom. Destroy the dining room table. Drink away his paycheck that week so we had nothing to eat. I did my best to protect my younger siblings from him and his rages, but he didn't stop until Alex was born. It was a terrible delivery, and it almost killed my mother. Scared him straight. So none of my brothers and sisters know how bad he *really* was, especially the twins and Alex. They were too young and missed it all. Lucky ducks."

She tried not to be bitter about how they were able to skate right past that one, unaffected by that trauma like she'd been. After all, she'd tried to protect them from it. She hadn't wanted them to know just how terrible Dad could be when drunk.

But still, a small part of her wished that someone had protected her too. Mom had tried, but…

"Your family seemed so normal when I met them," Zane said quietly. "I didn't know that about your dad. I never would've guessed. He seemed like the nicest guy on the planet."

"Oh, and he is," Louisa was quick to reassure him. "It's only when he was drunk that the devils came out to play. Alex is 13 years old, so my dad hasn't touched alcohol in 13 years. It doesn't mean he can never relapse, but it's not like he just sobered up last week. Every time we go to a party as a family and I see beer being offered up, though, I hold my breath. I don't know that I'll ever fully trust him again. There's always that chance he'll fall back into it."

She wished her aunts would stop serving alcohol at family parties, but then, her mother had done an excellent job hiding the truth from her three sisters. To this day, she wasn't sure if Carmelita, María, or Consuelo knew how bad it had gotten at home, and she was *sure* none of them knew that her father was an alcoholic.

Everyone had always told her mom how lucky she was to marry "such a handsome devil."

There was more truth in those words than anyone realized.

"So you think I'm a situational drunk?" Zane asked, his mind clearly drifting back to his own impending alcoholism. "So if I go out touring again, I can drink then without worrying that I'm slipping down that slope?"

"Yeesssss…?" she said doubtfully. "That's my theory. Like I said, I'm not a specialist in that field. Plus, ask yourself this: Why is it such a big deal to you that you still be able to drink? Your first question out of the gate is to ask when it is that you can start drinking again. Does that make you nervous? It sure as hell makes me nervous."

"Oh." He sat there, quiet, thoughtful. The minutes stretched on, and still, he was quiet. Then finally, he shot her a rueful grin. "I figured out how to get you alone for the weekend so I could woo you without my son right here observing every minute of it, and have instead spent it discussing alcoholism. Not exactly the romantic weekend I'd envisioned."

She laughed and settled back into the couch a little more, picking up on his not-so-subtle request to leave the topic alone, and more than happy to agree. There was only so much muck-stirring a body could stand in one go, and she figured they'd just about reached that limit. "We've been discussing some pretty heavy stuff tonight," she admitted. "I didn't mean to turn our date into a therapy session. Do you want to watch that movie after all?"

"On one condition," he said, snagging the remote from off the end table and flipping through the menu to get to Hulu. "You let me rub your legs and feet while we watch it."

"*Let* you?" she repeated incredulously. She rather thought this was akin to him asking her if it was okay if he paid off all of her student loans. Really, not a hardship.

"I've been fascinated with your calves since day one. I think it's all of that walking that you did as a nurse, but you have the sexiest legs of any woman I've ever met. Oh, and the sexiest ass. Has anyone ever mentioned this to you?"

She shook her head, mute. Matt wasn't much for handing out compliments. If he was really feeling effusive one night, he might've told her, "Lookin' good." She'd told him one time not to strain himself too hard.

The sarcasm had sailed right over his head.

"Well, obviously you've only dated blind men." He hit play on a thriller suspense movie and settled back against the couch, swinging her legs over onto his lap before pulling a small bucket filled to the brim with lotions out from the bottom shelf of the side table. He'd obviously come prepared. "You watch the movie and enjoy it, and I'll rub your legs and enjoy that. We'll both end the night happy people."

That, she thought as she snuggled deeper into the couch, letting her body conform to its contours, was a most excellent idea.

CHAPTER 31
ZANE

E HADN'T BEEN blowing smoke up her ass when he'd said that she had the sexiest legs he'd ever seen. As eerie music played and Louisa's body grew taut with expectation, Zane ignored the screen and instead kept his eyes focused on the delicate curves of her legs. She'd chosen that morning to wear a short pair of khaki shorts and a faded t-shirt that had *National Nurses and Health Professionals Conference of 2016* emblazoned across it. Not exactly the stuff of wet dreams.

It definitely wasn't the window dressings that took his breath away. That was for tomorrow night, and no doubt she'd look spectacular in whatever Buttons got her into.

No, it was just *her*. Everything about her, although he was starting to realize that he was particularly fascinated with her ankles. The way they curved into her calves just begged for him to kiss his way over them. Memorize their contours with his tongue.

Louisa let out a little yelp of fear as the music rose to a crescendo, hugging one of the throw pillows to her chest, and Zane chuckled to himself. Next time, he'd have to make sure to offer up himself as the pillow to hug.

Louisa settled back against the couch as the suspenseful moment faded, muttering to herself in Spanish, and he wished for the millionth time that he had more than a passing idea of the Spanish language. About the only words he'd retained all these years were the kind that Skyler had begged to learn. He hadn't mentioned that he knew swear words in Spanish during that conversation, because he knew his son wouldn't let up pestering him until he'd been taught them all. Louisa was much better at telling Skyler no, and him listening to her.

Just another reason why she made a better parent than him. Ironic, really, considering she wasn't a parent at all.

At least, not yet.

He tried to squash that possessive thought. He hadn't even convinced her to move past the "I like you" stage. He surely couldn't be planning his children with her.

His hands drifted up and down her buttery soft legs, smoothing the lotion in, her dark skin a stark contrast against his white hands. Unbidden, he remembered his skepticism when Kylie had first told him that the niece of the Mexican housekeeper was the nurse in one of the premiere spinal cord units in the country. God, he'd been *such* an ass. He wanted to bury his head with embarrassment at the memory. He was willing to share virtually anything about himself with Louisa, but he'd *never* share that thought.

Never.

She'd had to overcome so much – being Latina. Being a woman. Having English as her second language. Having an alcoholic as a father. And yet, she'd beaten every obstacle. She had a drive in her to succeed. She wasn't like Tamara or him, though. It wasn't a drive at any cost.

He admired the hell out of her for that. Somehow, she retained that drive to succeed *and* her humanity.

His hands began drifting higher and higher on her legs, the feel of her bare skin an aphrodisiac. His dick began to harden against his will. How could he be in the company of this beautiful woman and *not* be turned on by her? He'd always liked brunettes but Louisa was more than just dark hair and tanned skin and a J.Lo ass. She was…

Louisa.

"Yes?" she said, looking over at him, and he realized then that he'd said her name out loud.

"Come to bed with me," he whispered, his voice husky.

"Oh." The word slipped out of her mouth, her perfect cupid's bow mouth, and she stared at him for an endless moment and he was so damn afraid that he'd pushed too hard, too fast, and she was trying to find a way to tell him no, and then—

"Yes." It too was a whisper, but he felt the word deep in his soul. It was a yes to sex with him, but it was also a yes to a life with him. He knew that. Louisa was not one to jump into bed with someone she did not care about deeply.

Somehow, he'd won her over, despite the fact that she could probably name every one of his flaws, and maybe even some he didn't even know he had.

He grabbed the remote and hit the power button, killing the power to the TV, his hands trembling slightly with need. He couldn't make a fool out of himself by letting her know just how much he wanted her – she wanted to date a man, not an eager boy.

But still, it had been months…

He started at her toes, nibbling on the pads of them. How was it that the pads of her toes could be sexy? That's when he knew he was desperate. He was just this side of completely addled with lust and desire if he was obsessed with her toes.

She groaned, a guttural noise of lust that seemed to emanate from her toes, and sunk back into the couch, her eyes drifting closed. He swallowed hard as he kissed his way up her foot and over to her ankles. He'd wanted to make her look like that – that exact look of desire and lust and need –

virtually from day one. Maybe even minute one. He hadn't wanted to face up to it at the time – falling in love with your child's nanny was such a cliché – but it'd happened anyway. He ran his tongue in circles over her delicate ankle bones and her breath started coming in pants as she dug her hands into the leather of the couch.

"Zane," she groaned as he pulled her more fully across his lap. She seemed almost boneless as she laid there, draped over him, her neck and face flushing pink with desire. Did her breasts flush pink too? Oh, the answers he was finally going to discover. He flipped the button open and unzipped her shorts, his fingers drifting underneath the khaki fabric even as his tongue continued to make swirls up her shin bone and then to her knee, but it was her thighs that fascinated him. They were so damn muscular, she looked like she could climb a mountain before breakfast without breaking into a sweat. He wondered what they'd feel like, wrapped around his head as he licked her pussy.

Heaven, he guessed. Heaven on earth.

"Zane, Zane, Zane," Louisa panted, a chant of desire that rolled over him, his body reveling in the sound of his name on her lips. "Please, Zane, please…"

"Please what?" he rasped as he pulled the khakis off her and tossed them to the ground. She had on a pair of plain cotton panties, as down-to-earth and practical as her bathing suit had been, and so he didn't feel the slightest bit of guilt at tearing them off her. He would take her shopping when they got back to civilization. Only silk and lace from here forward.

"Please," she whimpered as he turned between her legs and began to lick the curls of her womanhood. Here, finally, was curly hair – the only curly hair Louisa would ever have. "Yes. I…please…"

Her words didn't make sense, but he didn't need them to. He knew what she wanted, because it was what he wanted too. He wasn't going to last much longer – his self control was slipping fast, and he knew that he'd look like a randy teenage boy if he didn't get himself wrapped up and inside of her soon.

He rolled off her and snagged a condom out of the lotion basket he'd put together earlier – he was nothing if not an optimist – and rolled it into place before moving back over Louisa again. Her hair was in a cloud of black strands around her head, and he thought as he slipped inside of her that she looked like an angel.

His angel.

"Oh! Oh! Oh!" Louisa was panting, her back arching, her head tossing from side to side as he drove ever deeper into her, withdrawing and plunging forward again, the rhythm of it as old as time itself. She screamed with pleasure, her whole body tensing, rigid, and then he was spilling his seed too, the world going dark around the edges as he felt himself come, wave after wave of desire washing over him, whispered pleas for lust and love and desire wrapping and swirling around them.

Time stopped then. They were floating on a plane of bliss, snuggled together, his nose buried in the crook of her neck, breathing in her scent. He realized belatedly that he hadn't even gotten her shirt off, let alone her bra. He still didn't know what color of pink her nipples were.

Next time. I'll look at them next time...

And then the world faded away completely and Zane was lost to sleep.

CHAPTER 32
LOUISA

I T WAS HER ARM that woke her up. It was doing that painful tingle that signaled that it was even more asleep than the rest of her body, and she sleepily tugged to free it from whatever it was stuck under…except it wouldn't move.

Her eyes fluttered open and then flew wide as she heard a snore that ended in a snort right next to her ear.

What the hell?!

She bolted upright, jerking her arm free in the process, and then stared down at the sleeping man next to her as pieces of the night before slowly reassembled in her mind. Zane. She'd had sex with her boss last night.

And not just once. Several glorious, wondrous, amazing times.

They'd ended up in his bed about halfway through – a bed she was never going to look at in the same way again.

Oh Louisa, you've gone and stepped in it this time.

Was she bound and determined to replay the same mistakes again and again? Was she destined to be stupid? What had she been thinking?

"Whatever you're thinking about," came Zane's groggy voice, "it's much too early in the morning to be that serious."

How did he know if she was being serious or not? She looked down at his sleeping form, confused, his face mostly covered with wild strands of blond hair and pillows. "And don't give me that look," he mumbled into the pillows. "It's too early for that look, too."

"How do you know what look I'm giving you?" she demanded tartly.

"I know everything about you," he said, his hands snaking out and snagging her, dragging her over to lay on top of him as she began to laugh. "For example," he said, snuggling her underneath his stubbled chin, her ear pressed against his chest where she could feel as well as hear what he was saying, "I know that there's that one spot on the back of your knee that when I suck on it, I make you cross-eyed with lust."

"Cross-eyed?" she protested. That made her sound like she was not completely with it upstairs.

He ignored her outburst, intent on listing all of the things he knew about her.

"I know that you love Skyler with all of your heart but that you also know that the best thing you can do for him is *not* spoil him rotten, something I'm only beginning to learn."

"Well, that was easy," she said. "For me, anyway. I grew up with way too many sib—"

He pressed a finger to her lips, stopping her from talking.

"I know that you have absolutely no idea how to just shut up and take a compliment," he said mildly. She wasn't sure if she wanted to laugh or smack him, or maybe both. "Of course, I still have more to learn about you. Last night was just the beginning."

"I thought you said you knew everything about me," she protested, except he still had his finger pressed to her lips so it came out sounding something like, "Ishawtusadunewederyshingoutme" instead. He pulled his finger away and she nipped at it playfully. "I thought you said you knew everything about me," she repeated.

"Everything important," he clarified, stroking her hair as she lay on top of him, one long pillow of muscle and bone and warmth. "I'm still trying to figure out the small stuff, like whether your eyes are a 90% cocoa brown or a 75% cocoa brown. Sometimes, I think it just depends on the lighting, but I need further study to know for sure."

Her shoulders were shaking with laughter. "I can see how this question keeps you up at night," she said dryly.

"It is one of life's great mysteries," he said mildly, his hands still stroking down her hair in long, even strokes. She realized why it was that animals loved being petted so much. She could just lay there all day, basking in his touch.

"But, alas, we have to do something more today than just compare your eyes to chocolate bars," he said with a heavy sigh, the rumble of his voice traveling through her body as he talked.

"We do?" She searched through her mind for what they could possibly be scheduled for that weekend but came up blank. With Skyler gone, she had nothing at all to do, and that just seemed decadent to her. Luxurious.

Lazy as hell.

"One of my friends from the music industry, Buttons, is on her way here from Tennessee," he said casually, as if talking about nothing more interesting than the menu at a restaurant. "Buttons did all of Tamara's dresses for her for all of the big events. She's going to do a fitting for you. Dress you up for a night on the town."

She jerked, her boneless body of just moments ago completely gone. She stared down at him in shock, only vaguely registering the *"oof"* of breath that blew out of him as she inadvertently dug her elbow into his stomach. "Night on the town?" she repeated.

Muttering something she probably didn't want to hear, he moved her elbow over, but she wasn't paying much attention to him anyway as her mind replayed his words, trying to actually understand them. He was flying a friend called Buttons – *who has a name like Buttons?!* – to Idaho to do a fitting so they could have a night on the town. The two of them.

She ran through the words frontwards and backwards, trying to wrap her mind around them. Was this for real? This couldn't be for real. Things like this didn't happen to Latina girls like her.

"Considering how late we slept," Zane said, pulling her back to the present, "I should probably warn you that Buttons will be here soon." He reached over and tapped his phone, peering at the screen. "In, like, ten minutes."

She scrambled, trying to clear his body and the bed and get dressed and do her hair and brush her teeth all at the same damn time and oh my God, there was a seamstress on the way over and she batted at the bedsheet, somehow wrapped up so tightly in it, she was surprised she could get one arm free enough to bat at it, and—

"Hold on, hold on," Zane said, his voice sounding suspiciously like he was laughing at her. She glared at him, but he just held his hands up in mock surrender. "Don't move. I'm going to untangle you."

Her whole body pulsing with anticipation, she stood stock still, letting him unravel the sheet from around her, until it finally fell to the ground and like a shot, she ran for the bathroom. She could not – *would* not – meet a designer with sleep creases on her face.

CHAPTER 33
ZANE

Z ANE FELL BACKWARDS onto the bed, helpless to hold his laughter in any longer. The look on Louisa's face when she'd realized what he was talking about…
Priceless.

He stacked his hands behind his head, listening contentedly to the sound of running water as Louisa readied herself in the bathroom. Last night was amazing. Stupendous. Mind blowing. Better than he could've ever imagined. He and Louisa were compatible on so many levels. *All* of the levels.

Sadly, he was *too* organized, and he just didn't have time for Round Four that morning before Buttons showed up, which was really too bad, because he'd been wanting to spend time sucking and licking the inside of Louisa's elbow. He was curious if it was as sensitive as the back of her knees were.

Just one more thing he needed to discover about Louisa.

With a grunt, he pushed himself out of bed and threw on a pair of jeans and a t-shirt. Buttons would be there any minute – punctuality was one of her best features – and as much as he liked her, he still didn't parade around in front of her in only his birthday suit.

The doorbell sounded just then, and Louisa let out a squeal of panic as Zane padded out of the room and down the stairs. Right on time, like always.

He opened the front door and pulled Buttons in for a hug and an air kiss on each cheek.

"Look at you," she said admiringly, pulling back and peering up at him square in the face. Even though he knew it wouldn't be there, there was still a part of him that was surprised when the cloud of smoke didn't follow her like it always had. She'd finally quit that spring after 42 years of smoking like a chimney, and honestly, it was a not-so-small miracle that no one had died in the process. "I think you've got yourself a tan. Finally spending time outdoors?"

"I am. Horseback riding, kayaking, short hikes around…"

"Good, good," Buttons said, but she was already peering around him, looking for Louisa. "Jeffrey, Cade," she barked. "Bags, please." The two men behind her, who hadn't said a word yet, turned and headed back towards the rental SUV. "Not enough coffee yet," Buttons said by way of explanation. "They'll wake up in a bit. If you'd had the good sense to try to find yourself while a little closer to civilization, the plane ride wouldn't have been so long, but I get it. I bet there are a lot of sexy cowboys in Idaho. Maybe I should try to find one– oh my."

She cut herself off and headed for the stairs, meeting Louisa partway up them. "Hi, I'm Alice but Zane here calls me Buttons," she said, holding her hand out to shake Louisa's. "I don't even think he knows my real name," she said in a stage whisper. Zane opened up his mouth to defend himself – he knew her name; he just thought Buttons suited her better – when she continued briskly, "You, dear, are even more gorgeous in real life than you were in the photos that Zane sent me."

Louisa looked past Buttons and down to Zane, the

surprise clear on her face. "You sent her pictures of me?" she asked, startled. "When did you take pictures of me?"

"He had to on the sly. That way, I knew which dresses to bring. I can't bring my whole business here, not even for Zane. It would take weeks just to pack everything up. Where are we doing the fittings?" This question was directed to Zane even as she continued to look Louisa over, her eyes darting over every curve and muscle, taking her all in. "The teal one is all wrong, all wrong," she muttered to herself. "Don't even know why I brought it. But the gold one…yes, yes…"

"There's a walkout basement downstairs," Zane said, cutting across Button's mumblings. "You can have the whole level to yourself. I'll stay up here until y'all are done."

"Excellent," she said, pleased. "That way, we can spread ourselves out." And in a whirl of expensive perfume and bags upon bags of dresses and makeup and jewelry and clothes, Buttons and Louisa disappeared into the elevator, Jeffrey and Cade dutifully carrying in yet more bags from outside.

Zane helped them bring the remaining items in, but then found himself with nothing to do, since he'd promised not to do the one thing he wanted to do more than anything – go downstairs and watch the transformation take place. It would be more dramatic if he didn't see her until Buttons was done, of course, but a part of Zane ached with the need to be close to her. Why, he hadn't even had a chance to decide if her hair was the color of midnight or obsidian yet.

Eventually, making himself crazy with the desire to do *something*, he found himself in his studio, his guitar in hand, picking at the strings, a new song bubbling up inside of him. Not just a change to an old idea, not just a variation on an old song, but a completely new melody teasing him around the edges, tickling his mind, begging to be written.

How long had it been since he'd been able to compose from scratch? Not just edit and modify but start from nothing and build a song? Too long. Longer than it'd been since he'd gone without drinking, he was sure of that.

He strummed the guitar and sang the refrain again. Yes. Yes, this would work.

He was writing again. Something he'd started to think he'd lost forever had come back.

He wanted to weep in gratitude but instead, he found a paper and pencil and began scribbling down the main chords, the refrain. He had to capture this on paper before it disappeared again.

CHAPTER 34
LOUISA

LOUISA DISCOVERED EARLY ON – roughly 45 seconds in or so – that there wasn't much to keeping up a conversation with Buttons. Talking was definitely not required, and in fact, she rather thought Buttons would consider it to be an intrusion on the flow of conversation. All Louisa had to do was say, "Ohhh..." and "Uh-huh" occasionally, and let Buttons do the work from there.

It would be exhausting to be around Buttons for any length of time, but in the short term, Louisa found her nothing short of fascinating, because here was a woman who knew Zane in his element. She knew him back when he was married to Tamara. She knew Tamara. She knew Skyler when he could walk. She knew Zane when he was packing the stadiums and selling out and his records were going triple platinum.

And somehow, Buttons and Louisa were in perfect agreement – Buttons only wanted to talk about Zane and what he used to be like, and Louisa only wanted to hear about Zane and what he used to be like.

Not surprisingly, Buttons' view of Zane's alcohol consumption was vastly different than it would have been if she'd been in close proximity to him since the car accident. She mentioned a couple of times how Zane was thought of as "the clean and sober one of the bunch" and when the rest of the band would go out drinking and doing drugs, he rarely joined in.

"I think he realized that it inhibited his creativity," she said with a shrug, flitting around Louisa, speaking around the pins in her mouth with apparent years of experience in doing so.

Louisa wanted to ask more questions – probe a little deeper – but Buttons was whinging off again, this time retelling a story that had that patina of having been told many times. The drummer's girlfriend had gotten into a wreck, and Zane flew the drummer back home in his private plane so he could be there when she went into surgery.

"Zane will never tell you these stories," Buttons said in a confidential tone of voice after delivering the end of the story: The good news that the girlfriend made a full recovery. "He is much too modest. Don't delude yourself into thinking that he's perfect, though, because he most certainly is not. After all, it was his stubbornness that almost destroyed his career." She said this last line with the air of someone who fully expected her audience to know just what she was talking about.

"It did?" Louisa asked, because really, she had no clue what Buttons was talking about.

"Oh yes. It was all over the news at the time. Did you miss it?" She was gaping at Louisa, stunned that she could've missed something so fundamental, but Louisa could only shrug. This didn't seem the time to mention that she hadn't even heard of Zane Risley before taking the job. Honestly, she'd never intentionally listened to country music before meeting him, and was only just starting to warm up to the genre. It was definitely an acquired taste for her.

"Well, Zane got into an argument with his lead guitarist,

Dan. They'd been together since the beginning, and Zane referred to him as the brother he never had. They were *tight*. And then, they started arguing about the direction of the band and which gigs they should say yes to and which ones they should turn down…it was nasty. Dan ended up leaving the band and taking part of the musicians with him. Zane refused to apologize. Said it was his damn band and he was the only one who could make decisions about it. Of course, news about this ends up in the gossip rags and soon, former backup singers and studio musicians with an ax to grind were all talking to reporters, happy to badmouth him. You can't get as high as Zane has gotten in the music business without stepping on some toes. Some of it was deserved; most of it was not. But still, in the end, Zane got the reputation that he was a bastard to work for. He *is* a hard driver, but that's because he's a perfectionist. He expects perfection out of himself, and out of everyone else. It doesn't make him an easy boss to work for, but he is fair, so there's that."

Louisa found this all to be mind-blowing. Zane? Hard to work for? She'd never had such an easygoing boss in all her life. Of course, she'd never had such an easy job in all her life, either. Taking care of one sweet, special, amazing child? She'd been right that this job was going to be a vacation for her.

She'd been wrong that she'd be able to keep her hands off Zane.

She let out a long sigh.

"What was that sigh for?" Buttons looked at her inquisitively, and Louisa was sure the older woman could see straight into her soul.

"Nothing," she said airily. "Just thinking about life." *And how I seem destined to make the same mistakes over and over again.*

Except – and this part she didn't want to admit, not even to herself – this time didn't seem like a mistake. Was she only fooling herself? Deluding herself?

Probably.

"You ought to know – I've never seen Zane act like this around a woman. Or, anyone at all," she added as an afterthought. "Him and Tamara…it was painful to be in the same room as them. They were sticking together for the good of Skyler but if you asked me, they needed to divorce for the good of Skyler. Watching your parents constantly going after each other, bickering and fighting and sniping at each other, can't be good for anyone. If she hadn't died in that terrible car wreck, they would've divorced – I would bet my business on it. They weren't good for each other. In fact, they were downright *toxic* for each other. But you…he's smitten with you."

She leaned forward, all cheerfulness gone from her voice as she stared Louisa threateningly in the eye. "If you toy with his heart," she said, enunciating every word carefully, "I shall crush you like a bug beneath my foot. Now!" she said, clapping her hands together once, acting for all the world as if she hadn't just threatened Louisa with death and destruction, "are you ready to see yourself in the mirror?"

Louisa felt a bit like she'd just suffered a mental whiplash but the idea of finally seeing how the dress looked on her pushed all other worries out of her mind. She nodded, breathing in deep, trying to keep the panic under control. She felt like Cinderella, getting all dressed up for the ball and her prince, but she wasn't Cinderella, she was Louisa, and for the millionth time, things like this just didn't happen to Latina girls—

With a flourish, Buttons pulled the sheet off the mirror the guys had set up earlier and then grinned with obvious self-satisfaction when Louisa gasped. Then she gasped again because the straight pins in the sides of the dress stuck into her – *ouch! Damn, that hurts!* – but she couldn't focus on that right now.

The dress was stunning. *She* was stunning. Where was Louisa Vargas? The woman in the mirror was not her.

The beauty of the dress was in its simplicity. The shimmering gold fabric skimmed her curves and then fell to the floor in graceful waves of shine and texture. Somehow, she looked sophisticated and ingenuous; regal and artless at the same time. She had no makeup on and her hair fell down around her, straight as a sheet as always, but the sharp dissonance between her and the dress was easy to ignore, at least for the moment, because all she had eyes for was the dress. She turned and twisted, swinging her hips back and forth lightly, watching as the dress clung and then fell from her curves. She realized there was a brush of cold air against her back and she could feel her hair, tickling at her spine, and so she turned, her back facing the mirror, craning her neck around as she tried to see.

"Oh," she whispered.

Her father would *kill* her if he saw her in this dress. There wasn't a back to it, at least none to speak of. There were two lightly glittering strands of gold that criss-crossed each other, holding the sides of the dress together but otherwise baring her back to the air. It wasn't that so much, though, as how *low* the back went. The small dimples of her back, right above her ass, were in easy view, and Louisa was sure her ass crack would show if she moved wrong. Her eyes flew to Buttons' face.

"My butt," she croaked.

"I know, right?" Buttons' eyes gleamed with satisfaction. "Zane is going to die of lust. He better check on his life insurance policy before he sees you in this dress. Now, before we wiggle you ever-so-carefully out of this dress so I can get to work on adjusting the seams, you need to pick out a pair of shoes to wear. Then the caterer will be here with lunch so you can eat and I can sew, and after that, the hairdresser shows up, and the makeup artist after that. I can only hope I get the alterations done in time. Jeffrey, Cade! Shoes!"

CHAPTER 35

ZANE

T ODAY WAS the longest day on record. He was sure that the scientists were all going to make headlines on the evening news, talking about the fact that the earth had slowed in its revolution around the sun and an extra couple of hours had been somehow shoved into the day. He'd managed to keep himself occupied for a while in his music – finally composing again was the sweetest feeling in the world – and then a phone call to Skyler – who'd spent the whole time trying to convince Zane that they needed to get a dog "just like Maggie Mae" – but after that, he was struggling to occupy his time.

Why hadn't he taken up oil painting? Or chainsaw art? Louisa could be gussied up while he went outside and attacked tree stumps with a chainsaw. It seemed like a manly-man sort of thing to do, not to mention that there were enough tree stumps around to keep him occupied for a very long time, and then he could sell his creations at charity auctions for ridiculously high prices. It was about time he got back at his friends, considering they'd done just that to him many a-time. There was a horrific oil painting packed away in a box somewhere that he'd bought from the lead singer of a rival country music band, and he was sure the singer had painted it while blindfolded, just to see how much money he could scalp off his fellow singers.

A chainsaw bear would be a terrific dose of revenge, since it wasn't something that could be hidden away in an unused room or the attic. No siree bob, it had to be placed outside, right in the middle of manicured lawns and patches of perfect blossoms. Nothing like spending tens of thousands of dollars on something that hurt the eyes to even look at.

The elevator door slid open and Buttons stepped out, her eyes filled with mischief even as she solemnly asked, "How does your life insurance policy look?"

"What?" he asked distractedly, trying to see around Buttons and into the elevator, but there was some sort of dark fabric hanging in midair – or at least that's what appeared to be happening, which just couldn't be right – and he couldn't see Louisa anywhere.

"Is it up to date?" she asked.

"Is what up to date?" He was on his tiptoes now, but he still couldn't see hide nor hair of Louisa. He kept trying to walk towards the elevator but Buttons was somehow in the way, no matter which way he tried to go. Finally, he looked down at her, giving her his full attention since the doors opened.

"And now," Buttons said, her voice ringing with satisfaction and mischief and pride, "I give you Louisa Vargas." She stepped to the side just as the fabric fell away and a part of Zane's brain realized that Jeffrey and Cade must've been standing on either side of the elevator, holding the fabric up in the air, but none of that mattered now.

His brain froze, his hands froze, his legs froze, and all he could do was gape.

Louisa was…

More than words. More than description. He'd never seen such a beautiful woman in all his life. Her hair was pulled up into a neat chignon, just a few loose strands trailing down her face and neck to break up the severity of the look. But she could never look severe in this dress. Or in that makeup. Her perfect cupid's bow mouth was painted a dark red and her eyes were a smoky world of eyelashes and brown irises that Zane wanted to spend the next year doing nothing but studying.

The gold of the dress was a warm complement to her skin, making it glow, and clinging to her breasts – her natural, perfect breasts, so unlike the balloons that Tamara had – and then shimmering and flowing to the floor like a cascade of physical light. Louisa was turning around then, and Zane heard faint instructions from Buttons to Louisa, telling her what to do, but it wasn't registering because when her J.Lo ass came into view, the world disappeared completely. The dress fell in folds, giving him a full and unimpeded view of the dimples at the base of her spine. He could see every inch of her back – the two tiny strands of gold offering no coverage at all – and he wasn't entirely sure he'd ever breathe again.

She was perfect. Absolutely perfect.

She was facing forward again and his eyes raised to hers. She was biting her lower lip, obviously worried when he didn't say anything. He needed to tell her how gorgeous she was. He needed to tell her how much he wanted her.

"Wow," he croaked out. Buttons laughed knowingly.

"Jeffrey, Cade, let's go. Our work here is done."

The men and Buttons began moving items towards the door, but Zane registered none of it. They could've been carrying out the sofa and the cabinet full of fine china for all of the attention he was paying them. He only had eyes for Louisa. Still, she was looking at him hesitantly, and he realized that "wow," although a perfect summation of how he felt, wasn't exactly eloquent. She moved forward and out of the way of the men as Zane moved forward too, picking up her hands and bringing them to his lips. Somewhere along the line, she'd even had a manicure done. Had he told Nina that he wanted that? He couldn't remember now. All that mattered was Louisa.

"You are gorgeous," he said hoarsely. "I've never seen a more beautiful woman in all my life."

She smiled then, those gorgeous lips curving into an arc of happiness and joy. "So," she said teasingly, her usual self-confidence back, "you got me all dressed up but you still haven't told me where we're going on our night out on the town."

"Surprise. It's a surprise." He cleared his throat, wanting to get his voice back to normal. He was a singer – his entire career depended upon his being able to control his voice to the nth degree – but right then, it was shaking with desire, just like the rest of his body.

"Ummmm…Is that what you're going to wear when we go out?" she asked, her voice innocent in a transparent bid to keep it free of judgment.

His eyes flicked down to his clothes – the jeans and t-shirt he'd thrown on that morning – and his face flushed. "Oh. God, no. Let me – I'll change. Don't move." He ran for the staircase, taking them two at a time, vaguely registering the sounds of Buttons saying goodbye and promising to send her invoice to his assistant. Whatever she wanted to do. Whatever she wanted to charge.

Tonight was worth it – worth it all.

CHAPTER 36

LOUISA

LOUISA SAT CAREFULLY on the formal loveseat, doing her best not to crush the gold fabric of her dress. Buttons had assured her that the gossamer fabric was tougher than it seemed and wouldn't tear at the slightest provocation, but Louisa still didn't think it was a good idea to get too comfy. This dress, these shoes…they didn't invite someone to sprawl out on the couch with a bag of chips.

She'd never been this beautiful in her entire life, she was sure of it. She'd been giving herself periodic pinches to the inside of her arm for a while now, trying to make sure that she really was awake and this really was happening, but still, it didn't seem real. None of it did. She was the daughter of Mexican immigrants. She'd grown up in a home where her father drank and there hadn't always been enough to eat.

And now…

"Are you ready?" Zane asked, his deep voice jerking her from her thoughts. She looked up and gulped, standing reflexively because she could not sit while in the presence of someone as godlike as Zane. His tux was the perfect complement to the glow of his tanned skin, his dark blond hair, his brilliant blue eyes. Even with her heels on, he was still taller than her and she smiled to herself. All her life, she'd been the tallest girl in her class, and she'd tended to beat the boys too. She'd worn ballet flats to every dance in high school, trying to shrink herself so she didn't tower over her dates.

So this afternoon, when she'd been picking out which pair of shoes to wear, she'd kept drifting towards the flats, instinctively going with the type of shoes she'd always had to wear. It was Buttons who'd encouraged her to "go big or go home."

"Zane is tall enough," she'd said. "You can get away with these heels when you couldn't with any other guy," holding up a pair of heels that looked like nothing more than straps of gold and light. There was *no way* Louisa could wear something so beautiful but even so, her hands reached for the shoes of their own accord, wanting – if nothing else – to simply hold them.

Buttons had been right about the shoes, of course. She was beginning to believe that there was nothing Buttons wasn't right about, at least when it came to clothing.

Zane held out his arm for her and Louisa slipped her hand through it, feeling shy and uncertain for the first time in a long time. This wasn't Zane, the guy she'd gotten into a water fight with at the lake, or seen coming downstairs with his hair mussed and sleep creases across his face, unable to do more than grunt a hello before his first cup of coffee.

This was Zane Risley, the country music superstar, and she was just Louisa, a nurse to a little boy.

What was I thinking? I can't pull this off. I don't care what Buttons says. I'm not a trophy girlfriend. I don't know how to act in situations like this.

They stepped outside, the warm glow from the setting sun bathing everything in a golden light that seemed to tell Louisa that it was okay. She was okay. This wasn't scary. It was wonderful.

Okay, maybe wonderfully scary.

A limo was sitting in the circular driveway, and as she watched, the driver got out and hurried around to the passenger side door, opening it up for them. "Mr. Risley. Ms. Vargas," the man said, giving them a little bow. Was she supposed to bow back? Ask him his name? Chat about his children with him? Zane inclined his head and murmured a simple thank-you to the man, and grateful, Louisa followed suit. Zane helped her inside and then slid in after her, the door closing behind them with a quiet thump, encasing them in the kind of silence that only truly expensive cars could ever achieve. They pulled away from the house and began heading towards town. Instinctively, Louisa braced herself for the jerks and bumps that were about to come, but the car purred on, gliding smoothly over the road.

"The suspension on this car is superb," Louisa said, partly because she wanted something to talk about but also partly because she was truly impressed. Even in the Audi, they'd felt the bumps and ruts and potholes.

"Oh, the road got filled in today," Zane said dismissively. "I've been meaning to do it ever since we got here, and I realized while I was making plans for tonight that I couldn't get you all dressed up and looking perfect, just to bounce and jostle you the whole way into town."

He really had thought of everything. She pinched herself again. *Ouch.* Yup. This was real.

"Thank you," she said softly. "For this." She gestured at her dress. "And tonight. Buttons was…delightful."

"Buttons is a talker," Zane said with a rueful grin. "I keep thinking she needs to marry a mute. I'm pretty sure she divorced her ex because he'd wanted to say more than ten words a month. Honestly, there's really no point in her significant other being able to talk."

Louisa snort-laughed at that, and then clapped her hands over her mouth. She really shouldn't laugh at something like that and in this dress, she really shouldn't be snort-laughing either—

"I like your laugh," Zane said softly. "It makes me want to laugh. And it's been a long, long time since I've wanted to laugh."

Louisa met his gaze for only a moment and then let it slide away. She still didn't believe this was really happening, and thus she couldn't let herself trust the moment. She was going to wake up and realize that she'd just had the most realistic dream of her life. Or Zane was going to wake up and realize that he could have almost any woman on earth and so why would he choose a Latina nurse?

And then it would all end and she'd have to go back to her boring life and just be Louisa Vargas again.

She was proud of who she was. She was proud of how hard she'd worked to get to where she was.

But tonight. This. It was a whole new level…

The car pulled smoothly to a stop and she looked outside, realizing that they'd somehow made it into Franklin already. Was this where their night out on the town would happen? She hadn't been sure what to expect. Franklin? Sawyer? Boise? Paris? With Zane's access to a private plane, she had no clue where they would be by the end of the night.

The driver opened the door and Louisa slid out, doing her best to appear graceful, as if she wore ball gowns and 3-inch spiked heels every day, Zane following on her heels.

"Let the *maître d'* know when you are ready to head home, and he'll get in touch with me," the driver said with a quick bow of his head, and then he was heading off into the evening twilight, the red tail lights disappearing.

"Are you ready?" Zane asked, holding out his arm, not thrown off in the slightest by the idea that the driver would be waiting all evening – and maybe all night – at his beck and call, just to drive them around.

She slipped her hand into the crook of his elbow, her

breath coming in choppy bursts. *Out of my depth, out of my depth, out of my depth…*

"Have you been here before?" she asked politely as they headed towards the front doors of an expensive-looking steakhouse.

"I haven't. My assistant, Nina, is the one who found it. She assured me that it was the nicest restaurant in Franklin. I didn't want to spend hours in the car, going to Boise and back. I wanted to spend the evening just focused on you."

Louisa found that her heart was starting to match her breathing, erratic and hard to control. Zane smelled so damn good, the clean masculine scent drifting off him as they walked sedately through the front doors of the restaurant.

But then, his scent was gone, buried under the explosion of flowers, a mixture of every floral scent imaginable. Louisa looked around, stunned. There were flowers *everywhere*. They'd entered some sort of tropical paradise. She glanced back towards the doors into the restaurant, wondering for a moment if they'd accidentally wandered into the wrong building. Maybe they weren't at a restaurant after all. Almost every table in the joint had flowers on them. There was no place for anyone to sit and eat, except one table up against a window that had been left open.

"Nina cleaned out the local florist," Zane said with a grin, clearly pleased with the look of awe on her face. "I've been told there isn't another flower to be had in all of Long Valley."

Louisa looked up at him, stunned but smiling. "But, where are the other guests?" she asked as he steered her towards the only open table. "We can't be the only ones eating out tonight."

"I bought out the house," he said with a shrug. "I wanted the place all to ourselves. No one to ask for autographs or call you a—"

He stopped.

She sucked in a quick breath. This *couldn't* be a dream.

Surely her dreams would allow her to live in a world where no one called her a spic.

Which meant that this was all real.

This. Was. Real.

Maybe fairytales did come true. Maybe sometimes, it was okay to believe.

Maybe – just maybe – she really was Cinderella, and she'd finally found her prince.

CHAPTER 37
ZANE

Z ANE MADE a mental note to give Nina a bonus. This was, quite simply, the most impressive move she'd ever managed to pull off on his behalf, and that was really saying something.

Louisa smiled at him from across the table, looking like she was practically floating on air, and he couldn't help but smile back. This was exactly what he was wanting – an evening of just the two of them where she could see what her life would be like on his arm. Last night was all about showing how he could be just as normal as the next guy, watching a movie and eating dinner on the couch. Tonight was all about showing her a world she probably didn't know existed.

The waiter was superb, keeping Louisa's wine glass filled while Zane stuck to a Diet Pepsi. His eyes had strayed to her glass a few times, a large part of him wishing for the easy glow of alcohol to calm his nerves – so very much was riding on tonight – but the more he craved the alcohol, the harder he was willing to fight the impulse. Somehow, Louisa had been right and he'd become an alcoholic when he wasn't looking.

There goes my reputation as the priest of the group…

Courses came and went, and the conversation flowed as easily as their drinks. He could tell when the alcohol started to really kick in, watching the flush in her cheeks grow a little pinker and her laugh a little easier. How was it that her asshole of an ex had cheated on her? She was breathtaking. More than just her beauty, her personality and wit and intelligence made her sparkle in the candlelight.

"I can't eat another bite," she protested when the waiter came out with a selection of small desserts. "They're beautiful, truly," she said apologetically. "I would love to, but…"

Zane caught the eye of the *maître d'* and gave a small nod, and the man headed towards the back, pulling out his cell phone as he went. The waiter backed off as Zane hurried around to help Louisa out of her chair.

"Oh!" she gasped as she stumbled a little, Zane automatically enclosing his arms around her and holding her up. She looked up at him and grinned widely. "My handsome prince," she said, the first hint of an accent in her voice that he'd ever heard from her.

She was still looking up at him, her eyes drifting closed even as she tilted her head back, and he was lost. He couldn't resist another moment. His mouth swooped down on hers and he tasted the wine on her lips and felt drunk…on love.

"I love you." He murmured the words before he could stop them but he didn't want to stop them anymore. He had to tell her how he felt.

She had to know.

He was kissing her way up her jaw when he felt her tremble slightly in his arms.

"Are you okay?" he asked, pulling back a bit to look her in the eyes. They were shining as she looked up at him.

"I love you too," she whispered.

He wanted to whoop for joy. He wanted to scoop her up

in his arms and carry her to the car. He wanted to kiss her and never come up for air again.

But instead, he pulled her against his chest, her arms wrapping around his waist and they stood, fitting together like two pieces of a puzzle. She fit him perfectly, like she'd been made for him.

And maybe she had.

"C'mon," he murmured into her hair. "Let's go home."

Home. What a lovely word.

CHAPTER 38
ZANE

H E ROLLED OVER with a happy groan, feeling more alive than he had in a long time. Last night had been magical – exactly what he'd wanted to show Louisa what a life with him could mean – but today was back to reality. They'd need to pick Skyler up and bring him back home. He seemed to be dealing well with staying with the Millers, but still, Zane had missed his son and was ready to have him back at home.

I've missed my son.

Just another miracle he could chalk up to having Louisa in his life. Skyler had always been someone Zane had to make sure was taken care of. Someone he had to ensure was happy, or at least not unhappy.

Not someone to miss and want to be around.

Before he and Louisa could pick him up, though, they needed to talk about what they were going to tell him. What if things didn't work out between him and Louisa? It was so damn strange to date someone and not only have to tell his son about it – something that he'd not had to do with the various one-night stands since Tamara's death – but to have Skyler know just as much about his date as Zane did.

They'd have to take this carefully. Really plan out a strategy before—

His phone buzzed on the nightstand and Zane shot an apologetic look at Louisa's sleeping form even as he rolled over to snatch it up. A stupid text message trying to sell him guitar strings was going to wake Louisa up, and after the night she'd had, she needed…her…

He blinked a few times. Something was wrong. His thumb scrolled down his lockscreen, where message after message, interspersed with voicemails, was lined up, some from close friends, some from people he hadn't talked to in years.

Automatically, he stopped on the message from Jacob Allen, the lead singer of the Jacob Allen Group, and one of Zane's closest friends. They hadn't really talked since Zane had flown out to Idaho, but honestly, Zane hadn't talked to anyone since starting his hideout in Idaho, so that wasn't much of a surprise.

Holy shit, Zane, what is going o —

The rest of the message was cut off so Zane swiped to open it, swinging his legs over the side of the bed as he sat up, trying to keep from disturbing Louisa. Whatever was causing his phone to blow up, it didn't need to include her.

Holy shit, Zane, what is going on? Are you seriously sleeping with the nanny? After what happened with Dan, this seems like a dumbass idea. Call me.

After what happened with Dan? What in the hell did Dan have to do with Louisa?

He stumbled out of the room and down the stairs to the merrily brewing coffee pot in the breakfast nook – thankfully set to auto-brew every morning – and swiping to call Jacob as he went.

"God, tell me it isn't true," Jacob said as way of greeting when he answered.

"I just woke up," Zane said curtly, rubbing at his eyes and

trying to stifle a yawn, "and saw your message. What the hell is going on? How do you know about Louisa?"

Jacob let out a string of swear words under his breath that'd make a priest's toenails curl. "Dammit, Zane, I was hoping maybe someone had just photoshopped the pictures. You really did go on a date last night with your Mexican *nanny*?!"

"Jacob, if you don't tell me how you know that in the next three seconds, I'm gonna hang up." He slid the coffee pot back into place and sucked at his black coffee. He normally liked to sweeten it up a bit but not right now. What he really needed was a caffeine injection straight into his veins, but this would have to be the next best thing.

"It's all over the news. Not just country music news – hell, not even just entertainment news. It's *everywhere*. It's sweet right now – you might as well start calling her Cinderella because everyone else is – but you know how this goes. The fairytale shit only lasts so long, and then the media starts looking for muck they can stir up. 'Country music star falls in love with serial killer' makes for a hell of a headline."

"Louisa is *not* a serial killer," Zane said, torn between laughing at the absurdity of the statement and wanting to scream at the unfairness of the situation.

"Right. Well, whatever she has buried in her past won't be buried much longer."

"Shit." As much as Zane hated to admit it, Jacob had a point. Damn his dirty hide. The press was probably already on the hunt for any dirt they could find on Louisa. The first website to scream a nasty rumor – unfounded or not – would get a hell of a lot of clicks.

Zane realized – right about the time that the coffee started doing its job – just how much this was going to change their lives. This was potentially catastrophic – the ruination of a lovely relationship before it really even started. Panicking, his mind started flitting through everything that needed to be done, but before he could hang up with Jacob, he had to ask. "Why did you compare this to Dan?"

"Because, dumbass, after the bad press you got because of the split with Dan, I thought you'd avoid close, personal relationships with your employees. Everyone already believes you're a dick to work for. What if you and Louisa breakup and she goes to the press? Makes up lies? Does a tell-all book where she talks about what it's *really* like to date a superstar? You *cannot* be this stupid, Zane."

"She's not like that," Zane said in a tight voice, "and if you say shit about her like that again, I'll rearrange that pretty-boy face of yours."

"Okay. Sure." Jacob's voice was a mixture of defeat and sarcasm. "Just keep in mind that they're never like that, until you break up with them."

Zane was staring down at his phone long after Jacob hung up, trying to wrap his mind around what just happened. His sweet, wonderful date with Louisa had been ruined, and now he had to figure out how to keep their relationship from being ruined just as completely.

CHAPTER 39

LOUISA

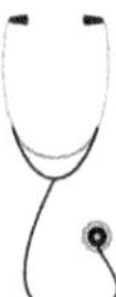

Z ANE WAS HOLDING his phone out, trying to talk to Louisa, but nothing was making sense to her. His words stopped having meaning. Now all there was was her phone – she'd wanted to look at the pictures on *her* phone, dammit, not his; it was her one lifeline to normality – and the pictures and the roar of noise in her ears.

There he was, feeding her a cube of cheese. Even with the terrible resolution of the photo – it'd obviously been taken from across the restaurant – the world could see the love in her eyes as she'd looked at Zane. She was the Cinderella of the modern age – the lowly servant girl plucked out of obscurity by her handsome prince.

Of course, that was exactly what she'd thought the day before, but it'd been sweet and touching when it had just been her thought in her own head. Now it was splashed across the internet and the newspapers for everyone to talk about and digest and speculate over.

"—fired him."

"Who's fired?" she asked dully, flipping to the next photo, this one of her and Zane kissing after they'd stood up to leave the restaurant. This was the moment he'd told her he loved her. The moment she was going to treasure for the rest of her life.

The moment she was now sharing with the rest of the world.

"The busboy." She could tell Zane was trying to keep a tight rein on his impatience as he stated information that he'd probably already said, but she couldn't seem to make her mind focus on his words. There he was with his hand at the small of her back as he'd guided her towards the front door. It was clear in the photo how low the back on the dress went, and how possessive his hand had been on her back.

My father is gonna kill me.

"The restaurant owner assures me that he'll never get another job in Franklin again. Of course, after the payday he probably just lucked into, I don't imagine he'll need to work for a good long while."

"Selling other people's lives is a lucrative business," she said quietly. The words were right, but still, there was a small part of her brain that wondered at her ability to say them. It sounded so intelligent. So calm. So rational.

She was broken, though. No matter what it appeared like on the surface, she was far from intelligent, calm, or rational.

"Does Skyler know?" Still, her voice was just as measured. Why wasn't she crying hysterically? She should be crying.

"Not yet. I told the Millers to keep their TV off and the boys off any electronic devices. Who knows what headlines will pop up as a notification. I do not want Skyler to find out we're dating from *Entertainment Tonight*."

It would already be enough of a shock that they were dating at all. She knew Skyler liked her. Hell, in his own twelve-year-old-boy way, he probably loved her. But there was a big difference between liking your nurse, and wanting your nurse to become a pseudo mother to you. Skyler had loved his mother with all of his heart. By all accounts, they'd been super close. Having Louisa fill that role was a touchy concept, at best.

And now having the whole world in on the discussion?

She pushed herself off the couch and ran upstairs, taking the stairs two at a time. Zane was calling after her but she blocked him out. She needed time away from Zane and Skyler and the news and the pressure of it all. She shoved her feet into her trainers, ripping at the laces, blood pounding through her veins, needing nothing more than space from everything. Zane was in the doorway, talking again, but she couldn't hear his words through the thudding in her ears. She snagged a hair tie from the dresser and brushed past Zane, slipping out of his hands, whipping her hair into a ponytail even as she practically flew down the stairs and out the front door.

She needed—

"Ms. Vargas!"

"Louisa!"

"We have a few questions for you—"

It was only sheer luck that kept her from plowing right into the crowd of reporters. She stumbled to a stop, looking around her frantically, trapped, and then made an abrupt U-turn and ran right back into the house, slamming the door closed behind her. She leaned against the front door, listening to the reporters banging on the heavy door, calling out her name, and wanted to whimper in frustration. All she wanted to do was go for a run. Clear her head. And now, she'd just given the bloodthirsty swarm of reporters another shot at pictures of her – pictures that were certainly going to be less impressive than the ones of her in her evening gown. She hadn't even looked in a mirror that morning. She probably had lipstick and eyeshadow smeared everywhere.

She heard Zane on the stairs. He was talking to her. He must've followed her. He was trying to apologize for the reporters out front, telling her that he had his security team flying in from Nashville but it'd be another couple of hours until they got there, but none of that mattered. Didn't he see that she needed to run? How could she ever breathe again if she couldn't run?

And how could she live if she couldn't go outside?

She remembered then the dusty, unused, unloved home gym that was in yet another room in the walkout basement. She'd found it one time while searching for Skyler. As far as she knew, it'd never been used the whole time they'd been there.

Well, it was going to get used today.

She brushed past Zane – he was still talking, this time about how this didn't change anything, as if she was really that stupid – and pounded down the stairs to the basement. She headed straight for the workout room, thinking how weird it was that Skyler wasn't on the couch, shooting something on the giant TV, red blood splattering the screen, but it was good that he wasn't there. He shouldn't see this circus. He was just a kid and he'd already lived through so much and it wasn't fair to ask him to live through more.

She slammed the door behind her, even more pissed when it just swung shut silently instead, the high quality hinge system keeping the door from being slammable – *is slammable a word?* – and robbing her of even that small bit of relief. She climbed onto the treadmill and began punching at the buttons, forcing it into the highest gear possible. She was going to run. Run until she couldn't think or breathe or hurt anymore.

CHAPTER 40

ZANE

Z ANE STOOD at the base of the stairs, listening to the whine of the treadmill set on high, the pounding of Louisa's feet as she did her best to run away from it all. He had to leave her alone. It wouldn't do a damn bit of good to talk to her right now anyway, considering that he doubted she'd heard anything that morning past his initial breaking of the news. She'd kept asking questions about things he'd already explained, and then asking about them again just moments later.

It wasn't difficult to ascertain that she was in shock.

And really, who could blame her? He felt betrayed and angry and disgusted with humanity, and he was used to this. He should've known stories about the most magical date he'd ever gone on would eventually leak. He just hadn't expected it to be reported on every channel in the free world, let alone within hours of it happening.

I went on a date with my nanny during a slow news cycle. Just my luck.

He heard three quick rings of the doorbell and knew that Stetson was there. Thank God. Zane hurried back up the stairs and opened up the front door just far enough to let the rangy cowboy in, and then shut it and threw the deadbolt, blocking out the horde of reporters, all shouting for his attention.

"Holy shit, Zane," Stetson said, eyes wide as he pulled his cowboy hat off and ran his fingers through his hair. "You weren't kidding. They're like a pack of bloodhounds. I've never seen anything like it."

Zane sent him an un-amused smile. "Bloodhounds is about right. Look, thank you for coming over. I know you probably have cattle to move or fence to fix or something—"

"It's okay," Stetson said, waving his hand dismissively. "It's what friends are for. Where's Louisa? Carmelita is worried sick about her. She's not answering the phone."

"Honestly, you're not going to get any better of a response in person. I've tried. She's in shock. Nothing is registering when you try to talk to her. It's like talking to a zombie. She moves like a human, but she's not processing anything. At the moment, she's downstairs, running on the treadmill. She tried to go outside to go for a run, but…" He gestured at the front door. "It didn't go well, let's just put it that way. I need to leave you here while I go pick up Skyler from your brother's house. Him and Juan are thick as thieves, and so I arranged for Wyatt and Abby to take Sky for the weekend while I woo'd Louisa." His lips twisted into a sarcastic smile.

Stetson was quiet for a moment. "I thought my introduction to Jennifer was rough," he said after a moment with a low chuckle, "but I think you have us beat to pieces. At least the national media wasn't beating down my door the day after."

"Fame ain't always what it's cracked up to be."

They were quiet for another moment, until a particularly loud demand for a comment made it into the house, loud and clear, jerking them back to the present.

"I best get going. Don't open up the front door for anyone, I don't care what bullshit they tell you. Everyone who is on their way from Nashville knows the key-code to get in through the garage. If someone's trying to come through the front door, they're not welcome here. Oh, and if Louisa makes her way back upstairs, tell her I've gone for Skyler and I'll be back soon, and to hold tight." He rather doubted she'd try to make another run for it – *terrible pun, Zane* – but he didn't want to take the chance.

They needed to figure out what they were going to do together.

Stetson nodded his understanding, and Zane took off at a jog for the garage door. He hadn't had to put on his media disguise for a while, but he hadn't forgotten the drill. Baseball cap low over the eyes. Sunglasses. Big coat with a high collar. The best shot the paparazzi could get would be of a man who could be him…or who could be any other millions of men in America. That didn't make for an interesting photo, and that was exactly what Zane was willing to give them.

He backed out of the garage, thankful that it was set on the side of the house, hiding its entrance from the front door. By the time the reporters realized he was leaving, they'd be lucky to get a shot of the backside of the Audi. Good luck trying to convince their editors to run with *that* picture.

He put the Audi into gear and then stepped on it, feeling the smooth roar of the engine as it gained speed, eating up ground effortlessly. A couple of reporters, probably getting bored with yelling at the front door, were loitering in the driveway, drinking coffee and laughing as they chatted with each other.

Zane didn't exactly point his SUV directly at them, but he also didn't exactly point it away, either. He buried the pedal as far as it would go and watched with satisfaction as people dove for the bushes, yelling at him as he tore by. Sure, it was best that he didn't run over a reporter – he'd be hard pressed to convince the insurance company that it was an accident – but still…

He let off the pedal with a regretful sigh. He had to keep his eyes on the road, and his hands at 10 and 2. Just drive calmly, and under the speed limit. All he needed now was to be pulled over by an overzealous cop and have *that* end up on the news that evening.

Don't worry Skyler. Get him home, and then decide how to proceed from there. Keep calm. Isn't that one of those stupid sayings that women hang up all over their houses? 'Keep Calm and Carry On'? Well, for once in my life, a trite saying is actually true.

After a mindless drive that Zane didn't remember a moment of, he pulled up in front of Wyatt's house and immediately, their dog came bounding over, tail wagging a million miles an hour, just thrilled to pieces to greet someone. Considering she was on their front porch, Zane was fairly sure that meant that Wyatt was actually inside, since Maggie Mae would never otherwise stay behind.

The front door opened and Abby came out onto the front porch, waving, trying to pin a cheerful look on her face, but Zane wasn't fooled and he was damn sure his much-too-observant son hadn't been either. She was just as worried as Stetson had been.

Smart people.

"Good morning, Zane!" she called out gaily as he stepped out of the Audi. He sent her a sarcastic look and she had the good grace to shrug and look a little guilty for the platitude. "Skyler's inside, gathering up the last of his stuff. He was a great kid the whole time. No problems at all."

"Good, good," Zane said, headed for the front porch. Suddenly, the overwhelming feeling of weariness washed over him. Had he really had a cup of coffee that morning? He suddenly felt as if his body had never even heard of the concept of caffeine before.

"C'mon in. You look like you need a cup of joe. Or three. You can sneak some into you while Skyler finishes up."

His lips curved at the corners, his best attempt at gratefulness, as he trailed along behind her. Wyatt had said that she was a cop, of course, and Zane could definitely see that in her. A no-nonsense straight shooter who stayed calm in an emergency.

He appreciated all of those traits, and counted Wyatt's taste in women in his favor. Marrying Abby was a damn smart idea.

"Hey, Dad!" Skyler called out, waving at him from across the large, comfortable living room before going back to a stack of cards that he and Juan were looking over. Although the home was new and had some upgrades to it that Zane was sure had cost a pretty penny, it wasn't pretentious or a showcase. It looked like a home filled with love. It was, Zane thought distractedly as Abby filled a coffee cup for him and shoved creamers at him, what he'd always wanted in a house, and yet had never had. Tamara had wanted a showcase once his record deals started bringing in the income to pay for one, and then there was the house they were renting this summer. It was even worse, at least in Zane's mind. Too much dark wood. Too much oppressiveness.

Too much old-man tastes.

"Morning," Wyatt said, coming into the kitchen and putting out his hand to shake. "You hanging in there?"

Zane smiled automatically, instinctually, even as a small part of his mind realized he'd just been spending his time thinking about the decorating tastes of the people who owned the house he was staying in, in the midst of a huge crisis.

No, he wasn't okay at all. He was barely hanging on by his fingernails.

"Of course," he answered smoothly. "Any…news?" He looked over casually to the boys. Skyler looked preoccupied, but Zane never knew how much little ears paid attention.

"Nope, we've been a news-free zone this morning," Abby said casually. "Haven't paid attention to a bit of it."

"Good, good." He sucked down the last of his coffee and then put the mug down, feeling weirdly nostalgic for a life that he'd never led. What would it be like to just stand around in the Millers' kitchen, chit-chatting with them without a care in the world? What would it be like to be able to go out on a date without it becoming headline news the next day?

Questions he'd never know the answer to.

"C'mon, Sky," he said, walking over and ruffling the straw-blond hair of his son. "We need to get going."

"Good morning, Mr. Risley," Juan said formally from his cross-legged position on the floor.

Zane shot Wyatt and Abby an amused look. They'd certainly raised a little gentleman. "Good morning, Juan. Did y'all have fun this weekend?"

"Yes, sir!" Juan said, his eyes glowing with excitement. "First, we—"

"Juan," Abby cut across what was looking like was going to be a point-by-point recitation of their weekend together. "Mr. Risley needs to get going. He's going to have to hear all about it from Skyler."

"Oh," Juan said, his face falling.

"I'm sure we'll be able to get Skyler back over here soon," Zane reassured him, and Juan brightened right back up.

They headed for the front door, Skyler rolling ahead of them, his backpack in his lap. Maggie Mae greeted them ecstatically as soon as the front door opened, as thrilled as she'd been when Zane had pulled up just minutes before, as if she hadn't seen a human being for years.

Not surprisingly, her love and enthusiasm immediately opened the "We really need a dog" floodgates. Zane listened with half an ear – the reasons all seemed to be a repeat of the reasons Skyler had rattled off the other night –

waved goodbye to the Millers, and began heading back home.

His shoulders were tightening with every passing mile, despite his attempts to stay calm, cool, and collected. He had to figure out a way to tell Skyler what was going on without freaking him out, while also making him understand the severity of the situation. It was a fine line to walk between telling Skyler everything and making him spaz, vs telling him too little and thus not giving his son the tools he needed to handle the situation.

"Dad, what's wrong?"

Zane almost drove into a ditch.

"Uhh…what makes you ask that?" he asked casually. So very casually. No one had ever been as casual as him in the history of the universe.

"You look like you ate a lemon for breakfast."

It was amazing how lovely small children were for a man's pride. He glared at Skyler in the rearview mirror. Skyler just looked back expectantly, waiting for an answer, apparently missing the whole I-might-have-just-insulted-you part of the conversation.

"While you were gone to the Millers this weekend," Zane started out carefully, testing each word before he said it, hoping he wasn't about to make a huge mistake, "Louisa and I…uhh…"

"Did you kiss?" Skyler broke in eagerly.

Zane almost drove into a ditch. Again.

It really was dangerous to drive while holding conversations with Skyler.

"I told Juan you liked her," Skyler said confidently. "She's really pretty so you'd be stupid not to."

Zane thought about lecturing Skyler on how a woman's appearance didn't matter as much as what was on the inside, but hell, who was he kidding? He spent ungodly amounts of money that weekend specifically to make Louisa feel as gorgeous as possible. Looks *did* matter, no matter how many trite sayings people came up with that said otherwise, but luckily for Zane, Louisa had stupendous looks *and* a stupendous personality.

Now if Zane could just keep her, he'd really be doing well.

"We started dating this weekend," Zane answered, sidestepping the kissing question, at least for now. It was going to have to come up at some point, considering the damn busboy had snapped more than a few pics of the two of them kissing after the meal ended, but as far as Zane was concerned, that moment could just wait its turn. "She's…I really like her a lot, Skyler. But first, I need to know how you feel about her."

"I like her," his son announced, no hesitation in his voice at all. "So does this mean that she's coming with us back to Tennessee?"

Well, he could say this about Skyler: He wasn't one for beating around the bush.

"I haven't actually asked her that yet," Zane said, feeling like he was tiptoeing through a minefield. Carefully, ever so carefully, he had to answer Skyler's questions while also not discussing "adult" topics with him. Topics he hadn't even discussed with Louisa yet.

"Do you want me to?" Skyler asked eagerly. "She likes me. She'd have a hard time telling me no."

That, Zane was sure, was the most truthful statement on the planet. Louisa did like Skyler very much, although she was better at telling him no when that was what he needed to hear. Better than Zane, anyway.

"The thing is," Zane said, deciding to leave that can of worms alone for the moment, "Louisa and I went on a date last night. We didn't know it, but the busboy took a bunch of pictures of us while we were eating, and sold them to the newspapers. Our date was all over the news last night and this morning."

"Were you naked?" Skyler asked, looking perplexed.

Zane only barely missed taking out a trash can on the side of the road. "No!" he roared, and then made a concerted effort to loosen his hands on the steering wheel. "Why would you ask that?"

"Because if you had clothes on," Skyler said slowly, as if explaining a simple concept to the dumbest of human beings, "why does it matter if they took pictures?"

"It's the…you don't always want the whole world knowing that you went on a date. Louisa isn't used to people prying into her life. She's used to having privacy, and really only her family and friends knowing about her. You know how after we got in the car wreck, you had a bunch of people all trying to break into your hospital room to ask you questions?" Skyler nodded slowly. "You didn't want them there, right?" Skyler nodded again, slower this time. "Part of that was because you'd just lost your momma, and part of it was because you didn't feel good at all, but part of it was also because it's a lot for a person to take in. You were raised in the spotlight, Skyler. You've always been my son, and so you've always had people interested in you when they wouldn't be otherwise. Louisa never has. She needs time."

Zane hit the blinker and turned down the long dirt road towards the house, so nicely smoothed out now. He rather wished he hadn't had the road graded the day before. Maybe if the ride wasn't as pleasant, more of the reporters would've stayed away.

"Wow, Dad, did you fix the road?" Skyler asked, his eyes wide as they met in the rearview mirror.

"Yeah. It was part of my surprise for Louisa. Part of our… date."

Talking about his love life, even in such vague terms, with his 12-year-old son had to be the most excruciating conversation of his life. The word *awkward* did not even begin to cover it.

But Skyler just nodded his head wisely. "Good call, Dad. You can't kiss her if the whole car is bouncing up and down."

Ex.cru.cia.ting.

"When we get to the house," Zane said, choosing to ignore yet another comment by his way-too-precocious son, "there is going to be a bunch of reporters out front. I want you to look out my side of the car as we drive in, okay? Don't look at them. We'll go right into the garage and they won't be able to follow us."

Skyler nodded, looking a little less certain about all of this. He'd been damn implacable while they had been discussing it in the abstract but now…

As they turned the last corner, Zane said, "Now, Skyler," just as he punched the gas. Normally he'd slow down as he got closer to the house, but not today. He jammed his thumb against the garage door opener as the reporters came rushing over, microphones and cameras waving as they went. Eyes straight, cap low, collar high, Zane zipped past them all and into the security of the garage, pulling to a hard stop and jamming his thumb against the button again to close the door. It slid silently closed, leaving them in the quiet of the garage, the muffled shouts of the reporters vaguely drifting through.

"How'd you do? Did you look at them?" Zane asked. Skyler shook his head. "Good. Let's go inside and talk to Louisa."

Hopefully, she'd actually want to talk to them. That wasn't exactly a given at that point.

They headed into the house, Skyler effortlessly transferring himself out of the Audi and into his wheelchair before zipping towards the service door. The door opened before he could get there, though, and there stood Louisa.

She'd come up from the basement. Thank God, she'd made it out of the basement.

"Louisa!" Skyler said, throwing his arms around her kneecaps. "Are you going to move to Tennessee with us?"

She let out a startled bark of laughter. "We didn't… uhhh…talk about that," she said carefully, avoiding Zane's eyes.

"That's what Dad said. But you should. Dad says you guys were wearing clothes when the busman took your pictures, so it really isn't all bad. The reporters get bored after a while and go away. Just ignore them."

"Busman…?" Louisa said, furrowing her brow and looking at Zane for the first time, who was still standing in the garage.

"I think he means busboy."

"Yeah, busboy," Skyler repeated.

Louisa pressed her lips together and Zane was sure that in that moment, she was trying to keep from laughing her ass off. *Welcome to having kids…*

"Glad you're back," Stetson said, coming up behind Louisa. "Hey there, pardner," he said to Skyler, pulling on the brim of his hat in greeting. "Now that you're back," he said, looking back towards Zane, "I'm gonna head on out. Y'all have got things to discuss anyway, so I'll just scoot on outta here." After a quick round of goodbyes, Stetson headed out the front door, his hat pulled low, pushing his way through the crowd, ignoring the shouts rolling in from every side.

"So I was thinking," Louisa said, once Stetson had left, "your dad and I really need to talk. What do you think about spending some time downstairs, playing some Xbox?"

Instead of squealing with delight and racing for the elevator, though, Skyler paused and then threw his arms around Louisa's knees again. "Don't make me move back to Tennessee without you *or* Juan," he said in a choked voice and then he was scooting for the elevator, not looking back as he went.

Zane felt a lump rise in his throat at Skyler's words. It really wasn't fair of him to set up a perfect summer where Skyler had a nurse who loved him and a best friend who wanted to hang out with him, and then tear him away from all of it and move him back to Tennessee without a backward glance.

Well, he couldn't do anything about Juan, but he was damn well going to do his best to convince Louisa that she had to move back with him.

He needed her as much as his son did, and he refused to give her up now.

CHAPTER 41
LOUISA

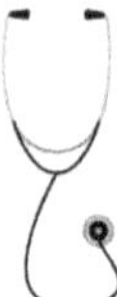

L OUISA STOOD THERE in the middle of the living room, the warmth of Skyler's embrace around her knees a branding iron of love. His thin little arms, his brilliant blue eyes so like Zane's…

He needs me. Dios mío, *he needs me. But I cannot base my whole life and what I do on what Skyler Risley needs. I have to do what's best for me too.*

Slowly, she raised her eyes and met Zane's gaze, forcing herself to look him in the eye. This was it. This was the turning point in their relationship. By the end of this discussion, they'd either be together as a couple, or they'd be over.

Which did she want?

Well, she knew which she *wanted*. That was a stupidly easy question to answer.

She wanted Zane. She wanted Skyler.

But at what price? And most importantly of all, was she willing to pay that price?

That, she didn't know. But she did know that she owed it to Skyler, to Zane, and most importantly to herself, to try.

Zane looked at her, his eyes begging her to give them a

shot. To give him a shot. He needed her just as much as Skyler needed her.

What price will I pay? What price will I pay? What price will I pay?

"I know," Zane said quietly, breaking the taut silence between them, "that we're moving damn fast. I know that I'm asking for a lot here. Maybe too much. But Louisa, *I love you*. I love you more than I realized I could love another human being." He snagged her hand and tugged her towards the uncomfortable sofas in the formal living room. They settled down onto the much-too-firm cushions and Zane pulled her hands to his lips. "I love you because of who you are, but also because of who you make me want to be. I'm a better dad and a better human being with you around. So, I want to ask you: Will you move back with us to Tennessee?"

She felt tears spring up in her eyes and this time, she *wasn't* angry. She really was heartbroken, because she was going to give up the love of her life, and oh, how she did not want to. "I'm sorry, Zane," she whispered, "but I cannot move to Tennessee. My family is here. I'm not moving across the country and leaving them—"

"But I have a private jet," he broke in, and she could tell that he'd already thought through all of this and was so sure he had the right answer to it all. "You can just zip right back across the country and visit them whenever you want."

"If that's true—" she countered, trying to keep her voice even and reasonable, brushing the tears away and straightening up on the couch. Melting into a little pile of goo wasn't going to help. She couldn't give into the grief. Not yet. "—then why don't you just zip over to Tennessee whenever you want? We'll stay here, and *you* fly to Tennessee whenever you'd like."

He gaped at her, and it was that open-mouthed stare which confirmed her theory that up to that point, he'd never once given even the slightest thought to staying in Idaho.

"But...but..." he sputtered. "Tennessee is where country music is made!"

"So you want me to move across the country to go live in a fishbowl, every eye pinned on me, in a town I don't know, in a state I've never been to, in an environment I hate – humidity is the absolute *worst*, in case you didn't notice – all to support *your* career. And in return, you give up...what is it that you give up again?" She tapped her chin as if thinking hard and then shot him an unimpressed look. "I've fallen in love with you and Skyler, but I am my own person, Zane. Here, I am Louisa Vargas, Carmelita's niece. I'm a damn good nurse. And now, apparently I'm Cinderella." She rolled her eyes. "But in Nashville, I'll just be your girlfriend. I couldn't get a job at the hospital there. It'd be too much of a distraction. I can just see it now – people intentionally hurting themselves in an attempt to get me as their nurse so they can slide a CD into my hands to pass along to you. Injury rates in Tennessee are gonna skyrocket overnight." She laughed sarcastically. "I'd be bad for the health of Tennesseans. But Zane, the people are different here."

"Are they really now?" It was Zane's turn to get sarcastic. "So the bus*man* last night, the people who swarmed us at the farmer's market and called you a spic," she winced, "does Idaho not have to claim them?"

"I was thinking about this while running on the treadmill," she said, holding up a hand to stop him. "Think back to every bad interaction that we've had so far. Where were we?"

"In Idaho," Zane said in his thickest southern drawl, sarcasm dripping off his words like honey off a honeycomb.

"No, in *Franklin*." She sat back and waited for a moment for those words to sink in. "When you went to the bar *in Sawyer* with the Miller brothers and those two firefighters, how many people swarmed you?" No response. "When you went to the therapy camp *in Sawyer* and watched Skyler ride, how many people accosted you, asking for your autograph?" This time, she didn't even wait for a response. "There was The Herd, of course, but they all stayed in their own little group and watched you from a distance. Really, you can't fault them too much for that. You *are* a superstar. But they left you well enough alone."

She sucked in a deep breath and plunged on. "The more I've thought about it, the more I've realized how different Franklin and Sawyer are. Franklin is a tourist town. There are probably more out-of-towners there than Frankliners on any given day, and especially on the weekend. These are people who have specifically come to be entertained, and in their minds, you're nothing more than a part of that entertainment. Sawyer, on the other hand, is a working town, full of cowboys and farmers and ranchers. While we were at Stetson and Jennifer's house for my aunt's birthday, I overheard Abby talking to Iris. She said something about how, 'That was a Franklin thing to do,' and it's been tickling at the back of my mind ever since. I didn't hear what it was exactly that they were discussing, but I started paying attention to the two towns and I realized that there's this gulf between Franklin and Sawyer. They're only 30 miles apart but they might as well be on different planets when it comes to personalities."

His eyes were glued to her face and she knew he was listening with rapt attention, trying to wrap his mind around the information just pouring out of her, but she needed him to understand with his heart, not just his head.

She needed to switch tactics.

"Think about Skyler. He can grow up in a huge city with hundreds of thousands of people stuffed into it, part of the country music scene, his dad *the* Zane Risley, or he can grow up out in the country where he's just another kid, and his best friend is Juan Miller. He can be here, close to my family. Close to the Millers. Close to the Whitakers. Maybe he'll never become an expert horseman, but he'll have true friends here; friends who like him for who he is, not who his father is."

"Now wait up a minute here," he said, holding up his hands to stop her roll. "I can see why *you* want to stay in Idaho but there's just no way that it's good for *Skyler*. He's in one of the top-rated schools in the country in Tennessee. Their math program is stellar. It's a launching pad to all of the top universities: Harvard, MIT, Yale—"

"But he hates it there," Louisa cut in.

Zane stopped. "He…he what? He does not. It's a great school—"

"Zane Risley," Louisa snapped, "have you ever heard your son talk about friends that he has in that school? About his teachers? About the clubs he can get involved in? Really think back. What positives has he *ever* mentioned to you?"

Dead silence. Zane had been thrown for a loop. She wasn't sure if he was ever going to start speaking again. He seemed to be stuck in permanent-mouth-agape mode.

"I know that all of the rich parents think that boarding schools are the Best Things Ever, and only the best will do for their children, but Skyler hates being gone from home. Even back when you two weren't real close, he still didn't like being sent away to school. C'mon, Zane, think about it. He's still a kid. Spending the night at a friend's house is fun, but being sent away to boarding school and not seeing your parents for months at a time? It isn't natural. After spending this summer with Skyler and really getting to know him, are you honestly going to be okay with going back to only seeing him during Christmas and spring break? Aren't you going to miss him?"

She fell quiet then, waiting, and still, Zane just sat there, his mouth hanging slightly agape, staring at her like she'd started speaking another language on him.

The silence stretched on, and she couldn't bear it any

longer. She had to keep talking. She had to get him to understand.

"Under your scenario, you get me, you get your career back, and you get to live where you want to live. Meanwhile, I lose my career, I live in a fishbowl, I live where you can practically swim through the air because of all of the damn humidity, and there's an entire country between me and my family. It doesn't work. I'm more than an appendage of you, Zane. I am my own person. I need to be here, where I can *be* that person."

"But...but you said how important it is for me to start touring again," Zane said, still watching her like he couldn't decide if she was being serious or not. "I can't make music in Idaho. Music is recorded in Nashville."

"Then you fly to Nashville and you cut a record. Or, you build a recording studio here. I'm fairly sure they'll let you record a music record somewhere else on the planet other than Tennessee. There's so much here in Idaho that we'd be giving up if we moved back east. Let's be real for a minute, Zane: I've fallen in love with you *despite* you being a famous country music star, not *because* of it. Life would be so much easier if you just worked down at the automotive shop, fixing engines. We wouldn't have a herd of reporters outside our front door, for starters. I'm willing to have some give-and-take to make this work, but it can't be all give and no take."

"I...it never occurred to me."

He still looked half convinced that she was pulling his leg and was going to yell out, "JUST KIDDING!" at any moment. He hadn't shut her down, though. He hadn't told her not a snowball's chance in hell. Not yet, anyway. They still had a chance at making this work, if she could just get through to him.

"Think about this," she said impulsively. "I know this house isn't your favorite."

"You do?" he interrupted her, looking – if anything – even more surprised than he had before.

"It's not hard to pick up on," she said dryly. "You wander around and mutter under your breath about all of the dark wood and how this is an old man's house. I get it – there can't be that many handicap-accessible mansions for rent in Long Valley, Idaho, so you had to roll with it."

"One. There was one. This was it," he put in. "Either we took it, or we didn't come. The guy who built it was in his late 80s, and he wanted a little 'hideaway' where he could be sure he could get around in his wheelchair when he came to visit."

"If this is your idea of a little hideaway…" Louisa mumbled, looking around the ornate formal living room. This room had to be her least favorite one in the house, and honestly, that was saying something. The competition was fierce for that particular "honor."

"My thoughts exactly." Zane flashed her a quick smile. "According to Nina who arranged all of this for me, the older man is hospitalized and most likely won't make it through the end of the year. He'd made arrangements beforehand to rent this place out since he wouldn't be using it. And I'm grateful to him for it – it made this trip to Idaho possible. But I could never live here full-time."

She tried not to sigh too impatiently, although if she was being honest with herself, she didn't try that hard.

"Do you know how cheap land is out here, especially compared to Nashville?" She cocked an eyebrow at him. "You could probably buy an entire working ranch up here, cattle and all, for less than what a mansion on a quarter-acre costs back in Nashville. I'm not saying you want to buy a working ranch – God knows you and horses aren't the best of friends – but you could buy a huge spread and build a house from the ground up. It can be wheelchair accessible *and* your style, at the same time. You can put in a private airport. You could fly from here to Tennessee and back again whenever you'd like.

And if you want, you could put up a nice security fence around the property to keep out the Franklin weirdos."

She swore she heard him then mutter something about skinheads under his breath but when she asked him what he'd said, he quickly waved her off. "Nothing. Don't worry about it. So we stay here, buy some land, build a house, and I fly back to Nashville whenever I need to."

We. It was such a lovely word.

"That's the idea," she said softly.

"Do you have any idea how different you are from Tamara?" he asked then, and shook his head, laughing. "In a million years, I didn't expect this to be an option."

She smiled in response to his little joke but didn't say anything. It was time for him to think through things. She'd given it her best argument.

He either saw the truth, or they fell apart.

CHAPTER 42

L IVE IN IDAHO.

Live in *Idaho*.

It was such an insane idea, he still partly expected Louisa to start laughing uproariously and admit that it was all just a joke. But she wasn't laughing, and it wasn't a joke.

Live in *Idaho*?

Granted, the idea had some merit to it. He could fly back and forth across the country just as easily as Louisa could.

And it was true that Skyler actually had friends here, whereas back in Tennessee, he couldn't remember Sky ever begging to go spend the night at a friend's house.

But public school? For Skyler? He couldn't send his kid to public school. Public schools had knife fights and gangs and—

Oh. Except that was Nashville. Now that he thought about it, the chances weren't real high that the Sawyer schools had knife fights and gang members in them.

But still. An elite private school for some of the richest residents of Tennessee *had* to have better programs than Sawyer.

But if his child hated that school? If his child was

miserable there? Was it better that it be a premium school with every opportunity and a miserable child, or a run-of-the-mill school with a happy child?

Letting Skyler leave for school and not see him for months…Louisa had forced him to think about that when he'd been doing a damn good job ignoring what was about to happen. He'd been dreading going back to Tennessee – although he wasn't about to admit that to Louisa – because he'd known that he was going to have to say goodbye to Skyler. No more chats over breakfast about what amazing insight he'd gleaned from Juan. No more discussions about Xbox vs PlayStation. No more kayaking around the lake and getting into water fights. Sure, they could come back next summer, but did he really only want to spend time with his son once a year? Now that he knew who Skyler was, he didn't want to send him away again. He was just starting to learn how to love his son.

And it was all because of Louisa.

He looked at her and wondered for a fleeting moment how long he'd been lost in his own little world. He hadn't said a word for probably a good ten minutes, and yet, she wasn't pushing and prodding him. She was giving him a chance to think through it all and make a choice. He tried to imagine Tamara doing that for a moment, and completely failed. She would've been no more likely to do that than she would've been to jump on a unicorn and fly to Paris. Tamara was *not* known for her patient nature.

"I hadn't thought about it like this before," he said, and immediately felt stupid. He'd already said that. He just…

The whole conversation was making his brain hurt.

"There's no way Tamara would've ever wanted to live here," he continued. He had to make her understand what a huge loop she'd thrown him for. "Even Boise would've been *way* too small. She only tolerated Nashville because that's where country music stars are 'supposed' to live. If it'd been up to her, we would've lived in New York City or LA." Louisa shuddered. Zane laughed. "I'm a people person. I would've been just as happy in New York City or LA as Tamara would've been. But, I was also happy in Nashville. I have plenty of friends there – friends who all think I've gone off the deep end for spending an entire summer in the middle of Nowhere, Idaho, by the way. If they could hear us discussing moving here permanently, I think they'd probably call for the men with the white straight jackets." Louisa laughed lightly at that like he'd intended her to, but he could tell she was getting nervous. Did this mean no to living in Sawyer? The panic was starting to grow in her eyes.

"I'd wanted to only ever give Skyler the best," he said softly. "You're right—" he gulped hard, "—that I've been dreading sending him back to school in just another week. I'm finally learning who my son really is. Did you know he doesn't like mayo?" he demanded, getting sidetracked for a moment by the insanity of it all. She bust up laughing. "Who doesn't like mayo? He says it makes his bread soggy. No, it makes his bread edible. His nut-and-seed-free bread, mind you. When we first arrived here, I couldn't have told you at gunpoint if he liked white bread, wheat bread, gluten-free bread, sourdough bread, or no bread at all. That wasn't something I had to worry about. Ask the chef – he'll tell you. It's his job, after all, not mine. There was so damn much that I didn't know about him – big things. Little things. Everything in-between things. Tamara was in charge of all of that. Of him. Of our home life. Tamara…"

His face screwed up with pain and the lingering laughter in the room dissipated, leaving Louisa just staring at him, eyes intense, waiting for him to tell her whatever he needed to get off his chest.

Damn good listener – he was adding that to her list of amazing attributes.

"She never really gave up on the dream of making it big."

There. He'd said it. He'd finally admitted the truth that he hadn't dared discuss with even Tamara.

"It was slowly killing her inside that she hadn't made it in the country music world. It was eating her alive, and she dealt with it through massive doses of retail therapy. When she died, she had clothes in the closet with the tags still on them. And not just a few – she had entire closets full of clothes with the tags still on them." Louisa's eyes went wide at that, and Zane chuckled ruefully. "It didn't matter to me – I didn't care. Money wasn't the problem for us. It was the drive she had to go shopping because she was trying to fill that hole – it was the fact that that hole existed – that caused the problems."

"Like you and drinking," Louisa put in softly, and Zane paused. Oh shit, she was right. "Your drinking never got bad enough that you were blacking out or making insane decisions or destroying stuff. But you also weren't dealing with the real problem because you were able to cover it up with the drinking. Paper right over it."

He just stared at her for a good long while. "I didn't… wow." He rammed his fingers into his hair. "You're right. I hadn't thought about it like that before. But back to where to live – you're right that I could fly out of here just as easily as I could fly out of Nashville if I go on tour again—"

"*When* you go on tour again," Louisa interrupted him. "No more punishing yourself. You need that stage. You need that feedback and that outlet of expression and that interaction with the crowd. I refuse to let you hide behind the walls of the house any longer."

His mind skipped back to Tamara yet again, remembering the many blowout fights they'd had on this topic. Had Tamara wanted him to stop touring because she knew it'd hurt him? Had she been trying to make him as miserable as possible?

Maybe.

Probably.

Did that matter now, though? That chapter of his life was closed. He could move forward with Louisa now, and *that* was what mattered.

"So we stay here," he said casually, as if this really wasn't a big deal at all, "buy some property, build a handicap-accessible home on it, put in a private airstrip, and fly out whenever needed?"

She nodded, looking almost scared to believe it could really be that easy.

"I think I can get behind that," he said with a grin, and leaned forward to kiss her.

He was finally home.

EPILOGUE

ZANE

MAY, 2021

THE ENERGY WAS THERE, beating hard and fast through him like an electrical current set on high. It was back. *He* was back.

And damn, did it feel good.

Louisa had been right, of course. Who was surprised? Not him.

But ever since that fateful day when they decided – together – that they should stay in Sawyer-freakin'-Idaho of all places, life had begun unfolding in ways he never could've imagined when he'd first spotted that online interview with Dr. Adam Whitaker. He'd come here as a last-ditch effort – a Hail Mary to deal with his out-of-control son because he had nothing left to lose.

And now…

"I'm your biggest fan," the woman was saying as she shoved her shirt at him to sign. He sent her a charming grin and she practically melted into the ground right there.

"Thanks for coming," he said, scribbling his autograph onto the t-shirt with only a small amount of struggle – years of practice always helped when wrangling fabric around – and handed it back.

"Zane Risley! Zane Risley!" A little kid was shouting and waving his paper above his head. He looked just like Skyler had as a kid. Zane missed that version of Skyler, not only because he'd been a damn adorable kid, but because he'd quite literally missed that part of Skyler's life, being gone all of the time on tours.

Zane bent over, chatting with the kid, his mother beaming, and then it was time to sign the autograph and move on. Making each person in a crowd feel special and singled-out was a talent not everyone could master. There was a trick to the chatting, the eye contact, a quick question, a signature, and then moving on. Not too long, not too short.

Today was the day – a fundraiser for the Sawyer School District the size that no local had probably ever seen. Jaxson Anderson, the local fire chief, had told him that their fundraisers tended to be baked potato dinners, chili cook-offs, and the occasional spaghetti feeds when a group was feeling particularly international. Zane had thought Jaxson was kidding but then the look on Jaxson's face…

Well, today wasn't a baked potato dinner or a chili cook-off, that was for damn sure. It would be so much more than that.

"Zane!" The cries for his attention were coming from every direction. He was thriving – reveling in the energy of the crowd. Right where he wanted to be. Signing autographs. Making people feel special because they *were* special. Posing for pictures.

Just then, Georgette Nash came hurrying over, a clipboard in her hand. "Zane," she said in a low tone of voice, "it's time to start moving backstage. The stage crew says they need the time to mic you up."

Zane flashed the woman in front of him his most charming smile as he handed her *Country Music Vibes* bumper sticker back to her. "Enjoy the concert!" he said even as he began winding his way towards backstage, following Georgette's gently round figure.

After he'd decided to make Long Valley his home, he'd met Luke Nash, a good friend to the Miller brothers, and Luke had told him about his younger sister, one half of a set of twins and somebody with more musical talent in her little pinky than most people had in their whole bodies. Zane had nodded and listened politely with half an ear – if he had a nickel for every time someone tried to convince him to give a hand up to a family member or friend or themselves, he could probably double his net worth instantly.

But when Luke started playing a video on his iPad of Georgette singing up on stage, her voice in a full vibrato, the hairs on the back of Zane's neck stood straight up. Hot damn, she really did know how to sing.

Except, she didn't want to keep touring and trying to make it on the big stage – Luke didn't share why and Zane didn't ask. Instead, she wanted to come back to Long Valley, and that was something Zane could get behind. He pulled a few strings and talked the superintendent of the Sawyer School District into hiring Georgette as the new music teacher for the district. She had talent in spades, and it showed.

Under her excellent tutelage, Skyler had moved up to the next level. Maybe Skyler would want to be just like his ol' dad when he grew up. Maybe he wouldn't. But Georgette's guidance and instruction would mean he had that choice.

Screw fancy boarding schools. Sawyer had the potential to be so much more than it had been before, and Zane was excited about the challenge. Georgette was his best idea thus far for improving the local school district.

It had been just what he'd expected: Normal. Problems because every place has problems, but no knife fights or gangs roaming the hallways. It also wasn't going to win any awards for its music program – at least not until Georgette started making shit happen.

Never stand between Georgette Nash and what she wanted to get done. *Force of nature* was one way of putting it.

Georgette left him in the hands of the makeup and hair team, the sound team darting in and strapping equipment to him whenever they could get close enough. "I'll be back later," she promised him as she melted back out into the crowd, off to fix yet another problem.

As Zane's crew did their job quickly and efficiently, Zane reached down and felt the round band of metal in his front pocket through his jeans and sucked in a breath. Today was the day.

His nerves were about to chew right through his stomach lining.

He took a swig of water, waiting for his team to finish up, and then jogged to the edge of the curtain, watching from the sidelines as The Boot Stompers entertained the crowd. They were just a local act and didn't have any stand-out performers, but they weren't that bad, either. Fairly impressive, really, considering they were only a local group.

Then Jacob was striding up on stage and the cheering began in earnest. "Jacob Allen Group! JAG! Jacob Allen Group! JAG!" the crowd chanted and Zane smiled to himself. The girls liked to use his nickname of JAG, and from the sounds of it, more than a few of his diehard fans were in the crowd. How many women would Jacob go home with tonight?

But not the one girl who matters…

He reached down to his pocket again, rubbing the ring like a talisman.

Today was the day.

They'd finally been able to move into their new home just days ago. After all of the planning and building and hard work, it was done. It'd taken on monstrous proportions there for a while, and Zane had started to wonder if it would *ever* get done, but finally – *fin.a.lly* – they'd been able to move in just as a late spring snowstorm hit the valley. Stetson had assured him that this would *probably* be the last snowstorm before summer took over for good, but Zane wasn't sure how much he believed him.

Then again, today's weather is gorgeous, so maybe he's onto something…

The local voice talent – *is Kurtis Workman his name? That seems right* – cut through the roar of the crowd. "Ladies and gentlemen, give it up one more time for JAG!" The crowd was roaring so loudly, Zane wondered for a moment if they'd still have enough voice left to cheer for him, but somehow, he was sure they would.

Jacob was jogging off stage and flashed Zane a grin as they passed. "Great crowd," he shouted over the noise and then he was gone, disappearing into the changing area to clean off the stage makeup.

Jacob had been one of the people who'd been most vehemently against Zane moving to Sawyer, and didn't mince words when he'd bluntly told Zane that he'd gone off the deep end. And trusting Louisa? Was he *that* naïve?

But when the two had finally met, Jacob had fallen under Louisa's spell just as neatly and completely as Skyler and Zane had. In fact, when Jacob'd found out that Louisa had twin sisters, he'd looked a little *too* interested. "They're barely out of high school," Zane had told him.

That'd squelched that thought.

"And now, what we've all been waiting for," Kurtis said. "The reason y'all are here. Welcome to our humble little town, Zane Risley!"

Zane jogged out onto stage as the crowd went absolutely insane. It was a damn good thing this was an outdoors concert – Zane would've had serious worries about the structural integrity of the roof otherwise.

He slipped right into *A Honky Tonk Life*, belting out the words, the crowd singing along with him. His eyes sought out Louisa's, looking for her in the shifting faces blending and weaving below. There she was. She blew him a kiss. Skyler was beside her, sitting in his wheelchair, clapping and singing along. Through damn hard work, Skyler had gotten to the point that he could stand and even walk a little, but he tired easily still, and an entire concert on his feet just wasn't an option.

The beat of the music, the energy of the crowd – Zane was coming home. He'd gone back on tour – he'd been around the world and had sung in sold-out stadiums. But being here, tonight, in this tiny mountain town that'd welcomed him with open arms, his gorgeous girlfriend, his handsome son watching him…

He'd come home.

The song ended and instead of moving into the next one like the crowd had expected, he paused and waited for them to quiet down. Every eye was on him when he said, "Y'all know that tonight is a fundraiser for the music program at the Sawyer School District. What you *don't* know is that I've written a song that I'm debuting tonight. It's for my son, Skyler Risley, but I hope that all y'all enjoy it."

He started singing then, the haunting words of love and pride in a child even when you aren't making the right choices yourself, swirling around the audience, and more than a few women began openly crying. It was when the refrain hit and he sang the one line of the song that would stick forever in the minds of anyone who heard it – *I gave him everything; everything but me* – that the men started tearing up too.

This. This was why he'd wanted to write this song. He looked at Louisa again, just for a moment, and found that she was wiping the tears off her face furiously.

The song drifted to a close, the last notes dying away, and then the crowd went absolutely berserk. They loved it.

The glow of pride flooded through him. He'd composed a song and the crowd had loved it.

He was back on top of his game.

Now, just one more piece to the puzzle and his life could be complete.

"Before I go on with the show, I wanted to bring my son and my girlfriend up on the stage for y'all to meet them. Would you like to meet them?" The crowd went nuts as Skyler and Louisa picked their way up to the front, Skyler walking slowly, carefully over the uneven grass. Dusk was falling fast, making it hard to see, and then the uneven footing…this was the worst possible combination of factors for Skyler, and yet he moved forward, never letting it show how hard this was on him.

That's my boy.

Zane's gaze slid over to Louisa and found that she was just a step behind and to the right of Skyler, ready to catch him if he stumbled, her eyes trained on his son. *Their* son.

No one loved Skyler more than Louisa. It was time to make it official.

They came up on stage, waving to the crowd as they crossed over to him, the crowd cheering and yelling hello back. It was such a small-town moment, and Zane wanted to chuckle at the quaintness of it, but he was mic'd and the sound would be projected far and wide. But there were some friends of Skyler's, yelling and pointing. There was Juan Miller, waving enthusiastically. There was Brooklyn Morland, another kid Juan had introduced Skyler to, jumping up and down like someone had attached springs to her feet. Skyler reached his side and Zane pulled him up close, feeling the fatigue run through his son's body at the strain of working so hard. Louisa stood on the other side, casually helping to keep Skyler propped up, hiding her help from the world.

It was such a Louisa thing to do, Zane wanted to tell her right then how much he loved her, but he didn't. Instead, he looked back at the audience.

"Everyone knows the story of how Skyler and I ended up in this tiny little town you've probably never heard of, called Sawyer, Idaho." The whoops and hollers went on for what seemed like days. "What you *don't* know is that Skyler wasn't the only one who was learning how to ride. I too borrowed a horse from Dr. Whitaker and went out riding. Needless to say, there's a reason why I'm up on stage singing, and not on the back of a horse riding in a rodeo." The laughter rolled over them in waves, and Louisa shot him a laughing grin along with a small shake of the head.

Your agent is going to kill you.

I know.

But he was done pretending to be someone he wasn't, trying to impress the world. He was taking a page out of Louisa's book. He was gonna be himself, and the rest of the world could love it or lump it, and he didn't rightly care which.

"There's something else I'm not sure you know," he continued, looking back at the waiting crowd. "You might've heard a rumor or two that I fell in love with my son's nanny, of all people." The crowd busted up laughing again. He shot them a knowing smile. "The world was only surprised by this because they didn't know Louisa. Anyone who's met her just loves her, and rightfully so. While we're sharing secrets with each other, though, I wanted to share one last one with you." He dropped to one knee as he pulled out the ring he'd been rubbing for good luck all night long. He would need all of the luck he could get in the next minute or so. He could hear the women in the crowd crying again as he held the ring up. "Louisa Vargas, will you marry me?"

"You better say yes!" Skyler put in, and the sobs from the crowd turned to choked laughter instead.

Louisa's shoulders were shaking also, and it took Zane a moment to figure out if it was from crying or laughing, and then realized that it was both.

"Yes, I'll marry you," she said clearly, looking him straight in the eye when she said it, her dark brown eyes – the color of the richest, deepest chocolate in the world – filling with unshed tears.

"Good job, Dad," Skyler stage whispered, and the crowd broke out into roars of laughter once again.

As Zane slipped the ring onto Louisa's finger, noting with pride that he'd managed to figure out her size without her having a clue of what he was up to, he realized that this was what life was made of – tears and laughter and joy and pain.

But most of all, love.

♫ ♫ ♫

QUICK AUTHOR'S NOTE

STRUMMIN' UP LOVE IS THE KIND OF BOOK that makes you grateful for all of the blessings you have in your life, especially the simple ones like the ability to walk.

I was particularly inspired to write *Strummin'* because during the final stages of finishing up *Baked with Love*, my niece got into a terrible car wreck between her junior and senior year of high school, and became an instant paraplegic. It was a complete and total coincidence that I was slated to next write a book about a little boy who'd become a paraplegic because of a car wreck.

Like, what are the chances, right?

I ended up "stealing" a lot of the information for Skyler from my niece's situation. She too had the entire force of the accident aimed directly at her T12 vertebra. She too did not know if she would ever be able to walk again. She too had to have the Jaws of Life used to cut the car apart around her so she could be pulled out.

But unlike Skyler, she had a system of family and friends around her who've helped her along the way and her progress has been remarkable. In fact, when she really pushes herself, she has already gotten to the point where she can sort of walk/shuffle along…as long as she has leg braces on and is using a walker.

But she's getting stronger and better with each passing day, and much of that has to do with her inner will and drive. She doesn't take no for an answer.

I love you, Heidi, and I'm so proud of you.

Also, a huge shout-out to the staff at the University of Utah Hospital in Salt Lake City. It's where Heidi ended up after her accident, and I spent several days following her around, asking lots of questions of the staff and making sure that the information that I included in *Strummin'* would be medically accurate. Every single nurse, CNA, and therapist was super patient with me, and I learned waaayyyy more about post-accident therapy than I ever expected I'd need to in this lifetime, lol. Any medical inaccuracies, however, are all on my shoulders.

And yes, in case you were curious, the University of Utah Hospital has one of the nation's premiere spinal cord units in place, and people really do transfer in from all over the US just to be able to take advantage of their knowledge and expertise. However, Dr. Matthew Funk is totally an invention of my imagination, I promise. The real head doctor of the spinal cord unit, Dr. Rosenbluth, is actually a wonderful human being.

Some other thoughts and notes:

I'm not Mexican and my handle on Spanish is about on par with Zane's, lol. So, I relied a *lot* upon amazing friends who were willing to critique my Spanish phrasing and help me find just the right words to use. Thank you, Geeta and

María. Please know that any mistakes in this arena are mine, not theirs.

Also, if you somehow stumbled onto *Strummin' Up Love* without having ever read any of my other books, boy are you in for a treat! Remember how Wyatt fell in love with his jailer? Yeah, that's all in *Arrested by Love* (Book 3 of the Cowboys of Long Valley Romance series).

Curious why it is that someone as young as Iris (Declan's wife) is walking around with a cane? That's *Returning for Love* (Book 4 of the Cowboys series). Oh, and don't forget about how it is that the veterinarian, Adam Whitaker, fell in love with his wife, Kylie – you'll find their story in *Bundle of Love* (that's Book 7!)

Then there's the firefighters, Levi and Moose. Yes, Moose's father did name his son Deere after his John Deere dealership and yes, it really is a rocky relationship between the two of them. If you're dying to know about that, you'll definitely want to check out *Inferno of Love* (Book 2 of the Firefighters of Long Valley Romance series) and then read Levi's story in *Fire and Love* (Book 3).

If you haven't picked up on it yet, all of the stories in the Long Valley world are intertwined. Characters from one book will "walk" through others, which means that you never have to say goodbye to anyone, and if you're anything like me, that'll make you very, very happy.

The next book in the Musicians of Long Valley Romance series will be *Melody of Love*, the love story of Georgette Nash. Y'all are gonna *love* her story – not only will you get to see lots more of the Nash family (both Luke and his wife Bonnie, and Georgette's twin brother, Gunner) but you're going to find out why it is that Georgette decided that she wanted nothing more in the world than to move back to Long Valley, Idaho. It's a hell of a story, because she's a hell of a woman.

But while you're waiting for me to get *Melody* written and out the door, travel with me back to where this all started.

Remember how Stetson talks about how he and Jennifer had a "pretty rocky start" but that his wasn't as bad as Zane and Louisa's was? You can judge that for yourself in *Accounting for Love*, Book 1 of the Cowboys series. (I think they're a pretty close tie, honestly!) It is available at your favorite book retailer or local library, so be sure to find it there and enjoy.

Love and hugs,

Erin Wright

Be sure to find my books at your favorite bookstore, retailer, or library 📚

Or, buy them directly from me at
https://ErinWright.net/My-Books

If you prefer, you can also scan this QR code with your phone:

ALSO BY ERIN WRIGHT

~ COWBOYS OF LONG VALLEY ROMANCE ~

Accounting for Love

Blizzard of Love

Arrested by Love

Returning for Love

Christmas of Love

Overdue for Love

Bundle of Love

Lessons in Love

Baked with Love

Bloom of Love

Broken by Love (TBA)

Holly and Love (TBA)

Banking on Love (TBA)

Sheltered by Love (TBA)

~ FIREFIGHTERS OF LONG VALLEY ROMANCE ~

Flames of Love

Inferno of Love

Fire and Love

Burned by Love

~ MUSICIANS OF LONG VALLEY ROMANCE ~

Strummin' Up Love

Melody of Love (TBA)

Rock 'N Love (TBA)

Rhapsody of Love (TBA)

~ SERVICEMEN OF LONG VALLEY ROMANCE ~

Thankful for Love (TBA)

Commanded to Love (TBA)

Salute to Love (TBA)

Harbored by Love (TBA)

About Erin Wright

USA Today Bestselling author Erin Wright has worked every job under the sun, including library director, barista, teacher, website designer, and ranch hand helping brand cattle, before settling into the career she's always dreamed about: Author.

She still loves coffee, doesn't love the smell of cow flesh burning, and is currently living out her own love story in a tiny town in rural Idaho.

Wanna get in touch?
https://erinwright.net
erin@erinwright.net

Or reach out to Erin on your favorite social media platform:

facebook.com/AuthorErinWright
x.com/ErinWrightLV
youtube.com/@ErinWrightLV
pinterest.com/ErinWrightBooks
goodreads.com/ErinWright
bookbub.com/profile/Erin-Wright
instagram.com/AuthorErinWright

www.ingramcontent.com/pod-product-compliance
Lightning Source LLC
Chambersburg PA
CBHW072029220726

48293CB00016B/577